Get Your
Coventry Romances
Home Subscription NOW

And Get These
4 Best-Selling Novels
FREE:

LACEY
by Claudette Williams

THE ROMANTIC WIDOW
by Mollie Chappell

HELENE
by Leonora Blythe

THE HEARTBREAK TRIANGLE
by Nora Hampton

CAROLINE

by

Barbara Hazard

FAWCETT COVENTRY ● NEW YORK

For Steven, David, and Scott

CAROLINE

Published by Fawcett Coventry Books, a unit of CBS Publications, the Consumer Publishing Division of CBS Inc.

Copyright © 1981 by Barbara Hazard

ISBN: 0-449-50225-2

Printed in the United States of America

First Fawcett Coventry printing: November 1981

10 9 8 7 6 5 4 3 2 1

Chapter One

"Mama, whether you want to admit it or not, I am an old maid!"

To look at her, you would never have said that Caroline Draper was any such thing. She was of medium height, and if she was not a striking brunette or stunning blonde, her soft brown hair curled charmingly around the perfect oval of her face. Although her nose was undistinguished, her mouth too generous, and her chin a little too determined for classic beauty, her large sparkling brown eyes more than compensated for such minor faults. Indeed they were her best feature, framed as they were with heavy dark lashes and set in the wild rose complexion of her face. Furthermore, her figure was excellent and her carriage graceful, and she had all the accomplishments any young lady could have desired. As the oldest of the four Draper daughters, she had a good deal of common sense and a straightforward way not only of looking at people, but speaking to them as well. Her mother had often bemoaned this quality, and wished that dear Caro would learn from her sister Lizzie the power of a blush and fluttering eyelashes, or even the charming toss of her curls that was so devastatingly effective when dealing with members of the opposite sex. At twenty-two she was hardly old, and she made an altogether charming picture as she sat on the window seat of a small salon of Draper House, engaged in repairing a small rip in one of her morning gowns. She was completely unconscious of the fact that the early spring sunlight touched her hair with accents of gold and created a most becoming halo effect.

"Caroline!" her mother said in a horrified voice. "I cannot have heard you correctly! An old maid? YOU?"

Her daughter looked up from her sewing to smile briefly.

"Now, Mama," she said in her decisive voice, "there is no use pretending any longer! I have had two seasons in London, and you will have to agree that I did not take! Oh yes," she added quickly as her mother opened her mouth to refute her, "I know I received two offers—if you can count as offers the one from General Bates, who must be all of sixty-five if he's a day, or the one from Mr. Kindle, who stuttered and blushed so I am still not entirely sure he *did* propose! But now it is Lizzie's turn, and then next year, Mary Martha's, and before you know it, Clorinda will be eighteen and ready to be fired off too!"

Mrs. Draper sighed. There was wisdom in her oldest daughter's statements, but to see her calmly announcing that she intended to remain at home for the current season was too much! She rose and began to pace the salon in an agitated way, managing as she did so to spill her needlework to the floor, drop one of Mr. Draper's books off a small table, and narrowly avoid upsetting a vase of flowers. Caroline watched her with a smile. Dear Mama! When she was upset, she was even more careless than usual, for she was one of those people who go through life spilling, dropping, losing, and overturning everything that came her way. After six children and a life of comfort and luxury, she had gained weight, and although you could see a trace of the pretty girl she had once been from the family resemblance to her

6

daughters, that prettiness was now blurred with middle age and the addition of a second chin. She sighed again and looked despairingly at Caroline.

"Indeed, Mama, I do not mind! You know Lizzie will be disappointed if she has to remain home again, now she is nineteen! Remember how she wanted to go last year and certainly might have if she had not fallen off the stile and broken her arm!"

"I do not see any reason why you both cannot enjoy the season!" Mrs. Draper said with dignity. "Why, I have been planning on it, Caro! You know what Lizzie is! I do not know how it is possible for one young girl to get in so many scrapes, but there you are! She may be nineteen, but she is not up to all the rigs of town by any means! Besides, you know I have promised your Aunt Wells that I would present your cousin Belinda this year, since her health is such she does not feel up to the bustle of town." She paused to get her breath and added darkly, "General Bates is only fifty-five, and young Kindle a trifle shy—they were perfectly good offers!"

Ignoring the last statement, Caroline sat with her head to one side, considering her mother's plan. It was true that Lizzie, who was such a dear, good girl at heart, was so often the one whose adventures never worked out, and there was a great deal of common sense in the notion that Caroline would be able to keep her in check more easily than Mrs. Draper could, for they would be so much in each other's company. Caroline had always felt that although she herself favored her father, Lizzie was exactly like her mother, and therein lay the problem. Even loving her dearly, Caroline had no illusions about her mother's intellect or superior sense, but it was not very flattering to be asked to go only as a chaperone. Suddenly she gave her warm, rich smile as she saw the humor of it.

"Mama, you are incorrigible! Now it is to help you watch Lizzie and our cousin that I am to go to town! You cannot fool me, you know, for I am more than two and ten! What you really have in mind is that I must go through yet another season, and all under the guise of helping my family!"

She laughed briefly and rose, folding her mending and putting her needle and thread away in her work basket. "Very well, I will *think* about it, but I still feel it would be better for me to retire from the lists and let Lizzie have a clear field, for I am sure she will form an eligible connection before the season is a month gone!"

"She is very pretty, is she not?" Mrs. Draper asked proudly, but for once was not to be swayed from her primary concern and added hastily, "But not a bit prettier than you, my dear, and if you were not so particular, you could have married in your first season too! I have often wondered what you are looking for, and why you discouraged Lord Grant—such an old, distinguished family!—and Viscount Sperling, who was so eager to pay you attentions—so handsome!—and even Mr. Rothley, whom you managed to freeze with a glare every time he came anywhere near you!"

Caroline was surprised, for she had never imagined her scatterbrained mother had seen so much, but she only gave a bitter little laugh and replied, "Yes, and they were so wonderful, were they not? Lord Grant is a rake, twice widowed; Viscount Sperling *has* to marry money; and Mr. Rothley only pursued me to try and get the better of Sperling, such bitter enemies as they are! It was not at all flattering, Mama! As for what I am looking for in a husband, I am sure I do not know, except it is most certainly not the likes of any of those gentlemen!"

Mrs. Draper took another turn around the room, inadvertently kicking Papa's book under a small settee, and as Caroline went to rescue it she said tartly, "Well, I assure you, my dear Caro, that you will not find the gentleman here in Hunstanton!" Caroline looked up in surprise as her mother continued, "There is no one eligible in the neighborhood unless you are thinking of the squire's son, and let me tell you it would not do, for your father has no wish to be connected there, and that leaves only the curate!"

Her tone was so gloomy that Caroline had to laugh again, which made her mother add, "And do not be expecting some handsome young lord, rich as Golden Ball, to ride up the lane some day to rescue you! I do hope it is not the result of reading too many novels that gives you such ideas!"

Caroline could have told her that it was Lizzie who devoured such gothic tales, her taste in reading being vastly different but she only went to her mother and hugged her.

"Indeed I know, Mama, and I do not in the least expect it! Alas, I fear I am not at all romantic. As for poor John and the curate, of course not! But I should like to stay and help Papa with the estate, for I am sure he needs me, with Ned away in Spain with Wellington, and Andrew still so young."

Mrs. Draper sniffed. "Your father has done very well without you for the past two seasons, and can continue to do so this year. He has a good bailiff and some excellent men under him, and if he does not desire to go to town with us, it does not mean he could not do so if he wished. Besides, Mary Martha can help him; it would do her good!"

"I am so glad it is Mary Martha who is to have the 'good!'" a gay voice from the doorway said lightly, and Lizzie came into the room, still dressed in her outdoor clothes. She had been to the neighboring village with a message from her mother for the vicar, and to see if the one village shop had by any chance a length of pink ribbon to trim her second-best bonnet.

As she was removing her pelisse and smoothing down her dark brown curls, which had been slightly disarranged by that same bonnet, her sister looked at her sharply. Her color was a little high, even allowing for the brisk wind blowing, and although Mrs.

Draper did not appear to notice anything unusual, Caroline thought her sister looked a little self-conscious, as if she had been doing something she knew would not meet with their approval. She sighed. Since Lizzie had been to the manse, she supposed it was the curate, poor man! Lizzie must have been flirting again, for she had only to see a young man before she began playing off her tricks. It was as natural to her as breathing, and she was much looking forward to her season in London and an ever-widening circle of admirers. The quiet countryside of Hunstanton did not give her anywhere near the scope she needed.

She was the same height as Caroline, but although you would have known them for sisters anywhere, they did not look that much alike when they stood together. Lizzie's hair was a very dark brown, her mouth a perfect rosebud, and her nose slightly tip-tilted in a delightful way. She had a much more voluptuous figure than her sister, and worried a great deal about her weight. Now she avoided her sister's eye as she told her mother what the vicar had said, and then she bemoaned the scarcity of anything slightly resembling the ribbon she needed in the village shop.

"I shall be so glad to go to London!" she sighed. "Just think of being able to find anything you need in any number of beautiful shops!" She frowned at her bonnet with its faded bow and asked eagerly, "Have you any idea when we are to leave, Mama? I do so long for it!"

"I have made no definite plans as yet, Lizzie, and there is no need to arrive before the rest of the ton, for the season does not open properly for some time. Your father has hired the same house we had last year. The location is excellent and it is very well appointed too. I wish I could talk him into *buying* a London establishment, but there! Men can be so stubborn!"

This was an old complaint with her, and Caroline attempted to turn the subject.

"Does Belinda come here to us, or are you to meet her in town, Mama?"

"Your Aunt Wells is only waiting to hear from me, my dears, and then she will send her on to join us in London in care of her old governess and a maid. I hope you will like her, Lizzie, since you are bound to be in each other's company so much, and I hope she is at least presentable! Perhaps it was hasty of me to agree to sponsor her when I have not seen her since she was five, but your uncle would retire to that huge pile of a house in Yorkshire! It is one of my foremost worries, girls!"

"The huge pile, Mama?" Caroline could not help asking innocently.

Mrs. Draper looked confused. "Of course not! Your cousin Belinda! Try not to be so difficult, Caro! Suppose she has spots? Or...or some other disfigurement? Or even a horrid local accent? You can see how worrisome it is!"

Before any of them could speculate further, the door of the salon was flung open, and a young girl came in, in a rush, shrieking at the top of her lungs and closely followed by a very young gentleman with a huge grin on his freckled thirteen-year-old face. The girl hid herself behind her mother's skirts just as another daughter arrived, still breathless from the chase.

"Hush, Clorinda!" Mrs. Draper said firmly, for after raising six children she had no illusions that her youngest child was in any way hurt or in danger. Mary Martha grabbed her brother by the arm and shook him.

"Naughty boy to frighten her so! Give it to me!"

"Give what to you, Mary Martha?" Lizzie asked, cautiously going to stand behind the sofa.

"A frog!" her sister said, shaking her brother again. "Come on, give it to me! I am so sorry, Mama," she added, "I meant to watch him, but Andrew left his books right after you came downstairs, and I could not find him anywhere!"

With five pairs of feminine eyes looking at him disapprovingly, Andrew reached into his pocket with a shrug and handed over a large frog, now slightly bedraggled and quiet.

"Ugh!" said Lizzie from behind the sofa as Mary Martha marched to the window and put the frog out on the terrace. Sobbing still, Clorinda clung to her mother and began to recite a litany of woes that Andrew had bedevilled her with that day, while her mother tried in vain to calm her. Caroline continued to put the room to rights as Lizzie and Mary Martha put their heads together and commiserated about the impossibility of ever civilizing a thirteen-year-old boy. Andrew, who had found a length of string in his pocket, was making a cat's cradle and whistling loudly.

"Behold the happy family group! How pleasant to see you all so peaceful, calm, and content!"

Instantly all hubbub ceased as Mr. Draper strode into the room. Even Clorinda settled down to a few watery sniffles and an occasional hiccup.

"Mr. Draper! Whatever can you think of us!" his wife exclaimed, "Andrew and Clorinda, go immediately to the schoolroom. I shall be up to see you shortly, young man! Lizzie, you go with Mary Martha! Surely the two of you will be able to keep the peace. Caroline, you will remain here; I wish your father to speak to you!"

As Mrs. Draper finished her stream of orders, the room emptied, only Lizzie grumbling a little because she had been sent off with the children. When the door had closed behind them and Mr. Draper had taken his customary place in front of the fireplace, he turned to his wife and said, "You are not going to tell me, my dear, that Caro is to blame for all that confusion and noise, for I shall not believe it; Caro is too good and sensible! Come, puss, what have you been up to that requires my censure?"

The twinkle in his eyes belied his stern tone; of all his children, he had a special love for his oldest daughter. He was a middle-aged man whose dark brown hair was just beginning to gray, and he was still straight and powerful looking, probably because he spent most of his waking hours on horseback and rarely went to town, no matter how much his wife pleaded with him to do so. Not for him the balls and receptions and clubs! Not when there was the estate to look after, and hunting to be had, as well as all the other delights of country life he enjoyed so much. He was perfectly willing to give Mrs. Draper a large draft on his London bank, that allowed her to spend as much as she wished, but she might look in vain for his company.

Now Caroline went to him and hugged him. "Indeed, Papa, it is not so bad! I have just been telling Mama that I have no desire for yet another season! It would be a waste of money, for it is obvious that I did not take, and to be sitting in a ballroom dressed in expensive gowns one more time is repugnant to me! Alas, Papa," she added with a rueful laugh, "I am afraid your eldest daughter is well on her way to being an old maid!"

"Stuff!" Mr. Draper said, frowning at her. "I have never heard such nonsense! When you are five years older and still unwed, then you might begin to think of settling down with a tabby and good works around the village, but I do not in the least expect it to happen, for I find it hard to believe that all the young men in England are blind!"

"Why, thank you, Papa!" Caroline exclaimed. "What a very nice thing to say!"

"It is nothing but the truth," Mrs. Draper chimed in. "You have the right of it, as always, my dear! Now please tell Caro that you wish her to go with us for the season, for nothing I have said has been of the least use in convincing her she should!"

Mr. Draper looked searchingly at his daughter before replying.

"I would not force you to go, my girl; in fact I hesitate to press you if you really have no desire for it, but let me assure you the money is of no importance! I do not mean to brag, for after all it was my grandfather who made the Draper fortune, but you are quite an heiress in your own right, you know. If your mother wishes your company, perhaps you should reconsider!"

"And then there's Lizzie!" Mrs. Draper added in a discouraged voice. "I do not know how I can bring her to London alone!"

"Lizzie?" he asked. "In that case, dear Caro, you *must* go! I had forgotten Lizzie was to make her come-out this season, and I should not have a moment's peace, knowing she was in town with only your mother to watch her!"

Caroline laughed at his horrified tone and promised to think of it seriously, for although she was glad her father had not ordered her to accompany her mother and sister, it was obvious he would feel much better if she were along. It was not only Lizzie, it was Mrs. Draper as well! Left to her own devices, there was sure to be trouble. Caroline sighed as she went to her room to put away her mending. It did look as if Miss Draper would once again grace the London scene, for the *third* time! And then she would have to escort Mary Martha, and eventually Clorinda as well! But of course, by the time Clorinda was ready to take the town by storm, Caroline would be an old maid in truth; sitting against the ballroom wall with the other chaperones, complete with cap or turban! How depressing! She went to the window of her room and looked out into the garden below. It was a lovely spring day, and the crocuses were making a brave display in a sheltered corner of the old brick wall. She gazed down, not really seeing them, and wondered, not for the first time: What is wrong with me? I know I am not homely or tongue-tied or gauche! Why isn't there a man who could love me, whom I could love in return? Perhaps Mama is right and I am too nice in my requirements, but surely it is not too much to ask that I find a decent man who is not also old or ugly or only interested in my money! She leaned her forehead against the cold pane and frowned a little. Very well, she would go, but on a condition that this must be the last time. And she would concentrate only on Lizzie and put her own dreams aside, since it was obvious that they were not to be! And then there was Belinda too. Caroline hoped she would be a steadying influence on her sister, for if her cousin turned out to be even remotely like Lizzie, she and her mother were in for a lively season!

That evening at dinner she announced that she would be pleased to accompany her mother and Lizzie to town, and Mrs. Draper sent her a warm, thankful smile, and her father beamed at her as Lizzie exclaimed, "Oh, famous, Caro! It will be so much more comfortable to have you with me, telling me how to go on and what to do!"

"What *not* to do, is more like it, Lizzie!" her father said sharply. "Let me hear of no madcap adventures, miss, or you will be home before the cat has time to lick her ear!"

Lizzie promised to be good, for she knew that tone of voice, but privately she confided later to Mary Martha that she was sure it was not her fault so many things happened to her; she certainly was not in the least adventuresome by nature! Although tacitly agreeing with her, still Mary Martha begged her to write often, since she said the letters from Mama and Caro would not be at all exciting, and she longed to hear every little thing that happened to Lizzie!

Mrs. Draper wrote to her sister the following morning, setting an arrival date in town a month hence and adding she quite longed to see her dear niece again, after all these years! As she sanded her letter, she wondered if that were not too blatant a lie, but, being very good-natured, she was sure she would love the young lady, and with Caroline to assist her, could even give her some town polish if that were needed. At least Lord Wells was wealthy; there would be no need to pinch pennies when she came to dress her!

She set Lizzie to sewing several new petticoats and chemises, to keep her occupied until the day of departure. Scatterbrained she might be, but she knew her second daughter! Mary Martha was allowed to help her, although Mrs. Draper had small expectations either girl would accomplish much, with their giggling and gossiping. Andrew's new tutor had arrived and she was pleased to see he had the young man under firm control, so she was able to take Clorinda away with her to pay some morning calls.

Caroline was thus free to spend the morning as she wished, and she was wondering if it was too cold for a long walk when her father came out of the library and asked her if she wished to ride with him to the squire's on a matter of business he had to transact. Assuring him she would enjoy it of all things, she flew upstairs to put on her habit.

As they rode down the avenue and turned onto the road leading to Hunstanton, Mr. Draper asked Caroline if she were quite happy with her decision to go to town. He was not an unkind man, and he did not want her to feel she had been pressured.

She smiled warmly at him. "Oh, yes, I am quite resigned to it, Papa, and I do not regret it! But I do hope that I will not be asked to perform the same offices for Mary Martha and Clorinda!"

Mr. Draper bit back the reply he had been about to make and kicked his horse to a canter, Caroline having no trouble keeping pace, and although she did not have his promise that she would not have to chaperone *all* her sisters, she was content that she had put the thought into his head.

When they arrived at Rillside, Squire Oglethorpe's estate, she went to pay her respects to his wife and pass the time exchanging family news until her father had completed his business.

It was some time later before they began their ride home, for the Oglethorpes had insisted they stay for a luncheon and then ride out to inspect a new colt the squire had acquired that he was sure would show to advantage in the hunting field.

As they finally came around a bend in the road near Draper House, they were surprised to see a smart carriage stopped in the road, and pulled up their horses when they saw that one of the wheels had come off. There were two men inspecting the damage, one in livery, who was obviously the groom, and the other a tall, handsome man with a mighty frown on his face.

"I see you have come to grief, sir!" Mr. Draper said cheerfully. "Allow me to assist you if I can!"

He swung off his horse and handed his reins up to Caroline to hold, while she gazed with interest at the man beside the carriage, with his hands on his hips.

"Thank you, sir!" the man said in a deep, somewhat harsh voice. "I shall have something to say to my carriage maker when I return to town! As you can see, the wheel was not properly attached, and the pin has worked loose!"

The three men bent over to look at the axle, Mr. Draper shaking his head as he saw the extent of the damage. "You'll not fix that easily, sir! May I suggest that I send out my wheelwright? He is a very good man and he might be able to repair it so you can be on your way shortly." He paused and then added, "By the way, I'm Draper; Edward Draper, at your service!"

The frown lightened as the tall man straightened up and shook the hand extended to him. "Thank you, I am grateful for your help, Mr. Draper. I'm Matthew Kincaid, the Earl of Cannock."

The two men shook hands, each sizing the other up, and Caroline was amused to see that her tall father had to look up slightly at the younger man. Suddenly he came to a decision and said, "But you must return home with us, m'lord, for it may be some time before you can be on your way. Come, I insist! My wife will be delighted to welcome you and hear all the town gossip, for she is shortly to repair to London for the season with my two oldest daughters." Suddenly recalling her presence, he turned to Caro and said, "Allow me to present my daughter, Miss Caroline Draper!"

Caroline, a welcoming smile forming on her face, was surprised to see the cynicism that crossed Lord Cannock's face, and the look of bored indifference that succeeded it. She stiffened as he bowed slightly and murmured, "Delighted," and wished she had the courage to cut him, so *un*delighted as he seemed to be. While he gave some orders to the groom and prepared to join them, she pondered over his attitude, but she had not solved the problem when he came back and prepared to walk by their sides. He had removed his many-caped driving coat and left it with his groom, and now she could see he was dressed in the height of fashion, from the beaver set on his dark brown hair to his bottle-green coat of superfine that fitted so closely across his powerful shoulders. His tight buckskins were complimented by a pair of glossy brown boots, obviously handmade by one of London's premier bootmakers. The face under the beaver's brim was strong-featured and as tanned as her father's, but there the resemblance ended, for his surprisingly bright blue eyes, half hidden by drooping lids, looked bored and discontent, and his thin-lipped mouth was tightened in a small grimace.

"It is not far, m'lord," her father said cheerfully, "or I would have sent a horse back from the stable for you!"

"It is of no importance, Mr. Draper," Lord Cannock said, striding along. "I am quite used to walking, although perhaps not in new boots!"

The Drapers kept their horses to a walk, and the three of them proceeded slowly to the gates of Draper House and up the winding drive. Caroline wished it were even longer to the front door than the half mile it actually was, for she had taken this arrogant young earl in great dislike, and was surprised to find she hoped the new boots were an exceedingly tight fit! Her father swung down from his horse and called for a groom as Caroline prepared to dismount. She was discomfited to find Lord Cannock reaching up to assist her, and with only a distant nod, slid down into his arms and as quickly as possible moved away. She saw him look around in some astonishment and knew that the size and the style of her home had surprised him. Suddenly she knew why he had looked so cynical; he thought Mr. Draper was trying to entrap him in a situation just so he could introduce his daughters and perhaps gain a peer's attentions to people so far beneath him.

"Not quite the country hovel you expected, m'lord?" she could not help murmuring as she gathered her riding skirt in one tightly gloved hand and prepared to mount the shallow steps leading to the front door. Lord Cannock swung around and stared at her, his dark eyebrows forming a straight bar across his forehead as he frowned. She smiled sweetly in return.

"I daresay we Drapers have been in England as long as, if not longer than, your own illustrious family, m'lord! Perhaps, if you have time, you might ask my father to show you the picture gallery. It is considered very fine, although quite a distance from the main part of the house, situated as it is, in the west wing. And you with new boots too! How unfortunate you will have to forego the treat!"

Nodding distantly again, she made her way up the steps to where the Draper butler stood by the massive door, attended by two footmen, leaving a bemused Lord Cannock wondering what he had done to offend the young lady, since he had only uttered one word to her directly since they had met!

By the time he and Mr. Draper had conferred with the wheelwright, and the horses had been led away by two grooms, Miss Draper had disappeared, and when the gentlemen were welcomed by Mrs. Draper in the drawing room, she was nowhere in sight. He was disappointed; he would have liked a chance to speak to the young lady again, if only to give her a setdown for her sarcasm! With Mrs. Draper was a very pretty girl, introduced as Miss Lizzie Draper, and Lord Cannock had no trouble recognizing a practiced coquette in her welcoming smile and graceful curtsy. Tea was brought and conversation was general until Mr. Draper was summoned by his butler and left the room. His wife lost no time in questioning their guest more particularly. She learned that Lord Cannock had been out of the country for the past few years, and that she was acquainted with his aunt, Lady St. Mark.

"And are you looking forward to your first season, Miss Lizzie?" he asked, when he could turn the conversation from himself. Lizzie blushed as she assured him she most certainly was!

"Do you go to town shortly, Mrs. Draper, all of you?" he asked next. "I have heard from your husband that you have a large family; surely a prodigious undertaking to move household in that case!"

"No, not at all, m'lord," Mrs. Draper said. "For you must know that Mr. Draper does not accompany us, nor any of the younger children. I cannot interest him in society, alas! 'Tis only Lizzie and I and of course my oldest daughter Caroline. You have met her?"

As Lord Cannock was acknowledging he had had that honor, Lizzie interrupted to say, "But you are forgetting our cousin, Mama!" She turned to their guest. "Do you know Lord Wells, m'lord? His daughter Belinda is to make her come-out with me!"

Lord Cannock turned to her mother. "You have quite a task ahead of you, Mrs. Draper, presenting *all* these young ladies!" His voice was tinged with a note of amusement, and Caroline, just entering the room, stiffened again. The insolence of him!

"My mother need have no qualms on that point, m'lord!" she said, as she crossed the carpet, "for I shall be with her to share the task!"

Mrs. Draper allowed a frown to cross her good-natured face. Why did Caro have to make herself out to be some sort of poor maiden aunt, especially in such handsome, august, and eligible company!

Before she could attempt to mend fences, Caroline continued, "The wheelwright has seen the damage to your carriage, m'lord, and regrets to inform you that it will be quite impossible for you to continue your travels today. He will get to work immediately, but it will take until sometime tomorrow to repair the wheel...."

"You will of course stay the night with us, m'lord!" Mrs. Draper interjected. "We should be delighted!"

Lord Cannock said everything that was proper, and blandly announced he was especially looking forward to seeing the Draper picture gallery, before he went away to give orders for his baggage to be fetched and his team brought to the Draper stables. Caroline's brown eyes were snapping as he bowed and left them to join Mr. Draper in the library for a glass of excellent Madeira and some masculine conversation.

In the drawing room, Caroline was being berated by her mother in angry whispers.

"For heaven's sakes, Caro!" she began, "whatever are you thinking of to be so cold and abrupt? Whatever can the young man have done to so alienate you? And it is the outside of enough to have you setting yourself up as some elderly duenna—well! I shall never understand you—never!"

Caro confessed that she did not know what it was, but she had formed a dislike for the man as soon as she saw him, and Lizzie looked at her aghast, her rosy mouth forming an o of astonishment.

"Can you be serious, Caro?" she finally asked.

"Why, he is quite the most handsome man I have ever seen! So tall and dark, so—"

"Just like all the heroes in your books, my dear?" Caro asked. "But to me he appears to fill the villain's role more neatly. Such a dark complexion, such frowns, such an air of consequence! Do not lose your heart there, dear sister, for I am sure he thinks the Drapers of Hunstanton of no worth at all compared to *his* exalted lineage!"

"I am sure the Drapers may look as high as they like for marriage partners!" her mother said indignantly. "I see he has incurred your dislike in no mean way, Caro, and he seemed perfectly easy to me, and not at all starched up! But come, I have some orders for the chef, and I want you both to go up and change for dinner. I will send Grandish to you shortly!"

She rose and left the room to be sure the chef was preparing a worthy enough dinner for one of the nobility, and Caro and Lizzie exchanged glances. Their mother's superior dresser was never sent to assist them unless there was an important ball!

"Oh, why was I wearing my old muslin today?" Lizzie moaned as they made their way arm in arm up the winding stairs to their rooms. "Do you think my yellow silk or the blue taffeta most suitable tonight, Caro? And what are you planning to wear?"

Their heads together, they continued upstairs, Lizzie talking excitedly to her strangely quiet sister.

Caroline was dressed well before time but she did not make her way back to the drawing room when the first bell sounded, choosing instead to sit by her window with a book. The less time she had to spend in Lord Cannock's company, the better!

She looked very handsome tonight, her mother thought fondly, when she finally joined the others. Grandish had dressed her hair in becoming waves, in a more sophisticated style than Lizzie's, as befitted her age. She wore her grandmother's pearls, and her beige silk dress trimmed with dark brown ribbons was most becoming, as well it should be, coming as it did from one of London's finest modistes. Lizzie felt a pang of envy that she had no smart London gowns as yet, and pouted a little in her old gown of yellow silk, shaking her brown ringlets as she did so. Lord Cannock was polite, and took Mrs. Draper's arm as the butler announced dinner, leaving Mr. Draper to escort his two daughters. Caroline was not surprised to see that none of the other family members were to be present, and commended her mother on her forethought. The entire family hoped that Mary Martha would soon outgrow her habit of helplessly giggling at the most inappropriate times, but until she did so, she was banished to the schoolroom party.

The dinner was excellent and the wines superior, surprising Lord Cannock yet again. Although he was treated with the deference due a guest, no one fawned over him or made him the main topic of conversation, and he soon found himself relaxing and enjoying the delicious meal. The Drapers seemed a pleasant family who had a great deal to say to each other and whose affection for each other was obvious, even to a stranger. When the ladies retired and left the two gentlemen to their port, he realized he had enjoyed himself very much.

He was also reassured to find, when at last they rejoined the ladies, that he was not to be subjected to an evening of music, performed by the daughters of the house. He had been steeling himself for amateur piano playing, or worse, perhaps a harp and singing, but instead he found Mrs. Draper with her children around her; the two young ladies he had met, busy with their needlework. He did not seem to mind Mary Martha's giggle as she curtsied, smiled kindly at Clorinda, whose eyes were wide with awe, and had a handshake for young Andrew, manfully on his best behavior. The schoolroom group was soon ensconced at a large table playing spillikins, and there was a great deal of merriment before the ad-

vent of the tea tray signaled their departure upstairs.

He had no opportunity to speak to Miss Draper
again, for although she was perfectly pleasant, she
did not allow him to seek her out but remained by
her mother's side. Lizzie was not so retiring, and
sent him a few yearning glances that fortunately he
missed, since he was deep in conversation with her
father about Wellington's strategy in the Pennisula
War and the coming campaign.

He was astounded to discover, as he made his way
up to the comfortable apartments assigned to him,
and the services of Mr. Draper's own valet, that he
had enjoyed himself tremendously. His own parents
had died so many years ago and his only brother
lived so far away that he was not used to family life
and had never imagined it could be so satisfying!

Chapter Two

The following morning, he rose at his usual time, and after a good breakfast, which he ate alone in the cheerful breakfast room, attended by the butler and two footmen and enough food for any number of guests, he made his way to the terrace and paced up and down admiring the view. Draper House was set on a small rise, and acres of lawns and gardens sloped gently down to a small lake which had a graceful white gazebo on its shores. He saw young Andrew with his fishing gear, rowing a boat, and sent him a cheerful wave. He was about to return to the hall and inquire of the butler where he might find his host, when he saw the two youngest Draper daughters coming towards him from the garden. When Clorinda called to him, he came down the terrace steps and strolled across the lawn to meet them and ask politely how they did. Mary Martha giggled and blushed, but Clorinda seemed to have lost her shyness and awe of him, and confidently took his hand.

"Would you like us to take you to the stables, m'lord?" she asked. "Mama said you would most likely wish to see how your carriage is coming along!"

Lord Cannock said he would be delighted for the

escort and offered his other arm to Mary Martha, which caused another fit of giggling.

"You must not mind her," Clorinda said gravely. "It is only when she is embarrassed, you see, or feeling shy."

"I am delighted that it is not some fault with my appearance that is so amusing, Miss Mary Martha!" he said, smiling kindly at her. "I used to laugh at the most inappropriate times too, when I was your age!"

"*You* did?" Mary Martha asked, quite forgetting her bashfulness. Lord Cannock told them both several stories of his youth, most of them completely untrue, which had the advantage of setting Mary Martha much more at ease, and it was a friendly trio who finally entered the stableyard, where the wheelwright and his assistants were hard at work, watched carefully by Mr. Draper and his steward. Lord Cannock was introduced all around, and the wheelwright assured him he could be on his way in an hour or so.

"But I hope you will not hasten away so precipitously, m'lord!" Mr. Draper said. "Indeed, my wife expects you for luncheon at the very least, and would be happy to have you remain with us for as long as you like!"

Lord Cannock thanked him and said he would be happy to lunch, but must be on his way immediately afterwards, due to appointments in town.

He did not see either Miss Draper or Miss Lizzie that morning, nor were they present at luncheon, something he found vaguely disappointing. He had planned to expend all his wiles to make Miss Draper smile and look more kindly on him before he left. He was not at all used to being snubbed; to be treated so by an insignificant miss was a wholly new experience for him. Mrs. Draper explained that the girls had a long-standing arrangement to ride that day with friends, and both had sent their regrets that they must miss saying good-bye to him. Lord

Cannock had no way of knowing that Mrs. Draper had bustled them out of the house early and sent them on various errands around the estate, with a picnic lunch and orders not to return until late afternoon. Lizzie was indignant at being so banished, but Caroline smiled at her mother's transparent ploy and wholely unexpected wisdom! Not, she told herself stoutly as she took up the reins of the pony cart, that she had any desire to see the man ever again!

She wondered idly if he planned to be in town for the season, and then had to concentrate on Lizzie's disappointed chatter until she was forced to call her sharply to order. She told her sister tartly that to show too much interest in any man was extremely provincial and bound to be fatal! Since Lizzie acknowledged Caroline's superior wisdom when it came to social niceties and was anxious to make as good an impression as possible on the ton, she was soon agreeing that their absence would only serve to pique his interest until next they met.

And so the two sisters went on their way, temporarily in harmony, and delivered a basket of food to a laborer who had injured his foot, before going to sit for a while with their old nurse, now pensioned and living in a small cottage on the edge of the estate. This accord lasted until they were driving home. Lizzie again mentioned the earl, and Caroline told her that when she arrived in town and met other young men, she would soon see that Lord Cannock was nothing out of the ordinary way, something her sister found extremely difficult to believe.

The gentleman being so hotly discussed took his leave of the Drapers at two that afternoon, shaking hands and giving Clorinda a hug. He said everything that was proper and assured Mrs. Draper that he would be delighted to renew their acquaintance when they arrived in town the next month; and, thanking Mr. Draper heartily again for all his assistance, was soon on his way. Mrs. Draper waved good-bye, happy in the knowledge that the Earl of

27

Cannock could never suspect *her* of pushing her daughters at any eligible man in the vulgar way some of the more desperate mothers employed.

The month before the Drapers were to leave for town passed much too rapidly for Caroline and dragged endlessly for her sister Lizzie. There were a few family visitors on their way to various parts of England, breaking their trips with a few days' stay at Draper House, and these visits served to distract her somewhat, creating, as they did, occasions for special dinners, picnics, and rides about the countryside. Caroline was delighted when a carriage came up the drive, for it protected her from much tedious conversation about the endless possibilities that a season in town provided and the many treats in store to say nothing of the daily tally Lizzie kept of how many days were left before they should make their departure. Caroline rode about the estate with her father as much as she could. Mrs. Draper, knowing how hard this month was on both her eldest daughters, often excused Caroline and set Lizzie to her tasks instead. Although they were wealthy, none of the Draper girls were exempt from helping with the running of the household, from planning the meals to arranging the flowers or mending torn linen.

At last the long-awaited morning arrived. Several of the servants had gone ahead in a large coach containing many boxes and trunks, as well as such items of the household as Mrs. Draper did not feel she could be without during her stay in town. Winsted, the butler, a most superior man, had also been sent ahead to open the house and interview such servants as would be needed to augment the staff, and his wife, in her role as housekeeper, had accompanied him. Mrs. Draper knew that everything would be in perfect order when she and her daughters arrived, although she was concerned that she deprived her husband of their services. Mr. Draper laughed at her worries, saying they would manage very well with the large number of servants remaining in the country. By the time the lengthy farewells had concluded and everyone had been kissed and hugged heartily one more time, Lizzie was in a state of acute impatience, and bounced up and down on the seat of the traveling coach until her mother took her sharply to task. Mr. Draper rode along with them for some distance, and when he finally turned his horse towards home after a last cheerful wave, Mrs. Draper felt especially sad and wiped her eyes a little. Caroline leaned over and pressed her mother's hands in sympathy. Although Mrs. Draper was cast down at parting from her husband, Caroline knew her mother's spirits would revive, the closer they got to town.

Because Mrs. Draper much disliked setting a spanking pace, considering it extremely ill-bred, they did not cover anywhere near the fifty miles a day that was considered standard at that time, and so it was fairly late in the day when they stopped at the inn near Ely where they generally spent the first night.

The lighter carriage, containing a footman, a young maid assigned to Caroline and Lizzie, and Mrs. Draper's dresser, Grandish, that accompanied them had taken the lead an hour before, so that when they stepped down from their carriage in the yard of the "Green Man," all had been made ready, and their host and his wife were there to welcome them and usher them directly to their private parlor. Lizzie looked around her in awe at the busy posting inn. There were so many carriages and so many people, all making a great bustle as they went about their work. She whispered to Caroline that she was sure she would not be able to sleep a wink for the noise. Caroline noticed her sideways glance at a handsome young buck who was ogling both the girls in a very offensive way and sighed to herself.

"*En garde,* Caro!" she thought ruefully as she followed her mother and sister into the inn, putting a small hand on Lizzie's back and propelling her forward firmly.

After an excellent dinner served in their private rooms—much to Lizzie's disappointment, for the young man had been exceedingly handsome—the party retired to bed. The girls' new maid, a country girl named Peggy, was as excited as Lizzie as she helped her young ladies to bed and prepared to sleep on the pallet provided for her in their room. She was glad to get away from Grandish, for that woman had almost ruined her first trip away from Hunstanton by instructing her in her now more-exalted duties, all day long. The footman had eyed her with sympathy, but as he was much in awe of Grandish himself, had not volunteered a word unless directly spoken to. He himself had been chosen by Winsted to accompany the Draper ladies, and was much on his mettle to give satisfaction. He did think Peggy a very pretty girl, with her black curls and fresh complexion, and even ventured to give her a wink as Grandish was descending from the coach at the "Green Man." Peggy had blushed but she had returned his smile.

Now she snuggled down comfortably with a little sigh and hoped Miss Lizzie would not continue to chatter, so she might go to sleep. Miss Draper must have felt the same way, for in a few moments she told her sister to hush, in no uncertain terms.

The early start the next morning came a great deal sooner than Mrs. Draper had anticipated. Suddenly they were all awakened by the sound of running feet and much shouting and noise. Caroline sat up in the dark, startled, but when she smelled smoke, she threw off the covers and shook her sister. In spite of Lizzie's fears that she would be unable to sleep for the noise, she was so soundly asleep it was several moments before she could be brought to a sense of their predicament.

Caroline shook her again. "Wake up, Lizzie! Fire!"

At the dreaded words, Peggy rose quickly, still

groggy with sleep, and, lighting a candle from the dying fire on the hearth, began to dress with no unnecessary delay. Caroline nodded approvingly, as Lizzie stumbled from the bed and began to cry.

"Stop that at once, Lizzie, and get dressed! Peggy, as soon as you are ready, go and see where the fire is, and which is the best way out of the inn. But stay! First call my mother and her dresser—they are down the hall and may not have heard the alarm!"

Peggy did as she told, although she was frightened when she opened the door and saw the billowing smoke. Covering her mouth with her hand, she proceeded to feel her way down the hall, knocking at every door since she had no idea which one was Mrs. Draper's. Suddenly she bumped into another figure and found herself gripped in a pair of strong hands. She cried out in surprise, and the man said quickly, "It's me, Stanley, Peggy! Thank heavens I've found you! Are the young ladies awake?"

"Yes, they are dressing now!" Peggy replied. "Where is the fire, and how do we get out of the inn?"

"It started in the taproom. A spark must have fallen out on the floor and caught. The landlord says they will have it under control shortly, for his dog woke him before it could really take hold, but for safety's sake he thinks all the guests should leave the inn. We can use the back stairs—go back and tell Miss Draper to make haste!"

He turned and hurried away, and Peggy went back to the room she had just left. By this time Caroline was dressed and was helping her still-weeping sister. Peggy saw she did not need any assistance and began to pack their bags quickly.

"Good girl, Peggy!" Caroline said with her warm smile as she buttoned her sister's dress. Peggy told her what Stanley had said and Caroline nodded again. "There, Lizzie, you see it is not so bad! Be a good girl and sit down and put on your boots!"

Lizzie did as she was told, although she continued to weep. In a very few minutes, all three girls were making their way down the steep back stairs, Peggy burdened with their bags, Caroline carrying their traveling capes and reticules, and Lizzie clutching their dressing cases. The smoke seemed less already, but they were glad to reach the kitchens, where they were met by the innkeeper's wife and bustled out into the stableyard. Lizzie saw her mother and ran to her to be comforted, while Caroline and Peggy pushed through the crowd of guests and servants assembled, to join them. Although it was still dark, Caroline could see a faint gray lightening of the sky to the east and knew dawn was not far away. She reached her mother's side and put down her burden on top of a pile of baggage, and then turned to make sure that all the Draper party was safely there. Stanley bowed to her from his position behind Mrs. Draper, and Grandish looked as superior as ever. It might not be what she was used to, no, not at all, but even such a frightening happening had not the power to ruffle her majestic calm. Caroline wished Lizzie had the same fortitude as she patted and soothed her.

"Grandish! My salts and vinaigrette!" Mrs. Draper demanded. "Oh, dear! Such a thing has never happened to me in all the years I have been traveling!"

Lizzie burst into a fresh flood of tears and Caroline shook her impatiently. "Do control yourself, Lizzie! Whatever did Mama say to so upset you?"

"But...but if it has never happened before, you will all think it all my fault!" Lizzie moaned through her tears. Caroline wanted to laugh but she controlled herself, and soon had her sister calmed down and wiping her eyes. She was not pleased when she looked up and discovered the young man who had stared at them in such a familiar way, bowing and offering his services.

"Allow me to be of assistance, ladies!" he said. "Archibald Quentin at your service!"

Caroline saw that Lizzie was smiling and peeping at him from beneath her damp eyelashes, and wished her sister had the more common failing of a shiny nose and red eyes after a bout of crying, instead of looking like a dew-drenched rose! She was also annoyed to see that in her haste to get Lizzie dressed, she had left a number of buttons undone, exposing a very tantalizing glimpse of her creamy throat and bosom, a sight that Mr. Quentin was eyeing with approval.

Before she could speak, her mother drew herself up and refused the young man's services. She was frigidly correct as she thanked him for his kind offer, but he was left with no illusions that his help would be in any way welcome, and, bowing slightly in embarrassment, he turned away.

The fire was soon put out, and the innkeeper vowed that his dog should have a special bone for warning him before it had a chance to really take hold. The servants were sent scurrying to air out the taproom and start the morning fires and prepare breakfast. When he apologized to Mrs. Draper once again as he was escorting them all back to their rooms, she was very gracious.

"Do not refine on it too much, Mr. Boyd!" she said. "It was not your fault, and since no one was injured and the inn does not appear to be badly damaged, I propose we all say a prayer of thanks!"

The Drapers gathered in their private parlor, but after eating a little breakfast and drinking some tea, Mrs. Draper sent Stanley to tell the coachman to prepare the horses.

"The smell of smoke will linger for some time, girls," she confided, "and although I am sure we would all like to rest after our fright, I think it would be better to be on our way. We will plan to stop earlier today to recover."

The bags were repacked more neatly, the carriages brought to the door, and shortly thereafter the Drapers' party was once again on the road to London.

That evening, in Buntingford, they were all glad

to sleep through the night with no unpleasant surprises, although Lizzie was disappointed that the handsome young man who had tried to be of assistance had not stopped at the same inn. Wistfully she imagined he was even now in town, and wondered if she would ever see him again. As the coach lumbered along the next day, she even dreamed of a chance meeting, although she was careful not to mention this to Caroline. Even dreams, however, could not keep her from exclaiming and leaning forward in her seat as they approached the metropolis.

It was a sight to intrigue even veteran travelers, but to a young girl from the country, seeing it for the first time, it was awesome. It lay under a great pall of smoke, from the many thousands of chimneys, and the noise and bustle were incredible as they reached the more populated streets. Lizzie's eyes were wide as she stared at the tall tenements, all of them seeming to lean against each other for support, and the great numbers of poor, ill-clad people who hurried about the streets and narrow alleys, trying to avoid the carriages and carts and wagons. She became a little pale from the smells that issued from the open drains, but they were soon in the more fashionable part of town, and at last she could gaze at the beautiful shops and the parks and imposing mansions of the rich. She was here at last! She squeezed Caroline's hand in excitement, and her sister smiled at her eagerness. As they reached the house that they were to occupy for the season, Winsted and two footmen stood ready to welcome them and take the baggage up the shallow steps to the front door. To Lizzie it seemed very small after Draper House, but upon her naively mentioning this to Caroline, was told it was one of the larger houses for lease, and even boasted a ballroom. Lizzie was delighted to see they were so near the park, and it was all her mother could do to prevent her from trying to persuade Caroline to go off exploring at once.

"Plenty of time for that, my girl!" Mrs. Draper said fondly. "First however, we must rest, for we have a vast amount of shopping to do tomorrow so you will be presentable when we begin to go out in society."

At the magic mention of new clothes, and London clothes at that, all pleading stopped, and Lizzie tripped happily into the house. The only other members of the party to be so impressed as they rode into town were Peggy and Stanley, but since Stanley was the elder by a few years, he was able to present a face of complete indifference, while Peggy leaned forward eagerly and had to be reprimanded by Grandish.

"Sit back in your seat at once, girl! Such a vulgar display I have never seen! And do shut your mouth; you look like a fish!"

As Grandish searched her bag for a handkerchief, Peggy sent her a glance of pure dislike. I do not never! she thought. *You're* the one what looks like a carp! By the time the servants' carriage had reached Whitcomb Street, Grandish had explained again, in no uncertain terms, the behavior she expected from any of the Draper maids, and since she pointed out there was nothing easier than to find a replacement if Peggy proved too difficult to train, the girl decided to keep her tongue between her teeth and be as amiable as possible. She had no intention of being demoted to a tweeny, not after she had tasted all the delights of being a lady's maid. Miss Lizzie had already given her a very pretty bonnet, and Miss Caroline was so pleasant and easy to please, and had inquired so carefully for her family, that she knew she would love taking care of them. Besides, the salary was vastly larger than her previous stipend, and that was important to Ma and her brothers and sisters back home in Hunstanton, especially since her da had died.

The following days were spent getting settled and in daily shopping trips. Lizzie was ecstatic, declaring each gown more beautiful than the last, for never in her wildest dreams had she imagined her mother would buy her so much—ball gowns, morning gowns, driving gowns, habits, capes, pelisses and reticules, several beautiful bonnets, and slippers and gloves and lacy underthings! Caroline would have refused any new clothes if she could, but her mother would not hear of it, and when she saw a particularly lovely gown of orange crepe that was so becoming, with her brown hair and eyes, she was glad Mrs. Draper had insisted. She was fortunate to find a pair of kid slippers in the same exact shade in one of the larger emporiums, but if she and her mother both had not exerted strong restraint, Lizzie would have left the store, staggering under the weight of all the folderols that she had seen and instantly decided were indispensable. Her father had given her some pin money, and, as she pointed out, the prices were so reasonable, it seemed a folly not to purchase the shawl and the feather fan and the necklet of coral and...Caroline took her arm and led her from the store as quickly as possible. She began to hope very fervently that Lizzie would marry an extremely wealthy man!

Mrs. Draper had not been remiss in making morning calls and leaving her card so that everyone would know she had returned to town. She always took one of her daughters with her, and sometimes both, if she considered the person she was calling on important enough. Caroline, after two seasons, was completely at ease, and Lizzie, with her sunny ways and happy smile, was soon a favorite with all her mother's friends. As they sat one afternoon in Lady Salton's drawing room, drinking tea and eating little cakes, the old lady said shrewdly, "You'll have no trouble with the second one, Mary Ann! Not as much brains as a hen, but pretty as a picture, and such winning ways as well!"

Mrs. Draper smiled at the latter part of the comment, and then Lady Salton added, "Too bad she will go off before Caroline, but mark my words, Caroline will make the better match! I notice a vast improvement in her; she is the kind of girl who improves with age, while Miss Lizzie is in full bloom now! I advise you to take the first respectable offer made for her!"

Mrs. Draper was not so pleased with this statement, but she nodded her head in agreement. It would not do to contradict Lady Salton, for she was a revered member of the ton and had more than once put paid to a young lady's chances by one of her sarcastic remarks if that young lady should have offended her nice notions of propriety. Mrs. Draper was sure she did not have to take the first offer she received for Lizzie, for she was positive that *this* daughter at least would not return to Hunstanton unwed!

Chapter Three

After the Drapers took their leave of Lady Salton and returned home, they were surprised to see a traveling carriage at their door, and the footmen busily engaged in carrying a number of trunks and band boxes into the house. Mrs. Draper descended the steps of her carriage as soon as the groom had them in place, saying over her shoulder to her daughters, "Come, girls! It must be Belinda who has arrived! What a shame we were not here to welcome her!" When they gained the front hall, she was stunned to see the confusion that abounded. Even Winsted looked slightly bewildered at the amount of baggage, and apologized to Mrs. Draper for the inconvenience. When she had reassured him it was of no importance, he said, "I have put the young lady and her attendant in the drawing room, ma'am!" There was an ominous tone to his voice which Caroline was quick to note as she followed her mother. As they entered the room, she was unable to see the occupants immediately, but she heard a deep voice intoning, "Vanity, vanity, all is vanity, and don't you forget it, Miss Belinda! Fine feathers don't make a fine bird, you know!"

The voice was so depressingly foreboding that Caroline was surprised when someone else answered gaily, in a light and lilting soprano, "Oh, pooh, Wig-

39

gleworth! I will not listen to you, for I intend to be a very fine bird indeed, and as gay and as vain as possible!"

As Mrs. Draper moved forward, Caroline was able to see the speakers. One was an elderly lady in very old-fashioned black. Her gray hair was dressed in severe bands, so tightly fastened to her head that it made Caroline's head ache just to look at them. The face under the severe hairdo and bonnet was long and sallow, the mouth set in a disapproving frown, while the lines across her forehead seemed a permanent feature. Caroline felt a chill of dislike, but then her eyes went to the other figure who had turned towards them, and they widened in astonishment. She had never seen such a little doll of a girl! Why, she must have been less than five feet tall! She was dressed in dusty rose, and although her gown was cut severely, as befitted a traveling outfit, it was extremely dashing. Obviously Yorkshire was not as provincial as her mother had feared! The girl was removing a very becoming bonnet adorned with matching dusty rose plumes, and Caroline was able to see her abundant black curls and a pair of sparkling blue eyes, fringed with black curling lashes. Her features were lovely, and if Caroline suspected the rosy cheeks and lips were not a gift of nature, she had to admit the effect was admirable. The little lady swept towards them, her arms wide.

"But you must be my dear Aunt Draper!" she exclaimed, putting her arms around Mrs. Draper as far as they would go and reaching up to give her a kiss.

"My dear niece!" Mrs. Draper said, in slightly failing accents. Caroline had to smile. It appeared that instead of giving a shy young miss some town polish, her mama might be required to remove some!

Belinda turned to her cousins and smiled as Mrs. Draper introduced them. Lizzie only managed to say hello, for she was busily assessing the quality and style of her cousin's ensemble, but Caroline greeted her in a warm, welcoming way. At a dry cough behind them, Belinda waved a careless hand and said, "And of course here is my governess, who was so kind as to travel with me. Aunt Draper, Miss Draper, Miss Lizzie—Miss Wiggleworth!"

Caroline could see that Lizzie was having trouble restraining a giggle at the lady's name, and she herself felt it singularly inappropriate, as Miss Wiggleworth curtsied slightly and looked more disapproving than ever at her charge's informality. Belinda ignored her, and when Mrs. Draper had begged them all to be seated, and had summoned Winsted to order refreshments, she began to speak again in her lilting voice.

"Oh, I am so glad to be with you at last!" she exclaimed. "You have no idea how tedious the trip was—days and days and days! But now I am here, and I can hardly wait to begin!"

"Begin, my dear?" Mrs. Draper asked, in some confusion.

"Why, yes!" Belinda said with a smile. "Begin finding the most handsome and wealthy gentleman I can, to marry! And of course he must be of the highest rank possible! Tell me, dear aunt, how many unattached dukes do you number in your acquaintance?"

"My dear!" Mrs. Draper exclaimed in shocked tones, as Miss Wiggleworth shook her head mournfully and said, "Pride goeth before a fall, mark my words, for the Good Book tells us, 'I know thy pride, and the naughtiness of thine heart'!"

Belinda, who did not ever appear to heed her governess, ignored this gloomy pronouncement and looked at her aunt expectantly. As Mrs. Draper seemed unable to comment, Caroline entered the conversation.

"I am sure Mama will do her very best, cousin, but you cannot expect her to conjure up several dukes and earls and marquises within moments of your arrival!" She smiled as she said it, for she had taken a liking to this forthright little miss. Although every young girl who was brought to town for the season was under no illusions as to why she was so feted, it was never mentioned, and she was supposed to act as if she had merely arrived to attend the balls, do some shopping, and see the sights, and wasn't it nice of her dear parents to afford her such a treat? Such honesty as Belinda's, so blatantly stated, was unheard of!

Belinda was not at all discomfited by Caroline's wry comment, for she said gaily, "Good! You have a sense of humor, cuz, and that is most important! I love you already! And dear Lizzie"—turning to her other cousin, whose eyes were wide with awe—"how well we will look together, all three of us brunettes! I can hardly wait for the first ball! We must be sure to coordinate our gowns so they compliment each other. Tell me, do you each have a pale yellow ball gown? It might be fun to dress alike once in a while!"

The two girls soon had their heads together as they discussed clothes and ensembles, and Mrs. Draper was able to turn her attention to Miss Wiggleworth. Since she appeared to have no control whatsoever over her young charge, Mrs. Draper wondered why she had been sent. Miss Wiggleworth handed her a letter from her sister, which she had retrieved from the depths of a cavernous black bag. Caroline inquired gently about the journey while Mrs. Draper, after excusing herself to do so, eagerly read her letter.

While seeming to attend to an account of damp sheets, uneatable food, and endless rain, Caroline could hear her mother's surprised exclamations as she read, and even one 'my Lord!' and was most anxious to learn the contents of the letter herself. At last Mrs. Draper folded it thoughtfully and said, "I see you are going on to stay with relatives, Miss Wiggleworth. I must thank you for my sister's sake for your chaperonage of Belinda on the journey, and I tell you that you may turn over your charge to me without any qualms! We shall do our best to take care of her!"

Since her mother seemed a little doubtful in spite of these brave words, Caroline added her mite. "Yes, indeed, Miss Wiggleworth—we look forward to it!"

"You won't!" that lady retorted as she gathered her bag and shawl, and rose. "I'll take my leave of you, then, Mrs. Draper, for I still have a way to go. Belinda!" she commanded in a louder voice, causing the girl to look up inquiringly. "I shall remind you once again of the precepts I have taught you, and implore you to behave as you should! Remember the poet tells us, 'Satan finds some mischief still for idle hands to do,' and also 'There's no repentance in the grave'!"

Belinda laughed as she rose and came to say good-bye. "Dear, dear Wiggles!" she said fondly. "I *have* been a trial to you, have I not? Thank you for your care; I shall be writing to you shortly!"

"Hmmph!" her mentor sniffed, and after another stiff curtsy, allowed Mrs. Draper to usher her back to the hall, where she charged Winsted with the task of summoning a hackney for the governess.

In the drawing room Caroline asked Belinda if she would like to retire and rest, since her journey had been so uncomfortable.

"Good heavens, no! It was nowhere near as bad as Wiggles made out! I am sure you would agree that she is hardly of a *sunny* disposition! Besides, I am never tired. If I go upstairs, I shall have to help Yvette unpack, but if I stay here and make my dear cousins' acquaintance for some time longer, she will have it all done!"

"Yvette?" Lizzie asked.

"My maid," Belinda explained. "I brought her back with me from New Orleans last year."

"From America?" Caroline asked with interest. "I have heard it is a city of much international elegance, and not at all the savage outpost that some of our former colonies consider metropolises!"

"That is true! I was delighted to visit after I left the Carribean, for there I could buy all the latest French fashions! That is most important, you know, since Napolean has closed the Paris shops to us! I only hope the other servants will not think Yvette is in sympathy with the revolutionists; she was born in America, and although she has French parents, considers herself as much a native of that country as any New England puritan!"

The three girls continued to chat, and Caroline was struck by Belinda's sophistication and educated conversation. She was only twenty to Lizzie's nineteen, but in experience and the ways of the world, she was far ahead of them both!

As Caroline showed her finally to her room so that she might change her gown for dinner, Belinda squeezed her hand in parting and said, "Dear Caroline, I did mean it when I said I was glad to be here—as an only child I have missed the fun of having sisters, but now I feel I have two! What fun we will have, and your mama is not to worry about me— my papa never does! I shall observe all of society's ridiculous strictures without complaint, but I do intend to marry as soon as I can contrive it! Married ladies have so much more freedom, don't you agree?"

Caroline went away bemused. She had never considered that the married state might set her free to enjoy herself. Rather it had always seemed like a door that was closing, not opening. What a very unusual young lady her cousin was! She was not surprised when shortly thereafter she was summoned to her mother's room. After dismissing Grandish, Mrs. Draper gave her her aunt's letter to read, saying faintly, "I do hope that Belinda will not be a severe trial, my dear! But there, read it for yourself!"

Skipping quickly over the family news, Caroline soon reached the heart of the letter, the part about Belinda. It seemed that Lady Wells bemoaned the way her husband had spoiled his only daughter, allowing her all kinds of freedom and letting her travel extensively anywhere she wished. She was not a *bad* girl, Lady Wells stressed, crossing her lines in an agitated way that was very hard to decipher, but she was in no way your ordinary young lady. As for Lady Wells, she had washed her hands of trying to bring Belinda to a more decorous deportment, but in all fairness had to admit that Belinda never crossed the line into unseemly behavior, such as would give the ton a disgust of her. It was her advice to let the girl have her head—indeed, she did not see how her dear sister could do otherwise!—and not to worry unduly, for like the kitchen cat, Belinda always landed squarely on her feet!

Caroline reassured her anxious mother by saying that Belinda had promised to be on her best behavior, for she really did intend to marry well, and that as soon as possible. She poured her mother a cordial and soon had her restored to a calmer frame of mind.

Now there were three young ladies to ride in the Draper town carriage every afternoon in the park at the fashionable hour when all the ton could be seen there. One young gentleman, who was introduced to them by a friend, exclaimed as he bowed, "What a beautiful posy of flowers you have surrounding you, ma'am!"

Mrs. Draper thanked him calmly as he blushed bright red at his temerity, and Lizzie and Belinda favored him with such warm smiles that he left them in a daze. Caroline, adjusting a button on her kid glove said to them, "He *is* a lamb, isn't he? What a shame he is only a second son!"

"Alas!" Belinda mourned, a dimple peeking out as she adjusted her silk sunshade, which had sent Lizzie into transports of envy when she first saw it, "you have blighted all my hopes!" As her cousins laughed, she added pensively, "I do find very young men so terribly *gauche!* Perhaps I shall look for someone older to marry, someone who will understand me better!"

"I implore you, Belinda," Mrs. Draper said urgently and in some distress, "do not be constantly talking about marriage! It is not at all done! You will become a positive antidote if you continue to call attention to the fact that marriage is your only reason for being in town!"

Belinda promised to be good, but Caroline, observing her cousin closely, felt she could do anything she wished and her charm and beauty, to say nothing of her wealth and family name, would carry the day.

As much as Belinda created a stir abovestairs, it was nothing to what occurred in the servants' quarters. Her maid, Yvette, was a very attractive redhead, with a tiny waist and swelling bosom, both accented by the black silk dresses she wore, topped by a tiny organdy apron trimmed in lace to match the pert cap she wore on her curls. Her English was excellent although she had an intriguing accent, and every so often a French phrase would creep into the conversation. She soon had all the male servants eating out of her hand; even Winsted wore a bemused expression when he looked at her. Grandish, however, had taken an instant dislike to Yvette since Mrs. Draper had confided what an excellent maid she was, and lost no time trying to put her in her place by explaining in a very haughty tone how she should do Miss Wells's hair.

Yvette listened patiently, and when Grandish had finished, said, "How very interesting! Of course what you describe is only suitable to older ladies and would not do for such a dashing piece as Miss Belinda! Me, I will continue to do it *my* way!"

As Grandish had no control over Miss Wells's personal maid, her wrath over such impertinence fell on Peggy. One day when the ladies had all gone out shopping, Yvette heard her berating the girl for sending Miss Lizzie out with her hair so badly dressed and Miss Draper's gown positively creased! Peggy knew it was no such thing, but she bit her tongue and said nothing. When Grandish had finally finished and swept down the stairs, Peggy indulged in a few tears. It was so unfair!

Yvette came out into the hall and exclaimed, *"Qu'a-t-il? Intolérable femme!* Do not attend her, ...Peggy, is it not? That one has no more taste than...than a chimney sweep!"

Peggy had to giggle at the comparison, and the two girls smiled at each other. She was not hesitant to pour out her troubles to Yvette, who nodded her head in sympathy and told her she would be glad to help dress the young ladies when she had finished with her own mistress, and even teach Peggy some new ways of dressing the hair that were all the crack! As for Belinda, Yvette said airily, "We are—how you say?—most deft now, and I am sure she would not object!"

From that moment, Peggy was her greatest admirer, and since she much approved the dash and style Yvette showed, determined to emulate her instead of that old war-horse of a Grandish!

Feeling much better, she took some linen down to the laundry and was surprised and pleased to meet Stanley on the stairs. He asked her how things were going on, and when she smiled at him and demurely said she was doing very well, thank you very much! he winked and replied, "Aye, I've only to look at you to know how you're bloomin'!"

Peggy blushed and would have passed him, but he put a restraining hand on her arm and said earnestly,

"'Ere now, Peggy! Would you...would you like to walk out with me, your next afternoon off? I know more of London now, since Mr. Winsted sends me about the town so much on errands, and I would be happy to show you the sights!"

Peggy considered the invitation, her heart beating a little faster. She had always thought Stanley very handsome! Then she thought of Yvette and wondered how she would answer such a proposal, and, tossing her head, teased gaily, "Why, I cannot say, not just like that! Maybe—and maybe not!"

Before Stanley could insist, she ran lightly down the rest of the stairs, feeling very sophisticated, and leaving a much perplexed Stanley behind her. Surely he had not misinterpreted Peggy's smiles and blushes and sideways glances, but what was this all about? Females! he thought as he went on his way. They were awfully hard to fathom!

Caroline was not surprised to discover during the following days that where the Misses Draper and their cousin were, there was sure to be a coterie of men, all anxious to dance, to make light conversation, fetch a glass of negus, or pick up a dropped fan or handkerchief. It amused her to see that all their dance cards were so promptly filled within minutes of entering a ballroom, but she did not notice that many of the gentlemen who solicited her hand never asked for Lizzie's or Belinda's. Because she had, or so she thought, removed herself from the matrimonial lists, she was much more at ease in masculine company, her conversation more sprightly and teasing; and instead of biting back a witty or intelligent comment, now had no hesitation in speaking her mind. It intrigued many a gentleman who only last year would have ignored her! She watched her young relatives carefully, for although Belinda had convinced her that she could take care of herself in the give and take of society and could be completely demure when the occasion demanded it, she had no such high hopes for Lizzie, and more than once had had to take her sister aside and remonstrate with her for going too far—in her conversation, her flirting smiles, and her exuberance on the dance floor. Lizzie accepted her condemnations in good part, for which Caroline was grateful. At the Johnson ball, she was especially on her guard, for it was the largest party they had yet attended, and the crowded room made it difficult to keep an eye on her sister. Her mother, as she had known she would be, was worse than useless, gossiping with her cronies and ignoring her daughters and her niece until it was time to go home. If only, Caroline lamented to herself as she danced with Lord Everest and tried to keep Lizzie in view, Mama would not assume that because I am here and I was never any trouble, I will be able to control Lizzie and she will behave as I have always done! It was to her credit that Lord Everest did not know he did not have her complete attention, for she smiled and responded at all the right moments. As the dance ended, she curtsied gracefully, knowing that in her new ball gown of palest ecru, with her grandmother's pearl and diamond set, she looked very well. Lord Everest would have amended that to "beautiful" without a qualm! As he bent his arm to escort her from the floor, she heard a harsh voice behind her.

"Miss Draper! What good fortune that we meet again!"

She turned to see Lord Cannock smiling and bowing. He was impeccable in his black evening dress, from his snowy white cravat and skintight coat right down to his knee breeches, silk stockings, and gleaming black pumps. He wore no adornments, and his hair was dressed most severely for evening, but somehow she found him more elegant than many of the other gentlemen, with their fobs and rings and quizzing glasses and enormous stickpins. He gave her another devilish grin, his teeth as white as his cravat in his tanned face, and she was forced to curtsy in acknowledgment. Lord Everest departed after only a few words, and Caroline looked around desperately for her next partner and was glad to see Mr. Sawyer coming towards her so promptly. The earl had been pleasant and easy, but she did not intend to spend any more time in his company than she had to!

"May I hope for a dance, Miss Draper?" he was asking now, and it gave her a great deal of satisfaction to tell him that she was *so* sorry, but her card was completely filled for the evening! Just then Mr. Sawyer bowed to her and the earl exclaimed, "George! Good to see you in town again!"

Mr. Sawyer bowed and then said, to Caroline's delight, "You must excuse us, Matthew. This is my dance with Miss Draper, you see."

The earl detained him with a languid hand. "Come now, George," he drawled. "I ask a boon, dear friend! Although I am acquainted with Miss Draper, it has been some time since we met, and I hope you will give up your dance to me! If you are so generous, why, you may name any favor you wish in return!"

Mr. Sawyer looked more than a little confused, for such a situation as this had never come his way. Caroline was indignant. How dare he! But she could not say she had no desire for his company without being excessively rude, and when the earl put out an imperious arm, she was forced to accept it, leaving a very confused and disappointed Mr. Sawyer behind.

"My thanks, George, for your generosity! Be assured you will be rewarded, if not in this life, then surely the next!"

Caroline was distressed to find that the musicians had struck up a waltz, and when the earl took her in his arms, had all she could do to seem contentedly at ease. She did not speak to him, however, and finally he said musingly, "I daresay you think me a trifle high-handed, Miss Draper? To the victor belong the spoils, however, and after all, all George had to say was 'no'!"

"How would he dare, m'lord?" she asked sweetly. "I am sure that when *you* speak, everyone hastens to do your every wish!"

Her voice was perfectly even and reasonable, but the earl frowned. So Miss Draper was setting up to put him in his place again, was she? He decided the young lady needed a lesson very badly and decided he would be delighted to administer it! He whirled her in a turn and then said with a light laugh, "Of course it was too bad of me, but with your card filled, what was I to do? How are your father and mother and all your delightful family?"

Caroline, who felt a little ashamed of herself for her pique, answered him with more warmth, giving him some news of her father, but the mention of her family recalled her sister to her mind, and, as unobtrusively as possible, she looked around the room, trying to catch sight of her. There was Belinda, flirting outrageously with a very young beau whose face was crimson with delight at this attention, but Lizzie was not dancing, nor was she seated along the wall with her mama.

A small frown crept between her brows, and the earl said lightly, "If you are looking for Miss Lizzie, I saw her leave the room with Rodney Crawford; perhaps you had better warn her about that young man! He is not at all the type of companion your father would approve!"

Caroline had heard of young Crawford—a gambler and a rake even at the age of twenty-four, and heading ever deeper into debt and dissipation. She missed her step and said anxiously, "M'lord! You must excuse me!"

As she made to pull away, he grasped her even more tightly and proceeded to dance gracefully between the other waltzers until they reached the edge of the floor.

"*That* is the way you leave the dance, Miss Draper," he said kindly. "Not tearing away and starting the gossips to wondering what on earth I have said to so insult you!"

Caroline was speechless with anger at his pointing out such a faux pas. As if she did not know how to behave in a ballroom! Before she could reply sharply, he took her arm and led her through the doors.

"But come! You are anxious to find Miss Lizzie! I am sure you will remember whatever blistering setdown you were about to give me, another time. I believe they went this way...."

Caroline swallowed her anger and meekly allowed him to lead her down the corridor, checking each salon as they passed. At the end of the hall, around a bend in the wall, was a small alcove, and it was here that she found her sister, sitting very close to the young rake and laughing in protest as he held her hands in his and tried to raise them to his lips to kiss.

"I do so hope we are not interrupting!" the earl said smoothly. "Ah, my dear Miss Lizzie, how delightful to see you again! I can see you are enjoying your stay in town!"

Lizzie jumped, her eyes going in a guilty start to her sister's face, as Crawford rose hastily and bowed, his color high. Before she could stammer a reply, the earl continued.

"We are of course desolated that you must leave us, Crawford, but you are awaited in the ballroom! Be assured that I shall take care of the ladies, perhaps not as intimately as you would yourself, but in a reasonably competent way."

Crawford frowned, but there was nothing he could do but make his excuses with as much dignity as he could muster, and leave them. The earl seated Caroline next to her sister on the sofa and began to talk of other things lightly, until Lizzie's guilty flush died down. Caroline took her part in the conversation, and it was not long before he was escorting them both back to the ballroom. Lizzie was immediately claimed for the next dance, and the earl paused a moment to speak to Caroline in a soft voice.

"Do not refine on it too much, Miss Draper. Given Miss Lizzie, young Crawford, and a deserted alcove, it was inevitable!" He smiled so understandingly that Caroline was forced to return his smile in gratitude, but when she would have thanked him, he stopped her.

"No, no, you must not become amiable! Not when

you have snubbed me so royally from the beginning of our acquaintance! However, I must admit my relief that it is Miss Lizzie who is to receive the blistering setdown this evening, and not I!"

He bowed, a devil lurking in those dangerous blue eyes, and left her. As she made her way around the ballroom, she wondered why it was that just when she was feeling more in charity with the man, he immediately found a way to annoy her again!

Belinda was seated with Mrs. Draper, and Caroline saw from her lifted eyebrows that she knew something was afoot, but fortunately she was too wise to ask, with her aunt sitting right there. When Lizzie came up to join them shortly thereafter, nothing was said of the matter at all, but from the scared look she sent her sister, it was perfectly obvious that Lizzie knew she was in for it as soon as she reached home.

And in for it she was, not only from Caroline, but from Belinda as well. This little lady sat pensively all through Caroline's lecture, and when she finally stopped speaking said musingly, "Yes, and one wonders why, dear Lizzie, *why* you did it? I know it is amusing to flirt, but surely a little discrimination could have been employed. You must correct me if I am wrong, but are you especially desirous of allying yourself with someone who is, from what I have heard, in debt, who cheats at cards, and is steadily drinking himself to death as well?"

Lizzie burst into easy tears and said she had not meant to be bad, but she could not help it! Caroline wished she could slap her, but Belinda only soothed her calmly, and when Lizzie had dried her eyes and promised to do better in the future, her cousin added, "You must try, dear Lizzie, very hard! There is no need for any of us to settle for fifteenth best, after all!"

Both Caroline and Lizzie had to laugh at this ingenuous way of putting it, and it became quite a password between them in the days that followed.

When Caroline saw Belinda with General Bates, who had quite forgotten the endless love he had at one time professed for Miss Draper, she whispered as she passed, "No, nor the twelfth, either!"

Belinda gurgled and had to hide her face behind her fan. When either of them saw Lizzie encouraging some suitor unworthy of her name and fortune, it was much more pleasant to depress her flirting by mentioning only a number, and since Lizzie took eagerly to this new pastime, it saved a lot of explanations as well. She also began to rate the gentlemen who surrounded them all so avidly, and was delighted to be able to tell Caroline that she thought Mr. Sawyer a mere nine, and as for Lord Everest, nothing below a seven!

Mrs. Draper was considerably confused, after returning from a cotillion one evening, to hear her daughters and her niece assigning each man they had met with a number, but when the matter was explained to her, she clapped her hands in delight at such ingenuity. She was unable to join in the fun, however, for she could never remember if a fifteen was good or bad, and only smiled fondly at the girls whenever they played their game, as she put it. She did warn them all most particularly, however, that no mention of it must ever come to anyone else's ears. She was very happy with the attentions they were all receiving, and she had not missed the attendance of the Earl of Cannock on Caroline. *That* pleased her very much!

But Caroline was not so pleased when Belinda, who had watched her chatting with the earl and who had come at once to her side so she might be introduced, murmured as the earl turned aside to respond to a friend's greeting, "My dear Caro! A definite one!"

Caroline raised her eyebrows and shook her head repressively, but Belinda continued to nod as she shook her curls and laughed at her cousin's vehement denial of the earl's attractions.

Chapter Four

The evening Belinda met the Duke of Darwood
was a memorable one. The occasion was a grand ball
given by Lord and Lady Jersey, and the preparations
for this event far exceeded any that had already
taken place for lesser galas. Yvette and Peggy
rushed from one young lady to the next, while Grandish shut herself up with Mrs. Draper and majesti-
cally pretended not to hear the noise and excitement
as first Miss Lizzie called for advice as to whether
the pearls or the coral set looked best with her white
gown, or Belinda could be heard to exclaim that
never had her gown looked worse, and where was
Yvette, for she wanted her this minute! Caroline
went from one to the other, advising and approving,
and managing as well to attire herself with a min-
imum of help in a lovely new gown of palest lemon
yellow. Its tiny puffed sleeves were trimmed in a
handsome braid of pearls, and matching braid outlined the low round neckline that showed off her
shoulders and graceful throat to such advantage.
Yvette, nodding sagely as she did Caroline's hair up
in a smooth, sophisticated style, told her she had
never looked so well, and Caroline shrugged even as
she smiled and replied, "But it is all due to your
skill, Yvette! My hair has never been dressed so well

since you have convinced Peggy to abandon the old-fashioned ways of Grandish!"

Belinda had chosen to wear a gown of deep blue. Mrs. Draper felt it was much too sophisticated for a young miss in her first season, but she had learned that although she might suggest and advise her niece, Belinda did exactly as she wished, in spite of listening so courteously. Mrs. Draper had to admit, however, that the dress was stunning with Belinda's bright blue eyes. It was made with a deep neckline and caught under her breasts with a pleated sash of matching blue velvet that streamed to the floor from an elaborate bow in the back. Lizzie was envious of the sapphire and diamond set that completed Belinda's costume, but she consoled herself with the thought that her pearls and the appliqued roses that trimmed the hem of her gown were all the latest crack. When Yvette tucked a pair of matching pink roses in her dark brown curls, she was sure she looked prodigiously elegant. Finally satisfied, the three girls ran down the stairs to where Mrs. Draper was patiently awaiting them, regal in purple satin with a matching turban. Peggy and Yvette followed them with stoles and reticules and fans, and the long white kid gloves that Lizzie had forgotten.

Although Caroline had been to grand balls before, the other two girls were amazed when at long last their carriage made its slow way through the crowded street, vying for position with sedan chairs and other carriages. There was also the inevitable crowd of sightseers, linksboys, and flower sellers, watching the arrival of the guests. What a bustle and stir of excitement ran through the onlookers as first a footman called, "Make way for her ladyship's chair!" or a groom cried, "What ho! M'lord's carriage!" When they finally reached the steps, there were footmen in livery to help them alight, and when they had given their wraps to the waiting maids, they climbed the winding stairs with the other guests to where their host and hostess were waiting. An impressive major domo announced them in stentorian accents, and as they moved into the already crowded ballroom, Lizzie gasped with delight. All the many chandeliers were ablaze with light; the richly brocaded walls also had their share of elaborate wall sconces, between which were large mirrors in gold frames. These reflected the brilliant company, so richly attired and bejeweled, the men no less than the ladies. Even the footmen, standing to attention along the wall, were dressed in satin livery, their powdered hair tied back with a black ribbon. Lizzie moved a little closer to her mother, but Belinda merely inspected the company with an expectant, delighted smile. As they strolled about the room and greeted their friends, several gentlemen came to claim a dance with one of the Three Graces, for so they had been named by Lord Everest, a sobriquet quickly picked up by the other male members of the ton. When Belinda heard of it, she clapped her hands and declared she could not wait for the next costume ball, for then they could appear as the three graces in fact as well as in name. Caroline had raised a skeptical brow.

"My dear cousin!" she said, trying to appear stern. "Perhaps you have not seen how goddesses are generally depicted in art? I very much fear Mama would not approve our emulating them!"

Belinda laughed. "Perhaps our draperies would not be so transparent and revealing, but we can wear wreaths of flowers in our hair, and Grecian sandals!"

Lizzie said that as far as she was concerned, she could not make up her mind whether the robes the graces wore reminded her more of nightgowns or winding sheets, and did Belinda really think they would look well, so attired? This ingenuous statement sent Caroline and Belinda into gales of laughter, with Belinda promising the final effect would be not only flattering, but memorable!

Now she smiled and added another name to her card. Caroline had turned away a little to greet Lady

Salton, when the Earl of Cannock appeared at her side.

"Evening, m'lady! Miss Draper!" he said. "I trust I am not too late *this* evening to secure a dance?"

Calmly he took the card from Caroline's unresisting hand and wrote his name in two places with a great deal of aplomb. Caroline silently gritted her teeth, while Lady Salton cackled. "It will take a royal setdown to depress the earl's conceits, my girl!" she said, for she had not missed the tiny frown Caroline had for the earl's high-handedness.

"But I have it on good authority, m'lady," the earl said easily, "that no one would dare oppose me! I believe the exact words were that everyone would naturally hasten to obey my every wish! Now, who said that, I wonder?"

He appeared to ponder the problem as Lady Salton laughed and Caroline flushed. Then she curtsied and said coolly, "You must excuse me, m'lady, for I have promised to attend my mother. Lord Cannock."

As she walked away, she was conscious she was being watched by the pair. "Nice gel," Lady Salton remarked. "Whatever are you about there, Matthew? She does not even seem to like you, and I have seldom seen you go so far as to actually cross a ballroom in order to gain a dance! Besides, you are never in attendance this early! I wish I knew why you young bucks think it is all the thing to arrive at any party hours after its start and still expect your hostess to be delighted to welcome you! Ragtail manners, I call it!"

The earl nodded his head. "But surely you cannot fault me on that this evening, m'lady! Behold me, one of the first arrivals!"

"Yes, I see you!" Lady Salton said tartly. "What I want to know is *why?* Can Miss Draper finally have broken down your up-to-now impregnable defenses?"

The earl smiled a little thinly. Trust Lady Salton to cut through the niceties to get the information she sought! They had been acquainted forever, so he knew the sharp interest she took in all the ton's doings.

"Perhaps it would be more truthful to say, where Caroline Draper is concerned, I stand more in the position of mentor. The young lady badly needs a lesson; I shall be delighted to administer it!"

Will you, now, Lady Salton thought shrewdly as the earl gracefully bowed and moved away. My, my! The season was fast shaping up to be extremely interesting; she was so glad she had decided to come to town again, for there was nothing she liked more than to watch the tangles that were inevitable as love affairs developed, and it would be most gratifying to see the mighty Matthew Kincaid, so long pursued and idolized, put in his place! She was sure Caroline was just the gel to do it! As she moved to join Mrs. Draper and ask a few adroit questions, she caught sight of Lizzie Draper, romping most indecorously with the young Baxter twins, and she shuddered. Thank heavens the earl had not set his sights on her! He would make mincemeat of her in minutes if he should turn on his considerable charm. Caroline, she was sure, was made of sterner stuff!

In the meantime, Belinda was chatting with Lord Everest, who, in hopes that she might remain by his side, had asked her about her travels in the Carribean. She had spoken enthusiastically of Jamaica and of Grenada, the tiny green island that was the farthest south of all the Windward Islands, where she had visited some of her relatives on their extensive banana plantation. Although pretending to be vastly interested in her descriptions of flowers and mountains that rose from a pale green sea, Lord Everest was more enthralled by her brilliant smile and sparkling eyes, so he was not aware of the gentleman who appeared at his elbow.

"My dear Everest!" a weary but authoritative voice exclaimed. "How many ages since we have had a chance to speak together!"

Startled, Lord Everest turned to see the Duke of

Darwood smiling thinly at him. Since the duke had never condescended to acknowledge him in any way during his four seasons in town, Lord Everest was considerably confused. At least he was until he saw the calculating, intent look the duke was giving Miss Wells. He hesitated, loath to share his prize, until the duke turned to him, his eyebrows raised.

"Have you lost your power of speech, dear boy?" he inquired idly, and Belinda smiled a little. She was not in the least discomfited by the close inspection she was receiving, and when the duke had insolently let his gaze travel from the tips of her velvet slippers up her figure to her face, he was a little startled to see her unconcerned smile. It was almost as if she were saying to him, "Feel free to inspect me all you care to, Your Grace! It matters not a jot to me whether you approve me or not!"

As Lord Everest reluctantly introduced them, the duke realized that Miss Wells was a new come-out indeed. Never had any young lady honored by his attention, so calmly curtsied and so easily given him her hand in such an assured way. Why, he thought in some amusement, it is almost as if she expects me to kiss it, in the French style! Here was no blushing miss, tongue-tied with delight at being introduced! How refreshing!

"Miss Belinda Wells," he repeated slowly. "I believe I am acquainted with your father, Miss Wells; that is, if your home is in Yorkshire."

Belinda agreed that it was, and Lord Everest intervened hastily, indignant that his prize was being stolen right in front of his eyes.

"She is a most inveterate traveler as well! Why, she has just been telling me the most interesting tales of the Carribean and America, which she visited last year!"

The duke turned back to the young man and raised his quizzing glass. The gesture had more than once sent young men fleeing at being so haughtily inspected, but Lord Everest bravely stood his ground.

Ignoring that steely glare, he said, "Please continue, Miss Wells, for it was interesting above all things!"

Good for you, Lord Everest, even if you are no more than a seven, Belinda applauded silently even as she shook her head. "I am so sorry, m'lord, but I must leave you now. My aunt will be wondering where I am, and I would not cause her to worry. M'lord! Your Grace!"

With another graceful curtsy, she left them before Lord Everest could offer to escort her. He was not long in quitting the duke's company, for the latter's sudden interest in their friendship seemed to have vanished with the little lady in blue. The duke retired to a position against the wall and watched Belinda's slow progress until she reached Mrs. Draper's side. His green eyes narrowed as he watched her curtsy to her first partner as the dancing began.

He did not approach Belinda again that evening, but his eyes were often drawn to the little figure in deep blue as she danced and chatted and flirted with the members of her court. If she were aware of his scrutiny, she did not let on by so much as a glance in his direction. But of course she was aware of it, for she had been out long enough to know what that sudden gleam of interest in a man's eyes signified, and the duke's eyes had positively blazed. She wondered, as she danced with Frederick Baxter, if she were also attracted to the duke, and could not decide whether she was or not. He was of no more than medium height, but his considerable air of consequence made him appear taller and more commanding. He had straight sandy hair, and pale green eyes that seemed to see a very great deal indeed. If she had to guess his age, she would have put him in his middle thirties, and although his features were regular enough, you would not have called him a handsome man. Belinda wondered why, even as she laughed at one of Mr. Baxter's sallies. Perhaps it was his rigid air of self-importance, or those tight lips and disdainful, cold green eyes that detracted from his looks. It was almost as if being a duke had convinced him he was far removed from the rest of the ton, and it was only with the greatest condescension that he acknowledged the rest of them at all.

Halfway through the evening, she found herself beside Caroline for a moment, and asked her if she were acquainted with the Duke of Darwood. Caroline, her eyes on her sister across the room, nodded and then turned.

"Have you met him, cuz?" she asked with interest. "Yes, I was presented to His Imperial Majesty last year, but I very much doubt that he remembers the occasion!"

For her, her tone was almost tart.

"You do not appear to be overwhelmed by the gentleman, dear Caro!" Belinda laughed. "How would you rate him, therefore?"

Caroline considered the question for a moment before she answered. "Definitely a one in rank and fortune, but...but no more than a ten in kindness and charm and concern for his fellow men! Why, what do you think of him, Belinda?"

Her cousin squeezed her hand. "I have not yet decided! But I must be gone, for here comes your 'one' to claim his dance!"

Caroline studied her dance card and saw the earl's bold handwriting and shook her head, but Belinda just laughed at her and melted away.

As the earl led Caroline to the dance floor, he asked, "And what is so amusing to your cousin, Miss Draper? Or perhaps I should not ask?"

Caroline smiled sweetly as he took her in his arms. "Oh, much better not, m'lord!" she assured him. Not at all discomfited, he grinned down at her as the waltz began, his teeth very white against the tan of his face.

"Girlish secrets, hmm? Very well, we will talk of other things. I see your sister has abandoned Rodney Crawford for the Baxter twins. What a relief it will be for the entire Draper family when Miss Lizzie finally drops the handkerchief!"

Caroline was forced to smile at his tone of weary concern. "But surely, m'lord," she said demurely, "there is safety in numbers?"

The earl laughed and then his hands tightened briefly as they turned. Caroline had to admit he was a beautiful dancer, even as she tried to draw slightly away from those strong, guiding hands. She looked up to see his eyebrows raised in amusement, and blushed a little.

"And I would like to know, m'lord," she said hastily, without thinking, for she was furious at herself for blushing, "how it comes about that whenever we dance, it is always a waltz!"

Horrified at what she had blurted out, she stopped in confusion, and even missed her step for a moment. The earl chuckled.

"Why, Miss Draper, it is either my very good fortune, or perhaps—and more truthfully—my excellent planning! You see, I have been to so many of these balls that I seem to know instinctively when the orchestra has played enough country dances and quadrilles, and is about to strike up a waltz! And it is so very hard to carry on a conversation when your partner is so often separated from you in the set, don't you agree? All that bowing and curtsying, and dancing around with other members of the figure! How are we to become better acquainted if we cannot converse—privately?"

At this provocative statement, Caroline nodded distantly, aware from the devil in his eye that he knew very well how she wished she might reply. The man was impossible! She wished there were some way to let him know, without being insufferably rude, that she had no desire to become better acquainted, especially with him, so arrogant as he was!

When the Draper carriage finally returned home in the early morning hours, only Lizzie was able to drop off to sleep easily. Caroline and Belinda lay in their respective beds and listened to the early-morning songs of the sparrows and watched the sky slowly lightening in the east as they considered the men who were so much on their minds. But dawn did not bring any solutions; and finally, worn out from the dancing and the late hour, they slept, and not even the noise of town woke them for the rest of the morning.

Yvette and Peggy had nothing to do until their mistresses called for their chocolate, so they settled down happily in the small sewing room to mend some of the girls' clothes and enjoy a brief gossip. It was here that Stanley found them. He had been sent upstairs with a note for Mrs. Draper, and when he found he did not have to wait for a reply, made so bold as to tarry. Old Winsted will never know, he told himself as he knocked on the sewing-room door. Both girls looked up as he entered, and he flushed a little when he saw the perceptive look in Yvette's eyes. She seemed to know he had hoped to find Peggy alone. Manfully he decided to ask the question he had come to propose, and now it was Peggy's turn to blush when he asked her to walk out with him that afternoon. She was a little annoyed that Stanley not only knew when she was free, but had asked her in front of Yvette. That young lady had her red head bent over her sewing in seeming disinterest, but Peggy knew she was listening to every word.

"Oh, Stanley!" she said airily, tossing her head as she had seen Yvette do, and peeking at him from under her lashes, "I am afraid I have other plans for the afternoon! I am so sorry!"

This was a complete lie, but Stanley had no way of knowing it, and he frowned. Had Peggy struck up an acquaintance with some other servant from another house? There was that very tall, very handsome young footman across the street, and he had caught him looking at Peggy one day when he was holding the carriage door for the young ladies and their maid as they were about to go off on a shopping expedition. He had glared mightily, but the other man had only grinned cheekily at him and laughed. Stanley was now as red as the dress that Peggy was mending, and he was very angry to be made such a fool of in front of the Frenchy maid. Suddenly Yvette looked up, and her eyes were so understanding and kind, he felt immeasurably better. Taking a deep breath, he said, "Perhaps Miss Yvette would like to see the sights, then!"

Horrified at what he had blurted out, he stopped in confusion. Peggy looked stunned, but Yvette smiled at him again.

"Thank you, *monsieur!*" she said with her intriguing accent. "I should—how you say?—be delighted, for I have not yet had a chance to explore the city!"

In a daze, Stanley completed the arrangements and left the room, trying to look satisfied at the change in the afternoon's companion. Peggy saw the smile on his face, and miserably decided he had wanted to ask Yvette all along! When the door closed, she laughed a little to show she was unconcerned, and Yvette said, "But I thought you liked Stanley, cherie. Why did you say you had other plans?"

"I'm sure I don't care for him one way or the other!" Peggy said lightly past the lump in her throat. "And I wish you both a pleasant afternoon; I only hope you won't be bored to death by him!"

Yvette bit off a thread, her eyes searching her companion's face intently. With a little smile, she changed the subject.

Every morning the servants were used to opening the big front door many times to receive the notes and flowers delivered in such great number to their young ladies, and although Winsted grumbled at the amount of energy he was forced to expend every time the brass knocker sounded, there was often a little smile of satisfaction on his face as he counted the floral offerings and cards. He was delighted to see Miss Caroline was holding her own, for she was a favorite of his, although there was no gainsaying the fact that both Miss Lizzie and Miss Belinda had the edge on her in the way of admirers. The younger footmen had a bet each day to see who would come out ahead, but they were careful to keep this from old Winsted!

The morning after the Jerseys' ball, Winsted himself accepted a very handsome bouquet of roses with a note attached. He knew from the seal that Miss Belinda had found herself a ducal admirer, and for someone of this consequence, he made the trip up the stairs himself, to deliver the flowers in person. Yvette answered his measured knock. She had just brought up Belinda's chocolate and was in the act of opening the curtains. When she saw Winsted, she raised her eyebrows and was rewarded by a conspiratorial nod, although all the butler said was, "Flowers for Miss Wells!"

Belinda, who was attired in a very bewitching lace peignoir and matching cap, much bedecked with pale blue ribbons, was stretching and yawning like a little kitten, but her blue eyes opened wide when she saw the magnificent roses in their silver vase, for there must have been three dozen of them at least, with the longest stems she had ever seen! Yvette handed her the note and went to place the flowers on a table near the window, where their deep red petals would catch the light, all the time watching Belinda's face as she slit the envelope and read the note inside. She did not learn very much, however, for there was no happy smile or expression of delight. Instead Belinda put the note down with a little sigh and looked out the window, her brow puckered in thought. It was not until her mistress was dressed in a lilac morning gown and had gone downstairs that she was able to find out who had sent the flowers. Belinda had left the card carelessly open on the bed, and Yvette read it without a qualm. She was still not much wiser, for all it said was "My sincere compliments! Darwood." She resolved to ask Stanley who this "Darwood" was, for she was much attached to her mistress, and took all her concerns very much to heart. She knew Belinda could take care of herself, but she had not appeared to be especially delighted to receive such a beautiful tribute, and Yvette wondered why.

Belinda found both her cousins and her aunt in the small salon they all used so often in the morning. There were no morning engagements that day, which was just as well, for Lizzie especially was still yawning from the late hours they had kept the night before.

Caroline and Lizzie were reading their mail, and Belinda idly leafed through the notes she had received that day, but she seemed so preoccupied that Caroline looked at her carefully. Then Lizzie distracted them all by asking if Belinda and Caro considered either of the Baxter twins as much as a four. Caroline laughed and said, "Eight!" and Belinda added wryly, "and a half—each!" Lizzie pouted a little. True, she knew they were madcaps and wild young Corinthians, up to every deviltry they could find, but their attendance on her at the ball last night had been very gratifying, and had caused them all much amusement since Lizzie could not tell them apart, and had no idea if it was Freddy or Ferdie who was paying her such fulsome compliments! Twins had never come her way before, and to have two such handsome and identical young gentlemen dancing attendance on her had doubled her enjoyment of the evening considerably. Besides, they seemed to be great rivals, each determined not to be outdone by the other, so an extravagant statement from Ferdie called forth an even more flowery phrase from Freddie.

Now, a little stung by Belinda's comments, she asked, "And what of the gentleman who sent you those beautiful roses this morning, cuz? Was he an eight and a half too?"

Belinda paused for a moment before she answered,

and then she took a seat near Caroline and said casually, "I have not decided as yet. They were from the Duke of Darwood, whom I met briefly last night at the ball."

Mrs. Draper looked up, her eyes wide with interest. "Never say so, Belinda!" she exclaimed. "My word, the Duke of Darwood! What a coup for you, my love, if *he* is interested!"

On Belinda asking why he was so important, she added, "Why, besides his title and his wealth, he has been on the town forever and he has never succumbed to any lures. Oh, the caps that have been set for him; the snares that have been laid!" She hesitated and then asked, "Did you like him, Belinda?"

"I am sure I cannot say, for we did no more than chat for a moment, and he never came near me again the whole evening. I was most surprised to receive his flowers this morning, I can tell you!"

"What did he say on the card?" Lizzie asked, the Baxter twins relegated to the background at her cousin's news.

"It was hardly lavish and adoring!" Belinda told her. "Merely, 'My sincere compliments, Darwood.'"

"I wonder what he meant?" Lizzie asked in a disappointed way, for she was used to much more explicit praises than that. Caroline laughed as she picked up the notes her mother had let slip to the floor and Belinda told them what Caroline had said about the duke last evening, which caused Mrs. Draper to say in disparagement, "Oh, Caroline! She is much too severe! I am sure the duke is a perfectly fine person!"

"With all kinds of redeeming human qualities, Mama?" her oldest daughter asked wryly. "Qualities he has never cared to show the world before? Well, for my part, I think him cold and callous and conceited!"

"But Caro," Lizzie said earnestly, "you do not like the Earl of Cannock, either, and both Mama and I have found him to be most kind and gentlemanly!"

Caroline had to smile. *"Touché,* Lizzie!" she said and picked up her needlepoint. "Perhaps you and Mama are right, and I am much too fussy. But there, that is the sign of an old maid, is it not?"

The cries of horror that greeted this statement amused her very much. Mrs. Draper declared that she did not know what she was to do about such an obstinate daughter, and Lizzie and Belinda were loud in their denials that she was any such thing!

Caroline sat stitching quietly, and when there was a moment of silence, said thoughtfully, "Perhaps that is what I wish to be, after all! To me, marriage appears to be a cage; for, once trapped in it, there is no escape. But if I remain single, I shall never have to answer to a man, or cater to all his whims, or be cheerful when he is in a bad mood, or entertain all his distasteful friends and difficult relatives! I can instead please myself! I have to admit that is a much more pleasant outlook to me than marriage, even to someone of the most exalted rank!"

Mrs. Draper said woefully she washed her hands of her, and went away to get ready for a shopping trip. Belinda was to accompany her, and although Lizzie had also shown some interest in the expedition, now she said she was very tired and preferred to remain at home. Caroline looked at her sharply. For Lizzie to give up a chance to shop meant there was something in the air, and she resolved to watch her carefully.

As Mrs. Draper and Belinda were seated in the carriage, the older lady sighed heavily, and when Belinda asked her what was troubling her, she replied, "My dear, I am in such despair about Caroline! Wherever did she get such notions? For I have been very happy in my marriage, you know, so it cannot be from my example that she speaks so vehemently against it! But to liken that blessed state to a cage or a trap—my dear!"

Her niece patted her hand kindly. "I would not worry about it too much, dear aunt! When Caro falls in love, her ideas will change in a trice! She is much more romantic than either Lizzie or I, you know. Indeed, therein lies the problem, but someday she will love—and very deeply, too!"

Mrs. Draper would never have called her eldest daughter romantic; why, Lizzie, who was constantly falling in and out of love, was the romantic one, she thought, but she brightened at Belinda's cheerful analysis of the situation, even if she was not clever enough to understand it. Then she said gloomily, "But since she takes a dislike to just about every gentleman she meets, how will she ever fall in love? I tell you, Belinda, it has caused me many a sleepless night of worrying!"

Belinda thought for a moment, and then said slowly, "I think Caro will never settle for second best, dear aunt, as perhaps I might, or Lizzie! But she will find her 'one,' never fear!"

"I do so hope you are right!" Mrs. Draper said fervently. "But there, there is nothing to be done about it now in any case! Tell me, my dear, was it a bonnet for your green walking dress or your peach gown that we are looking for today?"

That afternoon, Peggy miserably wandered around the shops and fashionable streets alone until she remembered that if she should chance to meet Stanley and Yvette, he would know she had no escort and had lied to him. She hurried home and spent the rest of her precious time off in the tiny attic room she was able to call her own. She was sorry she had ever come to London! It was crowded and ugly and boring, and she wished she were home in Hunstanton right now! She would have felt much better if she had known how unhappy Stanley was, until Yvette took pity on him and turned the conversation to the one subject he wanted to discuss.

By the time they returned home late that afternoon, they understood each other very well, and were well on the way to becoming the best of friends.

Chapter Five

Caroline was not at all surprised when both the Honorable Frederick Baxter and the Honorable Ferdinand Baxter came to call that afternoon, for in spite of all the activities Lizzie had ingenuously suggested she might enjoy, she had remained firmly at her sister's side.

The Baxters did not arrive together; Ferdie was first, but he had barely handed his hat and cane to Winsted and been ushered into the drawing room before his twin was on the doorstep as well. They glared at each other as they waited for Miss Lizzie to join them. It was well known throughout the ton that the two twins were forever trying to best each other. If Freddie won a point to point, Ferdie was sure to ride at the next meet hell bent for leather and with complete disregard for life or limb; if Ferdie won a large amount at Newmarket, Freddie more lavishly laid down his blunt at Ascot; Gentleman Jackson had forbidden them to spar together in his exclusive boxing salon, for he said they seemed set on killing each other to the exclusion of all the arts and sciences of the ring that he had so patiently taught them. Their father threatened and their mother sighed over each new episode, but no one could change them. Mrs. Baxter felt they had begun quarreling even before birth, for she had had a most unpleasant pregnancy and a difficult labor—almost, she thought, as if they were even then fighting each other for the privilege of being the first to arrive in the world. And yet they were inseparable, for if you saw Ferdie at a party, you were sure to meet Freddie shortly thereafter. They were handsome young men, tall and slim, with identical high-colored complexions and butter-yellow hair above bright blue eyes. They had never been in love before, and their sudden mutual attraction for Lizzie Draper boded no good for the peace and quiet of London.

Lizzie was only too pleased to play one off against the other, having no idea how dangerous a pastime that was when dealing with such highly competitive young men, and Caroline, who had come down to the drawing room with her, made a note to warn her as soon as possible. Freddie gracefully cut his brother out by asking Lizzie to join his party at Vauxhall in two evenings' time, and Ferdie indignantly wanted to know when plans for such a party had been made.

"For you know very well, bro, I am promised to Lord Haversome that evening!" he said forcefully.

"Know you are!" his brother agreed cheerfully. "Not asking you! I, however, have been so remiss as to neglect answering Haversome's invitation; therefore I can escort Miss Lizzie to Vauxhall—alone!" Catching sight of Caroline's astonished glance, he added quickly, "And Miss Draper too, of course!"

"Why, thank you, sir!" Caroline said, glad she was not of a sensitive nature, and trying not to laugh out loud at this backhanded compliment. "I am not sure that we are free; I shall have to speak to my mother and my cousin first!"

"Happy to invite 'em all!" Freddie said with a magnanimous gesture. "Most pleased to get up a party!"

Caroline was bubbling with laughter until she caught sight of Ferdie's indignant face, and then she hastened to smooth over these potentially dangerous waters by changing the subject adroitly.

Some time passed, and Caroline thought the twins would never take their leave. Both were determined to outsit the other, and if Mrs. Draper and Belinda had not come in just then, she did not know what she would have done to get rid of them. Both of them rose and bowed to Mrs. Draper, and in a few moments found themselves outside.

Freddie was beaming; Ferdie was furious.

"Think you've pulled a march on me, have you, twin?" he asked, shaking his fist and glowering. "You'll see!"

Freddie patted his arm. "Must be a gentleman, Ferdie, and take your losses with a smile! I was just too clever for you, nipping in ahead, that's all!"

Ferdie threw off the consoling hand. "You'll see, Freddie! That's all I can say! You'll see!"

Suddenly he whirled on his heel and strode away, leaving his twin to make his leisurely way to his club, well pleased with his afternoon's work and wondering what young gentlemen of his acquaintance he could call on to make up his party.

Lizzie was also gratified by the visit of two such handsome young men, so obviously vying for her favor. When Caroline pointed out the danger and told her of the Baxters' volatile temperaments and unceasing rivalry, she tossed her brown curls and giggled.

"I know! Is it not diverting?"

Caroline sighed and applied to her mother for help, but Mrs. Draper was preoccupied and told her she was making too much of nothing. She was much more worried about what Caroline had said that morning than Lizzie's conquests, for she realized the Baxters were much too young and careless to be serious contenders in the matrimonial race, and since this was so, had little interest in them. She agreed to attend Vauxhall with the Honorable Freddie and his party, after Lizzie teased her for her consent, but when Belinda was apprised of it that evening at dinner, she begged to be excused.

"I have promised to join Lady Salton at a small dinner party she is giving that evening, ma'am. She asked me at the Jerseys' ball, and I knew you would want me to accept."

"My, yes!" Mrs. Draper said enthusiastically, and when Caroline looked at her questioningly, she added, "I am sure I would not like to be forever in her company, for she has a very sharp tongue, girls, but it does no good to put up her back. If she is displeased, she can easily ruin a young lady's chances with only a word!"

"I wish you joy of the evening, Belinda!" Caroline murmured. "It does not sound at all diverting!"

"No," Belinda said, selecting a pear from the silver salver the footman was proffering, and beginning to pare it carefully with her fruit knife, "but she asked me at the very end of the evening, and as I was tired and unable to think of any other engagement, I was forced to agree!"

"I wonder who will be there?" Mrs. Draper pondered. "Lady Salton does not entertain at all these days; in fact I have heard it said that she considers it everyone else's privilege to entertain *her!* And most assuredly she did not mention it to me!"

Lizzie broke into the conversation by asking Caroline what she should wear to Vauxhall and what entertainments there would be at the famous garden. Caroline, remembering her one visit there with pleasure, soon had Lizzie's eyes glowing with her account of the music and the fireworks, and the many walks and gardens.

Unfortunately only Lizzie enjoyed herself the next evening. Mr. Baxter had indeed assembled a party. The two gentlemen that he selected to make up his numbers were so shy that they had very little to say, for he felt he had enough competition from Ferdie and wanted no handsome young beaux to distract Lizzie from his own charms. Caroline was distressed to find that Mr. Kindle, who had tried to propose to her last season, was included. He had not lost his stutter, or his devotion to Miss Draper, for he pressed her hand most meaningfully as he helped her into the boat that Freddie had hired to take them across to Vauxhall.

Mrs. Draper found herself trying to make conversation with a boy who seemed not much older than her son Andrew, and as she did not know his family, had very heavy going of it. Caroline made sure that neither Freddie nor her sister was allowed to wander off alone, and her mother was most helpful in keeping the party intact, since she was very unwilling to be left alone with Mr. Madson and his monosyllabic answers.

Belinda was driven to Lady Salton's at the appointed time and was only a little surprised to find the Duke of Darwood among the guests. She curtsied to her hostess and was introduced to several others, with whom she chatted easily until dinner was announced. She felt the duke's eyes on her most of the time but he did not come to her side, so she was unable to tell him what she thought of such scrutiny.

She was not placed near him at dinner, and since the party seemed to be composed of very elderly people, with the exception of the duke and herself, she was not particularly entertained by the elderly clergyman on her left or the retired naval captain to her right. The latter was very deaf, so any remarks addressed to him had to be delivered in loud tones, and Belinda was glad when he applied himself to his dinner, to the exclusion of all else. The clergyman tried to keep up a conversation until he was interrupted by a very old lady in purple across the table.

"Well, I'll grant you she's pretty!" this lady said, raising her lorgnette and staring at Belinda. "Not that that's anything to the point! At least it's a good family—that is, what I know of it! You, Missy! Who was your maternal grandmother?"

Belinda was astonished to be so addressed, and looked about her. The table seemed very quiet, as if everyone was waiting for her answer.

"My grandmother Rogers was a Markham before her marriage, ma'am," she said quietly and a little stiffly, and Lady Salton, at the head of the table, suddenly remarked, "That will do, Mabel! Let the gel eat her dinner!"

The elderly lady bridled but subsided. Stranger and stranger, thought Belinda as she helped herself to a plate on which some small pieces of chicken sat in a Spanish sauce. Was it possible that Lady Salton and the duke had engineered this peculiar dinner party for the express purpose of looking her over? She shook her head a little. Surely her imagination was running away with her!

After dinner, when the gentlemen rejoined the ladies, she was glad to see the duke coming towards her, for she had hardly been amused by the elderly ladies she had been sitting with. Their main topics of conversation concerned their gall bladders and livers, and even more unattractive organs. After dinner, even such a poor dinner as Lady Salton had provided, it was hardly conducive to digestion!

Without any fuss at all, the duke managed to send Miss Witherspoon on her way to join her brother, and assured Lady Wentworth that she must on no account miss seeing Lady Salton's newest figurine, which was placed on the what-not at the far end of the drawing room, and both ladies took themselves off while he settled himself next to Belinda, who was staring at him coolly.

"I hope you do not mind me routing the old dears, Miss Wells!" he said with his tight smile that never reached his eyes.

Belinda shook her head. "Not at all, Your Grace; I congratulate you! I have already been treated to a blow-by-blow account of Miss Witherspoon's last illness, and Lady Wentworth's retaliatory description of her husband's gout! One would not like to deprive the rest of the company of such amusement!"

The duke smiled again, and, looking around the room, said seriously, "Perhaps they are not the most entertaining of guests, but then, one's relatives so seldom are!"

"Relatives? Of yours, Your Grace, or Lady Salton?"

"Both, I'm afraid!" he replied. "You see, Lady Salton is a distant cousin of mine, and most of the people here meet somewhere on our family tree!"

Belinda was suddenly very angry. So she had not been wrong! She had been invited so the family might look her over and pass judgment! The arrogance of the man!

"They are a parcel of dowds and bores, but, being relatives, they cannot be banished from one's life, unfortunately!" the duke continued, unaware he had upset her. Suddenly he said more softly, "There is no one in this room worth talking to for more than five minutes, with the notable exception of yourself, Miss Wells!"

Belinda nodded distantly, and since he appeared to be waiting for her to speak, she said formally, ignoring his last comment, "I must thank you for the roses, Your Grace! They were very beautiful!"

"As beautiful as the receiver!" the duke said ponderously, and Belinda thought she had never heard such heavy-handed compliments in her life, as he added, "Do I have your permission to call, Miss Wells?"

She looked up, wishing she could deny him, and saw his eyes fixed intently on her face, with such a warm blaze in them that she was startled.

"Why, yes!" she managed to get out, "I should be pleased..."

The duke rose and bowed, his eyes shuttered again, and only a faint polite interest showing there. "I shall look forward to enlarging our acquaintance! Until then!"

Belinda watched as he made his way across the room to his hostess, stopping every so often to exchange a few words with the other guests. He spoke briefly to Lady Salton, who looked over at Belinda and seemed disconcerted to see her observing them, and then he took his leave. Belinda was indignant. If he had arranged the evening, he might have stayed a little longer and "enlarged the acquaintance" right then. It would certainly have spared her more tedious conversation with his relatives!

Lady Salton bustled over as soon as the door closed behind him, closely followed by Miss Witherspoon.

"Oh, do go away, Theodosia!" she said crossly, and poor little Miss Witherspoon did, shaking her gray curls at Cousin Salton's abruptness. The dowager sat down and smiled at Belinda.

"Well, gel," she said, "what do you think?"

Belinda was still angry, but she only asked politely, "About what, Lady Salton?"

"About the duke!" her hostess said, poking her with her fan. "Fine figure of a man, good family, wealthy...why, your father would be pleased and your mother in raptures if they knew!"

"What is there to know?" Belinda asked sweetly. "And, Lady Salton, if I may be permitted to say so, it is more to the point whether *I* am pleased than my parents!"

She stopped, afraid she had gone too far, but Lady Salton, after one indignant frown, began to laugh.

"So, you've got a temper, have you? Thought as much when I first saw you! But don't be too quick to whistle away Franklin Brownell! He is the catch of the season—has been for years! It would be quite a coup if you could pull it off!"

Before Belinda could tell her that she had serious doubts that she was interested in "pulling it off," some of the guests came up to take their leave. As Belinda prepared to join them, Lady Salton said in an aside, "I do not think I am exaggerating when I tell you that as far as Franklin is concerned, he has made up his mind and is determined to make you his duchess!"

Belinda nodded and curtsied, and went home in a brown study. She did not precisely dislike the duke;

but then, she did not know him very well. His formality and pompousness chilled her, but then she remembered that all-too-human blaze in his eyes when he looked at her, and that warmed her. She was home long before the Drapers, and was glad for once not to be subjected to exhaustive questioning about her evening, and she was fast asleep when they finally returned home.

The following morning she rose early and, taking a groom, went for a brisk ride in the park. There were few people about, and she felt much better after a hard canter in the fresh air. When she returned to the house, she found Winsted about to carry another large vase of roses to her room, and taking the card, she read it quickly. Although not as short as the first, all it said was that the duke would do himself the honor of calling on her that afternoon at three.

For a moment Belinda wished she had another engagement, just to teach him a lesson. She tapped her crop against one shiny boot as she studied the flowers. Had he never heard of any other kind, she wondered, or did he choose them because they were the most expensive? Shaking her head, she went up the stairs after instructing Winsted to place the roses in the drawing room, for she found the scent too heavy in her own rooms.

The duke was not especially pleased to see them there when Winsted reverently ushered him in at precisely three o'clock that afternoon. He paced up and down while he waited for Belinda, who was taking her time having her hair dressed. She had begged Caroline to accompany her, and Caro, finding out her caller's name, had raised her eyebrows.

"I know, I know!" Belinda said lightly. "He was at Lady Salton's last evening and asked if he might call. She seems quite sure he is going to propose, but I can hardly credit it! We have only met twice, and have not spoken above a dozen words to each other! Surely a duke—especially such a stiff and formal one—would not be so precipitous in committing himself to such a step. It seems almost foolhardy! Besides, Caro...I am not perfectly sure I...well..." her voice died away and she sighed.

Caroline did not appear at all confused. "I am sure he will be wishing me at the devil in a very few moments, my dear, but of course I will bear you company! It is the outside of enough for him to get his own way in everything so easily!"

Belinda hugged her, and the two girls made their way to the drawing room. If they had thought the duke would be disappointed, no trace of it showed when Belinda presented her cousin. She was not to know he applauded such modesty, and had never expected to see her alone. The conversation could hardly be called sprightly, but Caroline took her part in it cheerfully, sure that her gay, laughing cousin would never marry such a man—no, not even if he were royalty! He was staid, so sure of his welcome, so dull!

He stayed the prescribed fifteen minutes and rose to take his leave, after asking both ladies if he might drive them in the park the following afternoon. Caroline was impressed in spite of herself at his so graciously including her, but, ignoring Belinda's pleading look, she denied him.

"It is most kind of you, Your Grace," she said demurely, "but I am already engaged to ride in the park tomorrow."

Belinda was forced to say she would be very happy, but when Winsted had shown him out, she turned to her cousin in a whirl of skirts.

"Traitoress!" she cried. "How could you subject me to such a fate? You know very well he will make at least three very slow circuits of the park so everyone can see him, and I do not know what I shall find to talk about all that time! But stay! Perhaps Lizzie could go?"

Caroline dashed these hopes by saying that Lizzie was riding with Ferdie Baxter, and then she added,

"But Belinda, you must see him alone sometime, and you know it is perfectly correct to drive with a gentleman in an open carraige with his groom up behind! I shall look for you, and expect to see you conversing in a lively fashion! If he becomes too boring, treat him to a description of Yorkshire in winter!"

Belinda admitted she was resigned to it and went away to choose her gown for the theater party they were all to attend that evening. Although several gentlemen came to their box at intermission, the duke was not of their number, and neither was Matthew Kincaid. Caroline had seen him only in the distance since the Jerseys' ball, and found she missed the stimulation of sparring with him. If Belinda thought the Duke of Darwood was arrogant, she should become better acquainted with the Earl of Cannock! Mrs. Draper finally shooed both the Baxter twins from the box as the curtain rose on the second act and Lizzie's satisfied smiles.

True to his word, the duke appeared the next afternoon. Belinda had prayed for a downpour; the sky was maddeningly clear and blue. She wore a dashing driving dress of palest blue, with braids at the shoulders à la Hussar, and a very military hat that sat jauntily on one side of her black curls and was tied under her chin. The duke's expression seemed to admire the effect. Belinda stole a glance at the elderly groom attending the horses as the duke helped her up the carriage steps, and thought he looked as stiff as his master.

The duke discussed the weather, the London scene, and the play she had seen the evening before. When she found he had not attended it as yet, she told him in great detail what pleasure he had missed.

"I am afraid I take a dim view of the modern theatre," he said repressively. "There is so much levity, such carelessness..."

Belinda suddenly saw what she should do, and laughed lightly. "But how dull if one never enjoys something frivolous!" she exclaimed. "Now, *I* never miss a good play, for I enjoy it above all things!" There, she thought!

The duke nodded solemnly, and then he was forced to pull up when a party hailed him, and yet again for Caroline and Mr. Sawyer. Lizzie contented herself with a gay wave of her crop as she and Ferdie cantered by the slower-moving carriage.

"Do you attend the dance at Lady Wilton's, Miss Wells?" he asked when they were once again alone.

Belinda said that she had been invited, and the duke smiled. "Then I shall certainly be there too!" he said seriously. Conversation languished until Belinda thought to ask him about his home, and the time was spent, until he put her down again at the Draper home, in a description of his estate in Kent, the size of his holdings, and the magnificence of his house. Belinda was congratulating herself on finding such a mine of information to discuss, when a look on his face and one slip in a sentence told her he thought she was inquiring because she had a warmer interest in him. She was glad when he came around to escort her to the door. As they climbed the shallow steps, he said suddenly, "I think you are the most beautiful woman I have ever seen!"

Belinda smiled at him. It was the first impulsive thing he had ever said to her, and it made him so much more human. But even as she watched, his face reddened a little, and his bow was stiff and formal as she thanked him for the drive. As she went up to her room for a serious think, she wished there were some way to make him drop his serious pose and his air of consequence, for if he were plain Franklin Brownell instead of the Duke of Darwood, she knew she would find him much more attractive.

Chapter Six

When Caroline returned from her drive with George Sawyer, she ran lightly up the stairs to see if either Belinda or Lizzie was before her. But when she stopped in her room for a moment to remove her bonnet and gloves, she surprised Peggy, who was standing at the window, crying, her face buried in a handkerchief.

"Why, Peggy, my dear!" she exclaimed, coming in and taking the maid in her arms. "Whatever is the matter? You are not ill, are you?"

"Oh, Miss Draper!" Peggy sobbed, ashamed she had been found so; "No, no, I'm fine!"

Caroline led her to a sofa and made her sit down. "I would not call it 'fine' when I discover you weeping as if your heart would break! Come, tell me! Perhaps I can help!" She paused for a moment as Peggy tried to dry her eyes, and then she asked, "It's not Grandish, is it, that is making your life a misery? If it is, I shall speak to my mother without delay!"

"Oh, no, Miss Draper!" Peggy cried, horrified she would do so and make life even more uncomfortable.

"If you do not tell me, Peggy, I shall have to assume it is Grandish! I know what she is like, you know!"

Peggy realized she must tell Miss Draper the truth, and, taking a deep breath, she said shakily,

"Please, Miss, it's not that old battle-axe at all! The problem is Stanley..." She stopped and burst into tears again.

"Stanley?" Caroline asked. "Oh, you mean the young footman who came up to town with us? What has he done?"

She sounded so fierce that Peggy put out a restraining hand. Caroline had seen before what could happen to young maids, even in so strictly run a household as the Drapers', and if this Stanley had gotten Peggy in trouble, she would not hesitate to bring the matter to her mother's attention. She knew she would see to it that Stanley married Peggy immediately! Peggy knew what she was thinking, and blushed.

"No, Miss, it's not that," she hastened to say. "It's just that Stanley and I—well, I knew he liked me—but when he asked me to walk out with him, I said no because Yvette was there, and then he asked her, and she went!" This statement ended in a wail, and fresh tears began to flow.

Caroline sat down beside her and patted her shoulder. "I see; at least I think I do! And now you are sorry, are you not? Did Yvette say anything about her outing?"

She admitted Yvette had tried to mention it, but Peggy would not listen. She tossed her black curls as she added, "No, and I wouldn't so demean myself to show any interest; no, never!"

Caroline thought for a moment. "Perhaps, Peggy," she began slowly, "you will have to take the initiative now. Does Stanley still speak to you? Are there any times when you are alone together?"

Peggy shook her head. "Sometimes I catch him looking at me when we are together at the table, but he has not spoken to me since he took Yvette out. Oh, why did I refuse him?" She began to cry again and Caroline rose.

"Now, stop that at once, Peggy! It is only giving you a red nose and eyes, and it is not getting you anywhere. Let me think about this problem for a while, and then I may be able to tell you what you should do! But if Stanley should ask you to walk out again, do not refuse, for heaven's sakes!"

"Oh, no, Miss!" Peggy agreed, wiping her eyes and putting her handkerchief away. She felt so much better now that she had told someone, for she had had to listen to the other maids, and Mrs. Winsted too, speculating about Stanley and Yvette, and it had been almost more than she could bear to hear the gossip and the titters. She knew Yvette was pretty, and her figure was so much better than her own that she did not see how Stanley could help falling in love with her, and it was with this thought that she had crept into Miss Draper's room to cry where no one could see her. Now she straightened her cap and apron and went about her business, much relieved. Caroline shook her head a little. Whatever was she to do about this new tangle? she wondered. She heard Lizzie calling her as she came up the stairs, and went to meet her, putting Peggy and Stanley from her mind, for here was her major problem, all brown curls and rosy cheeks and sparkling eyes.

"Oh, Caro, it was famous!" she cried. "Ferdie and I had such a good ride, and then, just as we were heading back, who should we meet but Freddie!"

"Naturally!" Caro exclaimed. "It wouldn't be justice if you had not!"

"Hmmm?" Lizzie asked, and then she continued, "And he was so angry, Caro, because Ferdie was escorting me! I thought they would come to blows right on horseback!"

"Oh, Lizzie, why do you get in these scrapes?" Caroline asked in despair. "Don't you see what is likely to happen, encouraging both of them? I wish you would stop seeing them, for indeed, I am afraid of how this might end!"

Lizzie tossed her head. "I am sure I do not know

what you are talking about, Caro! Besides, I can take care of myself!"

She went into her room, somewhat indignant that her sister should so chastise her, instead of agreeing the whole affair was a tremendous lark and quite the most exciting thing that had ever happened to her! She decided not to take Caro into her confidence any more, for if she was only going to scold, she did not deserve to know all the delicious things Ferdie and Freddie had said to her, or the promises they had begged from her—no, she would keep her own counsel from now on!

The evening that they all went to Lady Wilton's dance, Caroline was glad to see the Earl of Cannock once again, although when he asked for a dance, most humbly, she agreed with only an absentminded smile. This caused him to look at her sharply, for he was not at all used to being treated so casually. Caro was more worried than she cared to admit, about her sister, for she had noticed that Lizzie seemed to be avoiding her, and when she questioned her about her activities, received only the barest of answers. She was determined to keep a close eye on her tonight, for both the Baxter twins were attending the party, and even now stood glowering at each other, one on either side of her sister, their handsome high-colored faces taut with anger, and their blue eyes positively blazing. Lizzie looked from one to the other and said with a little pout, "Ferdie! Freddie! You must not look so, for you are frightening me!"

Instantly both young men smiled.

"Never!" Ferdie breathed fervently.

"Impossible!" Freddie said simultaneously.

"Well, it is not very nice to be growled over!" Lizzie said, her blushes belying her fright. "I am not a bone to be fought over by two dogs, you know!"

"Must beg your pardon!" Freddie said, bowing deeply.

"Humble apologies!" Ferdie said, bowing yet more deeply.

Caroline relaxed as she saw Lizzie move away from them with her first partner, a young man so new to town that he was unaware that Lizzie had been claimed exclusively by the Baxter twins. He was to be apprised of his mistake shortly. No young gentleman asked Lizzie to dance unless he was a particular friend of either twin. Lizzie never noticed that all the men who filled her dance card could be so classified, although she knew she could only dance twice each evening with either Baxter. To do otherwise was to court gossip and gain a reputation for being fast. Lizzie did not care who she danced with, as long as her card was always filled and she never had to sit out with her mother, and she was unaware that the twins had schemed to make sure she was never approached by anyone but their own special friends. In one of their rare agreements, they had decided it was much safer that way. Until Miss Lizzie could make up her mind which one of them she preferred, there was no sense taking the chance that her fancy might favor someone else!

When the Earl of Cannock approached Caroline later that evening, she rose abstractedly. She had been searching the ballroom, and neither Lizzie nor either twin was in sight. The earl sighed audibly as she gave him her hand, and she dragged her mind back to her partner.

"I know!" he said kindly, as she looked up at him. "We are not to have our dance after all! Which way did they go?"

His tone was so weary and knowing, and his eyes so crinkled with amusement, that she was forced to smile weakly at him.

"I am not sure, m'lord!" she replied. "Lizzie did not go past me out of the ballroom, so therefore she must have left by the terrace. It is too bad! However, since both Baxters appear to be missing as well, all may still be well!"

The earl sighed again as he led her to the French doors and held one open for her to pass. "You did say there was safety in numbers, did you not, Miss Draper?" he asked. "And yet—I am afraid that where the Baxters are concerned, the word 'safe' does not readily leap to mind! And if I may say so," he added as they descended the shallow steps to the garden, leaving the bright lights and music behind, "I think it was a mistake to bring Miss Lizzie to town! There are so many men here, she will never be able to make up her mind! It would have been so much easier for everyone if your mother could have produced one eligible man at a time; that way she would have had no trouble falling in love. Indeed, I am sure one man would have done the trick!"

He sounded almost tart, and Caroline blushed, glad of the dim light. "It is very good of you to escort me, m'lord!" she said faintly, and then, feeling his observation merited an answer, added, "I agree with you completely that Lizzie is a problem, but I cannot let her fall into mischief, without making the least push to save her, you know!"

Just then, in the distance, they heard two voices raised in anger, and he led her down a gravel path in the direction of the sound. As they came around a bend, Caroline saw her sister between the twins, each one clutching one of her arms and shouting at the other.

"How dare you take Miss Lizzie into the garden alone?" one asked indignantly.

"And how dare you follow us? This was *my* dance, you know!" the other said, glaring back at him.

Both men pulled Lizzie's arms and she began to look most uncomfortable, as Caroline and the earl came into view.

"How very edifying!" the earl said wryly, causing both young men to whirl, dragging Lizzie with them. "Are you planning to pull her in half between you?" he continued in an interested way.

"Oh, Caro!" Lizzie wailed, and her sister went up to the Baxters, her eyes blazing.

"Release my sister at once!" she cried, raising her

hands as if she would strike them. Ferdie and Freddie were so astounded that Miss Draper could be so fierce that they complied at once, and Lizzie flew to her sister's arms. Over her head, Caroline said coldly, "What is the meaning of this? Be assured, sirs, that I shall tell my mother what has occurred this evening, and you may take it as read that neither of you will ever be welcome in the Draper house again, nor shall either of you be allowed to bother my sister any more. The very idea!"

"Oh, Caro, it was not so bad..." Lizzie began, horrified that both her suitors were being disposed of so summarily. The twins were straightening their ruffles and trying to look contrite and dignified, while the earl lounged against one of Lady Wilton's garden sculptures, sardonically at his ease.

"Bad ton! Very bad ton, boys!" he said, his cynical tone producing identical flushes on their faces. "I am sure we will be able to excuse you, you know," he added kindly. "You must be feeling very definitely *outré* by now, multiplied by two!"

Both Freddie and Ferdie had been wishing fervently that they might disappear, but they had no idea how to make an exit gracefully. Now they eyed the earl with gratitude.

"Humble servant!" mumbled Freddie.

"A thousand apologies, ladies!" muttered Ferdie.

When they had bowed themselves away, Lizzie burst into tears, and Caro wished the earl was not there so she could give Lizzie the slap she so richly deserved, as he came up and handed her a handkerchief.

"Come now, Miss Lizzie!" he said bracingly. "It will not do at all for you to arrive back in the ballroom drenched in tears. There is sure to be gossip enough over this evening, without that! Compose yourself, and then we will take you back to your mother, where I for one, devoutly hope you will remain!"

Lizzie agreed in a small voice, and was very subdued as the earl held out his other arm to escort her. As they reached the terrace again, they could hear the orchestra finishing a number, and he shook his head sadly.

"Alas, and it was a waltz, too!" he said.

Caroline was forced to smile, although she was mortified he had had to help her with Lizzie one more time. Whatever would he think of the Drapers after this? Surely he must be getting tired of rescuing her tiresome sister from her follies, and would soon find a way to cut the connection. With this depressing thought, they reached her mother, who, all unconcerned, smiled fondly at the earl and her daughters. As she spoke to Lizzie, the earl leaned down and whispered to Caroline, "I cannot tell you, Miss Draper, with what glee I shall wish your sister happy when *that* glorious day arrives! Perhaps then you will find yourself free to attend to...hmm...other matters!"

Caroline drew in a deep breath, her startled eyes going to his face. Although he was smiling, his eyes were serious as he stared down at her, and she, not knowing what to say, nodded faintly. The earl smiled again and left them.

In the meantime, Belinda was enjoying her usual popularity, and although the duke had signed his name to her dance card in two places, when he came up and bowed as the orchestra was striking up, he did not suggest they join the set. Belinda was aware that she looked very well that evening, in a new gown of palest pink. Mrs. Draper had bemoaned the deep neckline, but Belinda knew it was extremely becoming. It was obvious the duke thought so too.

Now she looked at him inquiringly as he led her to a pair of chairs somewhat removed from the rest.

"I do not dance, Miss Wells!" he said in explanation. "I have never seen the value of prancing around a ballroom with crowds of people pushing you and stepping on you and all talking so loudly you cannot hear the music. It is not dignified!"

He bowed and seated her. Of course, Belinda thought to herself, if it is not dignified, the Duke of Darwood would never indulge in it! Although she was annoyed at his high-handedness—could the man not even ask her if she wished to sit out?—she was completely at her ease. She had made up her mind that she would not be intimidated by the duke, no matter what he said or did. As he took his seat beside her, so calm and sure of himself, she spoke up quickly.

"But Your Grace, I find dancing most enjoyable! It is so exhilarating, and the music so gay! I should not like to spend an entire evening sitting against the wall while others danced!" There, she thought, what do you think of *that?*"

"I am sure, Miss Wells," the duke replied seriously, "this is mere youthful spirits, and as you grow older, you will come to agree with me. I do not object to *your* dancing, you know. However, when you are with me, I would much prefer to be able to talk to you in a sensible manner!"

Belinda snapped her fan open and waved it to and fro before her face, hiding her indignant eyes. The nerve of the man to tell her what she must do! She decided she liked this arrogant duke not at all, and when he mentioned he was leaving town for a few days, she only nodded her head distantly.

"And will you miss me, Miss Wells?" he pursued the topic. "I cannot tell you how much I will miss you!"

Belinda lowered her fan and looked at him. There was a look on his face that she had never seen there before, a pleading look that made him seem much more human, and a great deal younger. Again she thought how much more appealing he was when he forgot his rank!

"I do not know you very well, Your Grace," she said coldly. "I do not know whether I shall miss you or not!"

The look disappeared as he nodded his approval

of such maidenly modesty. "I shall call on you as soon as I return!" he continued. "Perhaps you will find you have missed me after all!"

Belinda was relieved to see Mr. Sawyer bowing before her.

"My dance, I believe, Miss Wells!" he said. "Servant, Sir!"

She rose and smiled at him as the duke bowed. She made her smile so warm and inviting that Mr. Sawyer was confused. Surely he had never flirted with Miss Wells before! He only asked her to dance because she was Miss Draper's cousin!

The duke did not miss the vivacity with which Belinda greeted her next partner, and he remained where he was, staring at her as she danced with Mr. Sawyer, the pink gown swaying with her movements and her regal little head nodding to the music. He wished there was some way he could tell her what was really in his mind; but of course, hampered by his rank, it was inconceivable that he should do so. He decided to return to town as quickly as possible. He did not fear she would fix her interest with some other gentleman; naturally she would wait for him, for he was, after all, a duke! But she was so beautiful, so desirable! He strolled away to chat with Lady Salton until it was time for him to return to Miss Wells.

Caroline told herself she was glad when she saw Matthew Kincaid leaving shortly after the supper dance. She had gone in with Mr. Sawyer, and although she tried to appear interested in the conversations around her, her mind kept going back to the earl's last remark, and the look that had been in his eyes. She must have imagined it, she told herself firmly. The earl had no interest in *her*, she was sure. She had merely piqued his interest because she would not fall for his charms, and trying to make her do so was just a way of amusing himself during the season. At least she had the good sense not to fall in love with such a man, she told herself stoutly.

Just imagine being married to such a person for the rest of your life! How unbearable that would be, always having your ideas and wishes overridden in the most arrogant way possible! She refused another helping of the Dunstable oysters but allowed her wine glass to be refilled, and decided to put the earl right out of her mind, as she chatted with Mr. Sawyer and the rest of the table. When she saw the earl leaving, she turned her back on him. Now she would be able to enjoy the rest of the evening, she told herself, wondering why she felt so depressed.

Lizzie stayed close by her mother, in a subdued frame of mind, and even when her new beau appeared to chat with her, her spirits did not revive. She supposed it had been very bad to go out in the moonlight with Ferdie, but he had been so very coaxing, and had paid her the most beautiful compliments! And she had been thrilled when Freddie appeared and the two brothers had begun to fight over her! She was sure she would have been able to handle them without the earl and Caroline's intervention, and it had only been mortification that had caused her to weep when they were discovered. She managed to send each twin—quite separately, of course—a small rueful smile as she was leaving the dance, and had been encouraged to see both young men brighten up immediately. Ferdie winked at her, and Freddie nodded his head eagerly. So all was not lost, she thought, as she settled her skirts in the Draper carriage for the ride home. Caroline was too busy thinking about not thinking about the earl any more to notice.

The next morning, when Peggy brought her chocolate, Caroline was reminded that she had promised to help her maid, and she was ashamed that all her thoughts of her problem had flown out of her head. She asked if Stanley had spoken to her yet, and Peggy sighed a little as she began to lay out Caroline's morning gown.

"No, Miss," she said, shaking her head sadly, "he 'asn't. Not one single word!"

She looked so woebegone that Caroline asked, "Has he asked Yvette to walk out again?"

Peggy brightened. "No, he hasn't! Last week Yvette and I went out on our afternoon off, so I know she hasn't seen 'im alone! Unless it were here in the house somewhere!" This dismal thought cast down her spirits again, and Caroline said encouragingly, "But there! He is waiting for you to make the first move, Peggy! Can you not smile or speak to him?"

"Oh, no, Miss!" Peggy said in a horrified voice. "Why, my mother would never allow me to be so bold! She always told me that men are like 'ackneys—if you miss one, there'll always be another one coming along! She don't 'old with girls chasing men, no, not at all!"

Caroline swallowed her retort that since Peggy seemed to want this 'ackney, to the exclusion of all the others, she had better make haste to hail it before someone else did!

"I see, Peggy!" she said slowly, and then an idea came to her mind, and she nodded her head decisively and threw back the covers.

"I shall wear the blue slippers with that gown, Peggy, and be so kind as to put out my cashmere shawl! I have an errand this morning!"

Peggy did as she was bid, but when she asked if she were to accompany Miss Draper, Caroline only said carelessly, "There will be no need, Peggy. I shall take a footman with me in case there are any parcels to carry. I know you have some work for Miss Lizzie this morning."

When she was dressed and had gone down to breakfast, she stopped for a moment in the hall and asked Winsted to please have Stanley ready to go out with her in half an hour. The butler nodded, wondering how his newest footman had made himself known to Miss Draper so quickly that she would ask for him by name. It was a definite step up for the boy!

As Caroline left the house, Stanley a deferential step behind her, she announced airily over her shoulder, "It is such a lovely day, Stanley, that I think I will stroll in the park for a while before I begin my errands!"

The footman nodded. True, it was a lovely day, warm without being oppressive, with only a few fat white clouds in the blue sky. The birds were singing, the grass in the park was a lush green, and the flowers bloomed brightly, but to him it might have been a heavy fog, his spirits were so downcast. Whatever was he to do about Peggy? he mused, even as he helped Miss Draper across the street and shooed away a dirty urchin who was about to beg for a penny. He opened the park gates and they proceeded inside. There was no one else about, for which Caroline was grateful. Of course it was permissible to talk to your footman, but not for any great length of time, and she did not wish to call attention to herself. Turning so suddenly that Stanley almost skidded into her, she asked, "Are you happy here in town, Stanley?"

"Why, yes, Miss, thank you Miss!" Stanley replied, somewhat astonished to be so addressed.

"I only ask," Caroline said, carefully tightening a button on her glove and not looking at him, "because my maid, Peggy, who is from Hunstanton this year too, does not appear to be at all content in London. Indeed, I am afraid we will have to send her back to the country if her spirits do not improve! I had thought that perhaps Grandish was bothering her, but she assures me that is not the case. Do you know Peggy, Stanley?"

"Oh, yes, Miss!" Stanley said eagerly.

"Have you noticed how unhappy she is?" Caroline pursued the subject, and then added daringly, "I would almost think she was in love, she is behaving so badly! But she tells me she has met no one outside the house, so it cannot be that!"

"She hasn't?" Stanley asked, quite forgetting not to speak unless he was directly addressed.

"No, she has not! I do not know what we are to do, and I should be sorry to lose her! Besides being such a good maid, she is a very lovely girl, don't you agree?"

Without thinking, Stanley said fervently, "The loveliest girl I've ever seen!"

Caroline stopped and stared at him. "So you are in love too!"

Stanley stood still, a pleading look on his handsome face. "Please, Miss Draper...do you mean that Peggy is in love? In love with me? I know I shouldn't ask you, but it means so much to me!..."

He stopped, feeling he would be instantly dismissed for his unthinkable behavior of actually daring to ask Miss Draper such a thing, but Caroline was smiling at him.

"That is why she is unhappy! She is so sorry she would not walk out with you the day you asked her, and then when you took Yvette, she was sure you preferred her. It has made her so very miserable, but she would never have told me if I had not found her crying one day in my room."

Stanley brightened up noticeably. "Crying, was she?" he asked.

"Yes, indeed, crying her eyes out!" Caroline affirmed. "But when I suggested she let you know how she felt, she said she could not do it, for it would not be seemly. I fear it is up to you to make the first move, Stanley, if you truly love her!"

"I will!" the young footman said, straightening his shoulders and grinning at her. "Right away, I will!"

Caroline laughed. "Then, since I have no errands this morning and this was all a ruse to find out your intentions, I suggest we return home. There's no time like the present, you know!"

Stanley agreed fervently, sure there was no mistress in all the world as kind or considerate as Miss Draper, and Caroline turned and began to walk briskly back in the direction they had come.

When they entered the house, she said casually, over her shoulder, "Please be so kind as to fetch Peggy to me, Stanley; I shall be in my room. I think you will find her in the small sewing room, for she has some mending to do for Miss Lizzie this morning."

Stanley hastened away, and Caroline went upstairs feeling a glow of satisfaction that she had been able to bring two such good people together. There was more to be said for this matchmaking business than she had imagined!

Stanley entered the sewing room on the heels of his impatient knock and was delighted to find Peggy alone, the sunlight dancing on her black curls as she bent over her mending.

She looked up from one of Lizzie's lacy petticoats and the blood left her face as she saw Stanley shutting the door firmly.

"Stanley!" she breathed, as he reached her chair and pulled her to her feet, the petticoat falling in a heap to the floor. He put both hands on her arms and stared down at her, wondering what on earth he was to say. He had been in such a hurry to find her, he had not thought of that, and now his mouth felt dry and there was a great lump in his throat. Peggy's mouth dropped open a little in astonishment, and, words forgotten, Stanley pulled her close and kissed her warmly.

"Why, Stanley!" she said weakly, when at last she was allowed to do so.

"I love you, Peg!" he said, putting his arms around her and holding her close. "I 'ad to tell you, for I 'ave been so miserable since you wouldn't walk out with me!"

Peggy sighed in contentment. "Oh, Stanley!" she said softly, as she snuggled close to him, "I was afraid it was Yvette you loved!"

"Never! Not that she's not a very nice girl, for a foreigner, I mean!" Stanley said fairly. "But I have loved you ever since we came to town together! Do you...do you love me back, Peg?"

"No, I never!" Peggy said, looking up at him with glowing eyes. "Great silly lummox! Of course I do!"

Stanley seemed to be delighted with his new nickname, and it was some time later before Peggy made an appearance in Miss Draper's room, all happy smiles and blushes. Caroline was writing a letter to her brother and had not expected to see Peggy for the rest of the morning, but she was very happy to put down her pen and give her a kiss and all her best wishes, and to agree she would be happy to attend the wedding as soon as they returned to Hunstanton after the end of the season, and the banns had been read.

Chapter Seven

Mrs. Draper was horrified when she heard of Lizzie's misadventures with the Baxter twins, and Caroline's story was interrupted many times by exclamations. "I never!" "Can it be possible?" "Whatever would Mr. Draper say?" "Oh, naughty girl!"

Lizzie was summoned to the small salon and a mighty peel was rung over her head. As always, she cried a little and promised to be good, and Mrs. Draper went away to her card party, feeling she had done her duty and Lizzie would now behave herself as a young lady should. Caroline was not so sure, as she confided to Belinda later.

The two cousins were driving to take tea with Lady Salton. "You see, Belinda," Caroline said in a worried way, "Lizzie is repentant now, but I know she does not understand what all the fuss is about! And I am sure she has no intention of giving up such attentive, handsome admirers! Somehow or other she will find a way to see them again, even if they have been forbidden to call or ask her to dance. I know Lizzie!"

Belinda nodded, but she was a little distracted today, and Lizzie's problems were beginning to bore her. Why had Lady Salton asked them to come to tea? Had the duke left town? Whatever was she to do about him? She was almost positive he would propose soon, and she was not at all sure how she would handle him. Now she tore her thoughts away from her own problems and smiled at Caroline.

"Perhaps you are making too much of it, Caro!" she said bracingly. "We must be sure to introduce Lizzie to some other men immediately! That will take her mind off the Baxters!"

The two girls bent their heads together and began to go over their acquaintance for someone suitable.

"Perhaps we should ask Lady Salton," Caroline suggested after they had had a good laugh at the possibility of interesting Lizzie in Mr. Sawyer or Mr. Kindle, or fat little Lord Anders, with his airs and graces and definite lisp. Belinda suggested Caroline sacrifice the earl to the cause, with a sidelong glance at her cousin's face, but Caroline did not even blush, but only said gloomily, "*He* won't want her! He has seen her in too many scrapes!"

By this time the carriage was drawing up to Lady Salton's impressive town house, and Belinda pressed her hand in warning:

"Let us first find out why we have been summoned by her majesty!" she said. "My, it is almost like a royal command!"

She closed her parasol with a snap as they went up the steps, and Caroline looked at her cousin more closely. She could have sworn there was something bothering Belinda, but since she had not been taken into her cousin's confidence, she had no idea what it could be.

Lady Salton was all smiles as the two girls curtsied. Caroline looked around, but it appeared that they were to be the only guests.

Lady Salton favored them with such positive statements as she felt constituted polite conversation, until tea had been brought and served and the servants had bowed themselves out. After she urged the girls to help themselves to the angel cakes and meringues, she settled back in her chair and favored Belinda with a beady stare.

"Well, Miss, and what have you to say for yourself?"

Belinda put down her cup and raised her eyebrows. She knew there was no point in pretending she did not know what Lady Salton referred to, although Caroline was looking from one to the other in complete confusion.

"I have not decided, m'lady," she said calmly.

"Well, you had better make up your mind without delay!" the older woman said tartly. "Franklin is not prepared to wait forever, you know!"

"Since the duke has just left town, I think I have a few more minutes before I make my decision!" Belinda replied.

"Hoity-toity!" Lady Salton bristled. "Watch your tongue when you speak to me, Miss!"

Caroline decided to intervene in this dangerous conversation. "I am all at sea, ma'am. Whatever is Belinda to decide?" And why are you so interested? she said to herself.

"The Duke of Darwood has confided in me that he wishes to marry your cousin!" Lady Salton told her. "We are distant cousins, you know, or perhaps you didn't—not that that has anything to say to the matter. But this gel seems determined to play fast and loose with him!" She turned to Belinda. "I do not know why you do not encourage him; you will not find another man like him, you know!"

Caroline was indignant and spoke without thinking. "And why should she want to, m'lady? I find it ludicrous that my cousin would even consider such a pompous, opinionated man as the duke!" She stopped abruptly, aware of the anger in Lady Salton's face.

"I do not know what the world is coming to," that lady exclaimed, "when young gels set themselves up against their elders in such a way!"

She waved her handkerchief in agitation as Belinda tried in vain to catch Caroline's eye.

"Well, they should not suit!" Caroline said in a

milder voice, aware of the inadvisability of annoying such a leader of the ton. "Belinda is so fun-loving, so happy in her outlook! How could you imagine such a vivacious girl could ever settle for the duke, so staid and set in his ways! It does not bear thinking about! Of course she will say no!"

Lady Salton proceeded to read them both a lecture on the folly of throwing such a prize to the winds, as well as her opinion of a society that allowed girls to choose their own husbands.

"It was not so in my day, I can tell you!" she said. "Then we did what we were bid, and I am sure marriages were as good as any that are made today in the name of love! If there is affection, good family, and the approval of your elders, that is all that is necessary when you begin to have children and make your way through life. Your station, wealth, and consequence are what matters, not love. Love! Bah!"

Caroline wished she might ask Lady Salton if she had had a happy marriage, but she wisely closed her lips. She seemed to remember her mother saying that Lord Salton's premature death, some years ago, had prevented the two of them from murdering each other. She had certainly never remarried!

Belinda pressed her hand warningly. "I know it must seem strange to you, Lady Salton, but it is true that most girls today do not choose to marry where they cannot give their hearts."

Lady Salton snorted. "Well, why cannot you give your heart to Franklin, Miss?"

"I...I don't know!" Belinda said with a frown as Caroline gasped. "I have not decided. Sometimes I think I could, but then..." She sighed in confusion as Lady Salton rose to dismiss them.

"I wash my hands of you!" she said. "If you will take my advice you will put all silly girlish dreams from your mind, and realize what a marvelous opportunity this is. The Duchess of Darwood! I daresay there are thousands of gels who would like to be in your slippers!"

Belinda promised calmly that she would think about it, and the two girls went on their way. Caroline was glad they had dismissed the carriage so they might walk home, for she very much wished to discuss the situation. Her brown eyes were snapping as she said, "Well, cuz, I have never heard the like! To have that old tartar try to browbeat you! Of course you will refuse him; it is not to be thought of!"

Belinda thanked her for her support, and then she said slowly, as they began to walk towards home, "I do not know my own mind, Caro. It was true what I said; sometimes he is different, and then I think I might accept him. But I have to wonder if I would be marrying him because he is a duke! You remember I boasted I would marry the highest rank I could find, when I first came to town. Can it be possible that that is why I contemplate an alliance with Franklin Brownell? I am so confused!"

Caroline begged her not to be hasty. As they strolled along, each deep in her own thoughts, she told herself that time would bring wisdom, and after Belinda was better acquainted with him, she would come to see that the duke was not for her. Caroline had become very fond of her beautiful little cousin, and she did not want her to be unhappy. Surely there could be only misery, married to the duke, and not all his wealth and consequence could make up for it! It quite took Lizzie's problems from her mind!

Her sister, in the meantime, had taken the opportunity to go shopping with Yvette, and as they were coming out of Madame Lorette's, on Bond Street, she was happy to see Freddie Baxter crossing the street and hurrying to her side. Not having heard of Mrs. Draper's banishment of the twins, Yvette fell back a few paces to allow them to converse.

"Miss Lizzie!" he breathed, sweeping off his beaver and bowing deeply. "The sun has come out at last!"

Lizzie blushed. "Why, sir, the sun has been shining all day! You are only being gallant, I fear!"

"But it has not shone so brightly until this moment!" he insisted.

He offered his arm, and, after hesitating a moment, she took it and they proceeded up the street, followed closely by Yvette. "You know, Freddie, I should not even be speaking to you," she whispered. "Indeed, I should not! My mother and sister are so angry with me!" She looked around nervously. "I do hope no one sees us!"

Freddie's brow clouded. "I would not bring any trouble to you, Lizzie, but we *must* see each other! Is there no way you can get away so we can be alone? There is so much to tell you...to ask you!"

Lizzie pretended reluctance, but by the time they parted at the top of the street, an assignation had been made for the following afternoon. Freddie had suggested the British Museum; Lizzie said it would seem most unlikely to her family that she had any desire to go there. She suggested a secluded part of the park; Freddie said he had no intention of skulking about, dodging behind trees, even in such a cause as this! They were at point-non-plus when Lizzie suddenly remembered that Mrs. Abernathy had been so kind as to ask the Drapers to a musicale.

"Surely we could meet there!" she said brightly. Freddie agreed reluctantly, musicales not being in his usual line.

"But your mother will be there, and your sister..." he said.

Lizzie interrupted him. "No, they will not; they have another engagement. It is only Belinda and I who attend, and if I slip away, saying I am not feeling well, she is bound not to suspect anything!"

Everything went as Lizzie had planned. Belinda had her own problem on her mind, and when Lizzie whispered to her, as a harpist was taking the stage, that she thought she would retire awhile, for the room was so hot and it was giving her a headache, she only nodded and remained in her chair, an expression of polite interest on her face although she heard not a single note.

All would have been well if Freddie had not let slip to his twin that evening in White's that he had had the good fortune to not only see Lizzie alone, but for twenty glorious minutes! Ferdie was only deterred from calling him out by the intervention of Lord Anders. "Not to be done, dear boy, most regrettable!" he lisped. "Bad ton to shoot a relative! No one would ever speak to you again. Not"—he added seriously—"even me!"

Ferdie went away indignant, and wrote Lizzie such a passionate note that she determined to keep it always. Such a turn of phrase, such compliments, such devotion! Since Ferdie said he would blow his brains out if she did not grant him an interview, Lizzie went about the house all day in a daze. All these clandestine meetings were beginning to tax her ingenuity.

Fortunately, before Ferdie could fall into despair and make good his threat, they met quite by chance in the park. Yvette was once again escorting Lizzie, and she smiled a little to see the same young gentleman bowing and smiling at her young charge. Ferdie quickly escorted Lizzie down a side path, with Yvette trailing behind, seemingly entranced by the flowers that grew along the path. When they reached a stone bench, Lizzie dismissed the maid lightly.

"Come back in a few minutes, dear Yvette!" she said, as Ferdie muttered, "Twenty-one minutes, to be exact!"

Lizzie's eyes widened as he went down on one knee and grasped her hands tightly. "You must fly with me, dearest Lizzie, for if you do not, I shall make good my threat and blow my brains out!"

Lizzie gasped in horror as Ferdie congratulated himself on remembering the line from the play so accurately.

"No, no, you must not, indeed you must not!" she

exclaimed, enjoying herself hugely. "Tell me you are only funning!"

"Funning?" Ferdie asked, bewildered. "Of course I am not funning!" This was not the way the girl in the play had replied. Lizzie was supposed to weep and promise to go away with him at once. He scowled and rose, taking a seat close beside her, telling her she was the most beautiful woman in the whole world, that he could not live without her, that he would most assuredly carry out his threat if she did not agree, and then his arm stole around her waist and his other hand tipped up her chin and he kissed her. It was decidedly pleasant to be kissed by such a handsome suitor, and Lizzie sighed and decided that perhaps Ferdie was the one after all.

Before Yvette came back, arrangements had been made for Lizzie to meet him the next morning. Ferdie had begged her to come to him that night at midnight, for he could not think that driving away in the bright sunlight, with maids shaking rugs, milkmen making the day's deliveries, and footmen walking m'lady's pug, was at all romantic, but Lizzie brought him back to earth by saying she had no intention of missing the Witton dance that evening; besides, it would be so much easier to escape the house while everyone else was sleeping late, and they would have several hours to evade pursuit. Remembering how very angry Freddie was going to be, to say nothing of Lizzie's family, Ferdie agreed.

He went away to borrow as much money as he could, for his last venture at the card table had just about emptied his pockets till next quarter day, and he would have to rent a team, and hire accommodations all the way to Gretna. All these unromantic details made him almost regret his impulsive proposal, for in thinking it over, he decided he really had no desire to be leg-shackled as yet. Besides, he would miss the cock fight next week, and Lord Anders's card party. Only remembering how furious Freddie was going to be, saved the day. There was no way he could top this coup! He managed to borrow almost enough from his long-suffering friends, and had the good luck to run into his twin at White's. Freddie had just collected a bet and was very plump in the pocket, and not at all adverse to sharing it with his twin. Completely unashamed to take the money for the purpose of duping his brother, Ferdie was careful not to explain why he needed it.

Caroline was surprised late the following morning as she sat in the salon, writing some notes, to have Peggy come rushing in, clutching a note.

"Miss Draper!" she said. "I am so afraid there is something wrong! I was not summoned by Miss Lizzie at all this morning, so I went and peeked in at her to make sure she was all right, and she was not in her bed! Some of her things are missing, and there was this note propped up on her dressing table, but I cannot find your mother, and..."

Caroline paled and took the note. "My mother is not here, Peggy. She has gone to a Venetian breakfast and I do not expect her to return till afternoon. Oh, that dratted girl! What has she done now?"

She read the note quickly and then she sat for a moment, thinking hard. Peggy watched her nervously. Suddenly she came to a decision and rose.

"Peggy, go at once and tell Stanley that we will need the light traveling carriage and the fastest team brought around as soon as possible! Then ask Miss Wells to join me in my room. You pack an overnight bag for us, and, oh yes, I will need you to come with us as well! That idiot sister of mine has eloped with one of the Baxter twins, and we must catch her as soon as possible! Not a word to anyone else, mind!"

Peggy did as she was bid, and Caroline wrote a short note to her mother, which she handed to Winsted with the instruction that it be given to Mrs. Draper as soon as she returned, for she and Miss Wells were called into the country to attend Miss Wells's ailing grandmother. The fewer people who knew of this, the better, and she knew she could trust Stanley and Peggy! She went upstairs to change and tell Belinda her plans, and that young lady instantly agreed to come and help her catch Lizzie.

It was not many more minutes before they were descending the front steps, followed by Peggy carrying two bags. Stanley was holding the door of the carriage just as the Earl of Cannock came driving by in his racing curricle. He pulled up and greeted them.

"Servant, Miss Draper, Miss Wells!" he said, eyeing the bags and their traveling gowns. "You are called out of town?"

Belinda was only too happy to tell him their plight, although Caroline was looking daggers at her. The earl laughed.

"I think perhaps it would be wise for you to join me, ladies! I am at your service, and I can assure you my team and rig will carry you much more swiftly."

Somehow Caroline found herself seated between the earl and her cousin, the groom ready to let 'em go, while the earl gave Stanley instructions as to the route he intended to take. Stanley was not at all adverse to following in the slower carriage, alone with Peggy, and nodded his head eagerly. The earl snapped his whip, the groom hopped up behind, and they were off.

Caroline was seething. Why does he always turn up at just the right moment, she asked herself. And how dare he arrogantly take over like this! It was no concern of his, after all, and when she thought of how he had taken charge and ordered *her* servants about, she was furious! The earl did not notice, for he was occupied with negotiating the busy streets, and Belinda seemed wrapped in a world of her own. When they were on the main post road north, the earl gave his horses a touch of the whip, and the pace picked up.

"Don't worry, Miss Draper!" he said cheerfully. "There isn't a rig in England that can beat mine, you know. We will come up on your sister before she knows it!"

Caroline did not answer, and he stole a glance at her profile, so sternly set. Whatever is the matter now? he thought in bewilderment. Surely she wants to find that silly little sister of hers as soon as possible! Belinda stirred beside her. "Caro, I have been wondering," she said. "Which twin did Lizzie run away with?"

Caroline thought back to the note. "Do you know, she never said!" she got out finally, and in only a moment the tension was broken, the three of them laughing so hard, the two girls had to wipe their eyes. "If that isn't just like Lizzie!" Caroline gurgled. "How ludicrous not to even mention her intended's name!"

"To tell the truth, I don't think it mattered which one it was," the earl said calmly. "Whichever proposed the scheme first, I should think. She is hardly a...a *selective* girl, is she?"

Unbeknownst to the trio, they were not the only ones who were racing after the elopers. Ferdie had not been able to resist leaving a note for his twin, and although he tried hard not to gloat too much, Freddie was gnashing his teeth by the time he finished reading it. He was in hot pursuit, some way ahead of the earl's curricle, and the way he used his whip on his fastest saddlehorse boded no good for his twin when he finally caught up with him.

Freddie did not know it, but Ferdie by this time was heartily sick of the whole adventure. First Lizzie had been almost an hour late to the rendezvous, and he was just about to give up and go home, when she came around the corner, clutching two bandboxes, her bonnet, and a cloak. It seemed she had had to wait until the front staircase emptied of maids and footmen and tweenies doing the early-morning housework. She had quite forgotten they would be working at an hour when she was always still asleep. Then, after he got her settled in the coach and tried to take her in his arms, she had burst into tears. He felt it was hardly an auspicious beginning to an elopement, but when he begged her to tell him what was wrong, she only cried harder. Eventually she fell asleep, lulled by the rhythm of the carriage, and Ferdie put his arm around her to keep her from falling. His arm was asleep now, which was very uncomfortable, he had no one to talk to, and he was sure the grooms knew exactly what was going on and were making all kinds of snide comments up on the box. He was not sorry when they pulled in at the first inn to change the team, and he woke Lizzie and helped her down for some refreshments. She was very quiet, and when the landlord had bowed himself out after bringing her some coffee, and a mug of home brew for Ferdie, he said bracingly, "You see how easy it was, dearest Lizzie? And before you know it, we shall be wed!" The easy tears threatened to fall again as Lizzie sighed heavily.

"But what is it, my love?" he asked in bewilderment. "Don't you want to be wed?"

"Of course I don't!" Lizzie wailed. "I only did it because you said you would blow your brains out if I did not! It is all your fault!"

Ferdie swallowed a few times, wondering how he could delicately suggest that they return to town before they were missed, when he heard a horse come thundering into the yard, and went to look out the window.

"Now we're for it!" he said, his handsome face paling a little.

"Oh, say it is not my mother. Or Caroline," Lizzie begged him.

"I'd rather face *them!*" Ferdie muttered. "'Tis my brother!"

Freddie lost no time joining the party, and it was not long before the landlord hastened back and began knocking urgently on the door of his best private parlor. From the sounds of the argument going on inside, he didn't have much hope for his furniture. The door was locked, and all his banging gained no response, but he could hear a table falling over, and the tinkle of glass above the bellows of rage from the two 'dentical men, and the wailing of the young lady.

Into this confusion came the Earl of Cannock with Caroline and Belinda. Caroline rushed to the door of the parlor, for she recognized Lizzie's voice, and demanded that she open the door at once. The landlord tried to explain to the earl what he thought was going on, but Kincaid put him to one side as Lizzie threw open the door and fell into Caroline's arms. Belinda peeped around the earl's shoulder and her eyes widened. Both the twins were rolling around the floor, landing many a good blow in between their shouted invectives. The earl strolled in and dropped his driving gloves on the one table that was still upright.

"That is quite enough!" he bellowed, and the twins, hearing such a voice of authority, ceased trying to kill each other and got to their feet. The earl closed the door on the protesting landlord, a gaping maid, and one of the grooms.

"Yes, yes!" he said. "I shall be with you presently! Now, if you will excuse us? There is a private matter to discuss!"

Ferdie, sporting the beginnings of a spectacular black eye, brushed down his coat and sent his brother a glance of dislike, which Freddie returned with interest as he tried to resettle his cravat, now liberally spotted from his bleeding nose.

The earl bowed sarcastically to Lizzie. "My compliments, Miss Lizzie! Surely you are the first young lady, to my knowledge, who has tried to elope with two gentlemen at once!" Over her protests, he turned again to the twins.

"May I suggest the two of you repair to the stable-yard and finish your...hm...conversation? You are distressing the ladies! And I think I may say for all of us that you may feel perfectly free to beat each other to a bloody pulp! It can only save someone else the trouble, somewhere down the road!"

"It was his fault!" Freddie said, wiping his still flowing nose. "He was the one who eloped with Miss Lizzie!"

"And if you had taken your loss in good spirit and not followed us, bro, this never would have happened!" Ferdie said, wincing as he touched his eye. "As soon as I have straightened the matter out, Lizzie, we can be on our way again. Never let it be said that Ferdinand Baxter does not honor his commitments!"

"Oh, go away, do, both of you!" Lizzie said with loathing. "I never want to see either of you again!"

Both the twins' mouths dropped open at this callous remark from their lady love. They were soon put out of the room by some dexterous method of the earl's which left them no choice, for which Caroline was extremely grateful. While the earl called for refreshments, she settled Lizzie in a chair and demanded to know the whole story.

It was soon told, and Caroline shook her head in despair. The earl listened quietly, and then he said, "I think we have brought her safe out of it, Miss Draper, for I am sure neither of the Baxters will be eager to tell the world of this morning's work!"

He was so easy, so matter of fact about the whole matter, that Lizzie soon recovered her spirits. By the time they had had a light luncheon, the coach with Stanley and Peggy had arrived. Caroline put her sister inside and would have followed her, except the earl suggested she ride back to town with him, leaving Belinda to see to Lizzie. Caroline would have refused—there he went again, managing everyone! she thought—but Belinda urged her to go, her blue eyes dancing as she said reasonably, "Do, Caro! It will be so crowded if we all travel in our coach. Besides, now the earl's horses are rested, you will make better time than we can, and reassure your mother that all is well that much sooner!"

Knowing her mother would be vastly upset by this time, and waiting anxiously for news, decided the issue, and Caroline allowed the earl to hand her up into the racing curricle. Where the Baxters had gone, she had no idea, but she sincerely hoped they would not pass them on the road.

The two twins had indeed gone out to finish their business in the yard, as the earl had suggested, but the sight of Freddie's bloody nose and Ferdie's black eye had been too much for them, and they had collapsed with laughter before they repaired to the taproom to enjoy the landlord's ale. Ferdie repaid him handsomely for the damage to his private parlor with some of his elopement money, and everyone was in high spirits. The twins promised each other they would never fall in love again. It had turned out to be such a tedious business and took up all too much valuable time, when all was said and done.

"Let us confine our interest in the female sex to the racing fillies at Ascot!" suggested Freddie.

"I rather think Newmarket, old chap!" replied Ferdie.

Chapter Eight

If the earl thought the return journey to town would give him an opportunity to further his relationship with Caroline Draper and cause her to look at him with more kindness, he was vastly mistaken. Although she answered all his questions calmly and easily, she volunteered no comments on her own. There seemed to be a thin sheet of glass between them, in spite of his very best efforts and most charming smiles. He quirked an eyebrow at her as he helped her down at the Draper house later that afternoon. He had never felt so unimportant to anyone in his life, and he had no idea how to change the situation. Although she was very polite and thanked him graciously for his assistance once again, he had no illusions that he was making any headway in breaking down her barriers. She seemed determined to hold him at a distance, and it made him extremely impatient. Caroline Draper was becoming more than a challenge; he was now determined to make her fall in love with him, no matter how she fought to remain aloof. She would learn that it did not do to treat Matthew Kincaid so nonchalantly!

She asked him if he cared to come inside, for she said she was sure her mother would wish to add her thanks to her daughter's, but he declined.

"There is no need for any more thanks, Miss

Draper. I only did what any other man would do to assist a lady in distress!" He smiled at her warmly as she held out her hand in farewell, and added, "Besides, your mother will be wanting to hear all the details, which she would never dare ask about with me standing there!"

Caroline dropped him a curtsy and went inside without trying to persuade him to change his mind. As Winsted closed the door, the earl stood there a moment, perplexed, and then he dismissed his curricle. "Take 'em back to the stables, Bardsley!" he told his groom. "I shall walk home!"

The groom tipped his hat and the earl strolled away, lost in thought and wondering what his next move should be. If he had realized that Caroline was furious with him for always turning up when there was trouble, and for so calmly taking over the management of her family's affairs, he would have been astounded. He was a man used to command; he did not realize that Miss Draper was also used to running matters without the help of any mere man, thank you very much!

When the slower carriage arrived back in town an hour later, the story, down to the last detail, had been reported to Mrs. Draper, who told Caroline that she did not know what she was to do with Lizzie; she was beginning to think it had been a horrible mistake to bring her to town! Caroline let her go on and on, knowing that by the time Lizzie arrived, her mother would have calmed down a bit, and the subsequent lecture would be that much lighter. Not that she did not agree with her mother, for she was getting very tired of her sister's escapades and the need to constantly rescue her. She also had a headache, which she put down to the events of the day and the rattling back and forth to and from town in the earl's racing curricle.

After she had seen Lizzie and Belinda settled in the drawing room, where Mrs. Draper was waiting, vinaigrette and salts in hand, and an indignant frown on her face, Caroline begged to be excused, saying she was rather tired and would like to rest. Belinda looked at her thoughtfully as Mrs. Draper urged her to go and lie down on her bed. "For, my love," she said, "there is no wonder you are tired, such a to-do as there has been, and all the fault of that naughty girl sitting on the sofa!"

As Caroline closed the drawing room doors behind her, she heard her mother say tartly, "There is no need to cry, Lizzie; it will do you no good, no good at all! And do not promise to be good! We all know where *that* leads!" Caroline shook her head and went slowly upstairs, sure that with Belinda in attendance, her mother did not require her presence as well. Frankly, she told herself, I am tired of the whole affair!

She fell into a restless sleep, and it was not until the first dressing bell that she awoke and called Peggy so she might dress for dinner. The Drapers had no engagements that evening, for which she was thankful, for she was still feeling out of sorts. As she dressed, her thoughts returned to the earl and his incredible arrogance, and her lips tightened again in annoyance.

At the table, she learned that Mrs. Draper had decided to return to Hunstanton with Lizzie, just as soon as she had attended all the events she was promised to for the next two weeks. She would accept no more invitations, she said; she would take Lizzie home! That young lady was not at the table, having been banished to her room in disgrace, so there was no way of knowing how she felt about it, but Belinda sat there calmly eating and saying nothing.

"But Mother!" Caroline protested. "How can you do that? Belinda and I cannot remain here alone, you know; it would be most improper, for even though I am older, I am sure I would never be accepted as her chaperone. Do you mean we shall all return to the country?" Two months ago, such a prospect would have filled her with delight; now she felt a sinking feeling at the thought of leaving town.

"No, my dear, not at all!" her mother said. "Belinda and I have discussed it, and she tells me she is sure Miss Wiggleworth would be agreeable to coming to chaperone you both, and I am sure Lady Salton would be happy to take you around to balls and evening parties. I see no reason why you should have to forego the season because your sister is bad! Besides, you are both dear, good girls, and I know I can trust you to keep the line!"

Caroline looked wildly at Belinda. Miss Wiggleworth? Lady Salton? Oh, dear! Belinda smiled at her and said, "Since it is impossible for your mother to leave before the Abercrombie ball, and that is still two weeks away, dear Caro, there is plenty of time before those two ladies descend on us! We shall see!"

She winked at her cousin, and Caroline felt better. Surely in two weeks' time, her mother's anger might have cooled, if Lizzie were very, very good. She could not look forward to welcoming Miss Wiggleworth, and as for being constantly in Lady Salton's company, that was not to be thought of with any great anticipation either. But two weeks had to pass before that unhappy time became reality. She began to eat her dinner with more appetite.

The next day, Mrs. Draper received a very interesting communication in the morning post from her sister, Lady Wells. It was unusual that she did not immediately show the letter to Belinda, for the contents did much to revive her spirits. To think her niece was to be Duchess of Darwood! Dear child! Lady Wells had written that the duke had come to Yorkshire expressly for permission to propose to Belinda, and she for one was in heaven at the thought! Such a good, steady man, and of such high rank as well! Lord Wells had also thought the duke most personable, and very well able to handle his daughter, with her weird quirks and high spirits. How she longed to see her sister, Lady Wells went on, so she might thank her personally for bringing Belinda out so successfully, and seeing her so satisfyingly settled! She said the duke would be calling as soon as he returned to town, and begged her dear Mary Ann to give him every assistance, and a sincere welcome to the family.

Mrs. Draper generously smiled in delight for her niece, quite forgetting her own errant and unsatisfactory daughter. As soon as that is settled, she told herself, I shall tackle Caroline's affairs! She knew that the Earl of Cannock had driven the girls in pursuit of Lizzie; indeed, she had sent him a most effusive note of thanks, and she was aware that he had insisted on driving Caroline back to town alone, just the two of them. And the groom, of course, but he didn't count, Mrs. Draper told herself, so this tête-à-tête was a most promising development!

Lizzie had been forbidden to leave the house unless she was accompanied by either her mother or Caroline and Belinda both, and Mrs. Draper had set her to the task of making a chair cover in needlepoint to keep her occupied. Lizzie sighed over the work, praying her mother would relent in time. It was not very exciting, after all that had happened to her.

True to Lady Wells's letter, the duke arrived one morning and was closeted with Mrs. Draper for some time. It was agreed that he would call on Belinda that very afternoon, after she returned from a picnic at Richmond, where she had gone with Caroline and a party of young people. He had frowned a little when Mrs. Draper told him of this, and she hastened to assure him it was quite unexceptional, and a large group, all of whom he knew, and since she was with her cousin and...but before she could become embroiled in any more explanations, the duke took his leave. As she said good-bye, Mrs. Draper promised to have Belinda in the library at four.

Perhaps it would have been better if Mrs. Draper had prepared Belinda for the meeting, but she thought it would be much more romantic to surprise her, and so when the summons came, shortly after the girls returned from Richmond, Belinda paused only to remove her chip straw bonnet with the blue satin ribbons before she tripped down the stairs to the library, still dressed in the sprigged muslin gown she had worn to the picnic, to see what her aunt wanted.

She threw open the door and said gaily, "Here I am, dear aunt, and...oh, it's you!"

The duke rose from the velvet sofa, where he had been waiting impatiently, and came forward. "Did I not promise to call as soon as I returned to town, Miss Wells?" he asked, smiling down at her and taking her hand. Belinda blushed and curtsied, and then, her heart beginning to beat in a very disturbing way, she asked the duke to be seated. She herself took a small straight chair across from him.

"I had thought you might welcome me with more enthusiasm," he said playfully, taking the chair she indicated. "I hope I am not any more conceited than the next man, but as a duke, you know, I am seldom greeted by the comment, 'oh, it's you!'"

Belinda tried to smile. "I beg your pardon, Your Grace, but you startled me. I thought my aunt was waiting for me here, and did not expect you!" She paused but the duke remained silent, although she noticed he never took his eyes from her face, so she continued, "I trust you had a pleasant journey, sir?"

"Most pleasant! And most worthwhile!" he said. "I am sure I do not have to tell *you* where I have been, or what my errand was! Indeed, I am sure you have been waiting most anxiously to hear!"

Belinda was becoming confused at all this heavy raillery. She could not remember the duke ever being so coy before, but said she would be delighted to know, if he wished to tell her.

He smiled again. "I have been in Yorkshire, Miss Wells, visiting your father and mother! I must tell you they were very happy to welcome me."

"Visiting my family?" Belinda asked slowly.

"But of course you knew I would do so, my dear Miss Wells," he replied calmly. "It would be a gross impropriety to speak to you about our marriage before I had your father's permission to do so."

Belinda rose and began to pace the library, her hands in two tight little fists. "I am afraid you go too fast, Your Grace," she said coolly. "I was not aware that our marriage was an accepted fact in your mind. It is most certainly not so in mine!"

The duke rose and came to her. "But of course you are funning, Miss Wells," he said. "Surely you have been aware of my intentions; consider my attendance on you, my great interest in you, and you alone, among all the other girls. There could be no other interpretation of the matter by anyone who knew me, except marriage. I salute your modesty, but the time for all that is past. Now we have your father's blessing, we can announce our betrothal to society at once!"

"One moment, Your Grace!" Belinda said, holding up a delaying hand when he would have taken her in his arms, assuming that of course she must agree. Such complaisance angered her, and she said, "I have not said I wished to marry you, you know, no matter what my father and mother say! My feelings are the most important, and the final decision is mine."

The duke allowed a little frown to cross his face. "Whatever are you talking about, my dear?" he asked. "Of course we shall be wed! I know Lady Salton has spoken to you, and you have never given me any indication that you wished to repulse my attentions. What missishness is this?"

Belinda clasped her hands tightly before her, to keep them from trembling. This was much, much worse than she had imagined. "I am sorry you have been so misguided, Your Grace," she said, as calmly as she could. "I do not know you very well, after all, and I am not at all sure we should suit! And I think it most arrogant of you to think that all you have to do is mention marriage and I will fall into your arms!"

"I have not held them out, Miss Wells!" the duke riposted sternly, his face now flushed. "That would be most improper until I have your consent!"

"But that is the problem!" Belinda blurted out without thinking. "It seems you are very cold, Your Grace, for a man in love! I take it you are in love?" she asked, and then hurried on when she saw the look in his eyes. "But perhaps you have merely decided on a marriage of convenience, after all, and that is why you checked my family and connections, to be sure I was worthy of being your duchess! I am afraid I will have to decline your offer, flattering as it is! I do not care to marry where I do not love, or am loved in return!"

The duke appeared speechless, so she curtsied. "And now you must excuse me, Your Grace. There is nothing more to be said!"

She turned to the door, her head high, but she did not reach it before she felt the duke grasping her shoulder and turning her around. Furious, she tried to raise her hand to strike him, but he held her arms firmly while he stared down at her, his green eyes intent, and blazing with suppressed fury.

"How dare you, Belinda!" he said in a tight voice. "A marriage of convenience, indeed! You know that I love you—I want you—and I tell you now, my girl, I intend to have you!"

She would have spoken, but suddenly he put his arms around her and pulled her close to him before he bent his head and kissed her. Belinda was no innocent; she had been kissed many times before, but never had she felt such a response as now rose in her breast. Is it possible that I love him after all, she thought wildly as he lifted his lips from hers and stared down at her triumphantly. No, it cannot be! He is so stiff, so conscious of his rank! I am sure he would lead me a life of misery, for all he professes his love, and kisses me with such ardor! Before she could speak, the duke began to kiss her again, and all coherent thoughts left her mind. When he finally let her go, she would have stumbled if he had not caught her and led her to the sofa.

"Now you see I was right!" he said, a little unsteadily. "And you love me too! It is not possible that you do not, not after such a display of warmth! Come, my dear, say you will marry me, and soon! I do not intend to wait for that happy day a moment longer than I have to!"

Realizing that there was indeed a passionate man beneath the pompous façade, Belinda hung her head and tried to organize her thoughts, and he took her chin in his hand and tipped her face up to his again. When she saw the pleading look in those intent eyes, she could only nod.

It was some time later when the duke took his leave, and Belinda went to find her aunt and tell her the happy news. She was still feeling very confused, but the sight of Mrs. Draper's fat beaming face did much to reassure her. Caroline came in as the two of them were sitting there making plans, and was soon apprised of Belinda's new status.

"But my dear cuz!" she said, much horrified. "You cannot be serious! Marry the duke, after all you have said about him? I do not believe it!"

Belinda blushed prettily. "I find I have changed my mind, Caro! I did not realize—I mean, he is not at all what he seems—oh, do wish me happy, dearest Caro!" she wailed; and, slightly ashamed of herself for her unkind thoughts that Belinda had been swayed by visions of ermine robes and diamond tiaras, Caroline came and kissed her.

"Of course I shall wish you happy, my dear, if that is what you truly want! Perhaps we were all misled by the duke's personality, for if you want to marry him, I am sure he must be delightful!"

There was not much conviction in her voice, and Mrs. Draper hastened to assure her that not only was her cousin making an excellent match socially, it was a love match as well! Belinda blushed again, remembering the way the duke's mouth had felt on hers, and said quickly, "And you must be my maid of honor, dear Caro, and Lizzie a bridesmaid! The duke will want a state wedding, of course. I shall have to see to my bridal clothes without delay, for he wishes the ceremony to take place as soon as possible!" She blushed yet again, and Caroline held her tongue although her heart was heavy. She went away to tell Lizzie the news, Belinda calling after her gaily, "And now we must find your 'one,' dear cuz! I do so wish you to be as happy as I am!"

Caroline shook her head and left Belinda and her mother with their heads together, discussing the relative merits of Westminster Abbey, the Chapel Royal, or an elegant home wedding in Yorkshire, as well as whether Belinda preferred white satin or a figured silk for her wedding gown. Mrs. Draper assured her the family bridal veil would be vastly becoming with either.

In the days that followed, they were all much involved with the coming nuptials. Lizzie had been delighted to hear the news, and took to calling her cousin "Duchess Bel," which, although Belinda declaimed such pomp, seemed to please her nevertheless. Mrs. Draper continued ecstatic, but not to the point of forgetting Lizzie. She had been very good, but for once Mrs. Draper was not to be lulled into complacence, for she wanted no more contretemps before the wedding. All thoughts of retiring to Hunstanton, however, left her mind, for which all the girls, especially Lizzie, were grateful.

The duke sent flowers to his betrothed every day, and as soon as the announcement appeared in the newspapers, gifts and congratulations poured into the house. The duke now escorted Belinda to every function she attended, personally calling and driving her and the Drapers in his own carriage. Belinda was delighted with this attention, and with the beautiful gifts he showered on her with such regularity.

He had first presented her with a magnificent sapphire ring, encircled with diamonds. It was so large and heavy that she told him she was afraid it would be impossible for her to raise her hand!

He kissed her, and then held her left hand up to her face and murmured, "I thought it would be perfect, but now I see that its blue does not quite match your eyes. But then, nothing could compare to their beauty; the sapphire is but a poor copy of their loveliness!"

It would have been a much colder young lady who would not have been delighted with such lovemaking and compliments, and even Lady Salton's complacence and tart comment, "I told you you would, gel!" did not annoy her. She drove out every afternoon with the duke, and was happy to be introduced to all his friends; she went to church with him; she accepted any suggestions or plans of his with smiling good humor.

Of course it would have been marvelous if they had not had a few words occasionally, even as much in love as they were. When Belinda felt annoyance at a pompous statement he made, or an assumption that she agreed with all his thoughts and wishes and had no opinions of her own, she had only to come into his arms and be kissed, and all was well. I know I can change him, she thought to herself, after we are married. If he is too pompous, it is only because he has been fawned over for so long. Soon I will be able to brighten his outlook and show him that there is no need to treat life so seriously; that it does not belittle him or his rank to show a little kindness and good humor, to laugh and be gay occasionally. And since I know he loves me, it will be easy to bring him around to a happier frame of mind!

Caroline watched her cousin anxiously, still not entirely sure that Belinda had made a wise choice. One morning when the Earl of Cannock called on her to ask her to ride with him the following afternoon, she answered him almost absent-mindedly.

"Thank you, that would be delightful!" she murmured, staring out the window to where Belinda was being assisted from the duke's carriage. She watched her laugh up at the duke and take his arm closely, and saw his answering smile. I cannot like him, she thought to herself. Of course he is pleasant and attentive now, but after the wedding, I am so afraid he will revert to his former state, and then what will Belinda do? And he will want her to be just as formal, just as starched up as he is himself!

She came back to earth speedily when the earl came to stand beside her at the window. "What can be of such interest, Miss Draper," he asked in a stiff voice, "that you have not heard a word I have said?"

Caroline turned, bewildered, to see his heavy dark brows meeting in a ferocious frown. "But I have, m'lord!" she insisted. "I should be delighted to ride with you; did I not say so?"

"That was some time ago!" he replied. "Since then I have addressed several unexceptional remarks to you, all of which have been ignored! I hope I am not boring you, Miss Draper?"

Caroline wished she might laugh, he sounded so indignant. As if everyone must of course hang on his every word, just because it is *he* who speaks, she thought, trying to keep a straight face.

"Now I see where your thoughts have been," he continued, watching Belinda and the duke stroll up the front steps, close together. "I wonder why? Your cousin is engaged, and to a duke, no less! And she seems to be very happy. What is there in that situation that upsets you?"

He sounded so much kinder, suddenly, that Caroline found herself telling him all her fears about her cousin's coming marriage, and would have continued to expound on it if Belinda and the duke had not come in to join them, thereby putting an end to her confidences. The earl watched the happy couple closely. He could see why Caroline was disturbed, for they were such disparate types, but he himself thought Belinda would be very good for Franklin Brownell. He had never been a particularly close friend of the duke, but he knew nothing in his disfavor except his haughty contemptuousness and overbearing conceit. He was sure that such a merry little lady as Belinda was, could soon coax him out of such attitudes, for it was obvious that the duke was head over heels in love with her. His eyes never left her face, and there was a warm glow in them that was unmistakable, even as he chastised her for so quickly acknowledging Mrs. Crosley, who according to him was no better than she should be, and not at all the kind of woman he wished his betrothed to be connected with.

Belinda quite sternly replied that she would do exactly as she wished; and for herself, she found Mrs. Crosley most convivial and amusing. The duke sniffed a little and remarked that of course for one in her position, he imagined conviviality was a prerequisite. Belinda pooh-poohed him and called him stuffy before she changed the subject.

Since it was obvious that the two of them much preferred to be alone, Caroline walked to the door with the earl after he had taken his leave of them.

"You see what I mean?" she whispered, as the door closed behind them. "How *can* she marry him? And Mrs. Crosley is nowhere near as bad as he makes her out to be, as you must know too! Why, only the highest sticklers do not acknowledge her. I am sure it is not her fault that Mr. Crosley divorced her, no matter what the ton says, and I am positive she is about to marry Lord Rogers, who is a most acceptable man!"

The earl took her hand in farewell. "My dear Miss Draper," he said, trying to lighten his tone, "as far as Mrs. Crosley, Mr. Crosley, and Lord Rogers are concerned, I find it hard to interest myself in such an affair in any way! And may I point out to you that what Miss Wells and the Duke of Darwood do is their business! It is your cousin's life, after all! I do not know why you feel you have to matchmake, or perhaps I should say 'unmatchmake' in this case! Come, forget it! Miss Wells is a capable young lady, and she knows what she is about!"

Caroline wished she might sink into the ground, for she knew it was none of her concern, but she wished the earl had not felt called upon to point it out to her. It was extremely unpleasant, she realized, to be reprimanded by a man who was not only beginning to dominate her thoughts much more than anyone else had ever done, but who had the ability to make her heart jump in such an alarming way whenever he turned that sardonic white grin her way as well!

When he took her hand in farewell and smiled down at her, it was all she could do to curtsy politely, her thoughts were in such a turmoil.

Unaware of her feelings, Matthew Kincaid walked briskly to his club, a frown on his dark, handsome face. It seemed there was no one in London that Miss Caroline Draper was not concerned about...except, of course, himself!

Chapter Nine

Early the following afternoon, as Lizzie sat sighing over her needlepoint, bemoaning the fact that her mother had made her stay at home instead of accompanying the others to inspect designs for Belinda's wedding gown, she heard Winsted's voice exclaiming in the front hall, and rose hurriedly. Whatever could it be to make that superior butler so forget himself, she wondered, nervously smoothing her gown with suddenly shaking fingers as she hurried to the door of the salon. Oh, pray there was nothing wrong at home, she thought, not the children or her father, hurt or sick! She ran through the hall to the front entrance and saw a footman assisting a young gentleman into the house, Winsted hovering about, wringing his hands and advising caution. One glance was all Lizzie needed.

"*Ned!*" she shrieked, "my dearest brother! Is it you?"

She ran to him as he lifted his head and smiled weakly. "As much of me as there is left, dear Lizzie!"

Lizzie was shocked, and one hand stole to her throat. Could this truly be her brother, this pale, thin young man in the torn scarlet regimentals, with the dark circles under his eyes, and his forehead creased with pain lines? Ned had always been so strong, so gay! He had gone to war with his head high and a song on his lips, and he had promised to return the same way. Now tears came to her eyes when she saw how he limped, and with what care he held his left arm, bound in a dirty sling. He stopped for a moment to catch his breath, leaning more heavily on the footman, and tried to smile again.

"I'm all right, Lizzie, really I am! A few small wounds, that is all, and even though I am not the cleanest I have ever been, I find it most distressing that you will not even give me a kiss!"

Lizzie went to him and kissed him gently, not touching him. At his questioning look, she said, "I am afraid I will hurt you! Oh, Ned, my dear, whatever is the matter with you?"

"Just about everything, I'm afraid," he answered ruefully. "But I am on the mend now. Alan is in much worse case than I am!"

Suddenly he turned to Winsted and said, "I forgot! There is another gentleman in the coach, a Captain Carter. Please send two footmen out to help him, Winsted, for he is sorely wounded. Tell them to be as gentle as they can!"

He allowed Lizzie to lead him to the porter's chair while they awaited his companion.

"But who is Captain Carter?" Lizzie asked. "And why does he come here if he is in such bad case? Should he not go directly to a hospital?"

"He wanted to, but I insisted he come home with me!" Ned replied. "You know the hospitals, Lizzie! He can get much better attention here, and since all the surgery has been done, there is no need for him to be crowded in a ward and neglected. He saved my life; now I have a chance to save his, for he has no relatives living except for some distant cousins, all elderly. But enough of that!" He sounded tired, and Lizzie swallowed all her questions and summoned Mrs. Winsted. When that good lady saw Master Ned, as she called him, she wasted no time sending the housemaids to prepare rooms, and insisted Lizzie send for a doctor at once. She had known the oldest Draper since he was a baby, and loved him dearly, and to see him like this was most upsetting.

"Where is Mother?" Ned asked, when he was able to speak over the orders and instructions that issued from the housekeeper's lips.

"She is out shopping with Caro and our cousin Belinda; you remember we wrote and told you she was staying with us for the season," Lizzie said. "She will be so sorry she was not here to greet you, Ned, but perhaps it would be better if we get you and the captain to bed before that happy reunion. I fear it would be a great shock to Mama if she should come upon you in this state!"

Ned laughed a little. "Yes, a bath and some clean bandages would help! The ship that carried us from Spain was crowded; there was no time for such niceties."

Suddenly he broke off as the footmen reappeared with another soldier, even more grievously wounded than Ned. They had to lift him into the house, and Lizzie's heart went out to him, barely conscious and with his head covered with bandages.

"Carry him upstairs immediately!" she ordered the footmen, "and then return for my brother! Winsted, send someone at once for Doctor Booth! Tell him it is an emergency, and he must come to us now!"

Mrs. Winsted preceded the footmen as they carried the young officer upstairs. "Can I get you a drink, dear Ned? Or something to eat?" Lizzie asked next.

"Thank you! A glass of wine would go well, for my throat is coated with road dust! I made the best time I could, for I do not like the looks of Alan at all; he needs special nursing, and I only hope the journey has not worsened his condition!"

Winsted himself went off to get the wine, and Lizzie knelt by her brother, patting his unbandaged hand. "Do not try to talk too much, Ned," she said decisively. "Just rest until the footmen return and we can help you upstairs!"

Ned winked at her, in quite his old way. "You have become vastly competent, little sister!" he said. "When I went to join Wellington, you were still a scatterbrained girl; now I find you taking charge, a grown-up young lady! You will have to tell me all about your beaux, one of these days—I am sure you have many of them!"

Lizzie had seldom felt less like talking about beaux, and as for feeling competent, it was no such thing. Her insides were fluttering with nervousness, and she had to keep swallowing to preserve any semblance of calm, but since her mother and Caroline were not home, it was clearly up to her to see both men disposed of and cared for. She watched Ned drink his wine, and was grateful to see a little color come back into his pale face; and when the footmen came back, she promised to come to him as soon as he was bathed and put to bed. She went with Mrs. Winsted to the housekeeper's room to make a list of things they would need for the invalids, and reminded her to have plenty of hot water and fresh bandages ready for the doctor. Mrs. Winsted smiled kindly at the second Draper daughter.

"It will be all right, Miss Lizzie, dear!" she said comfortably. "I have seen men much worse than that, who have recovered completely, so don't you go fretting about your brother or the other officer. We'll take good care of them! And let me tell you, your mother and father would be proud of you, the way you handled everything! Good as Miss Caro, you were! But there! Here I am chatting when there is so much to do!"

With a final smile, she whisked away, and Lizzie sat back in her chair and tried to relax. Let Mrs. Winsted be right, dear God, she prayed. If anything happens to Ned, I do not know what will become of us! And of course, the captain too, she added hastily.

She went back to the front of the house and told

Winsted to call her as soon as her brother was in bed, and to send the doctor to him immediately he arrived. Winsted nodded solemnly, and she went back to her needlepoint to wait. Not a stitch did she take in the half hour before she was summoned; then she flew up the stairs at once to Ned's room.

When Mrs. Draper returned home some time later, it was to learn that the doctor was with her son and his friend, and that Miss Lizzie had handled everything most competently. Lizzie herself came down to prepare her mother and the girls, and the three Drapers hurried back upstairs to see the invalids and hear what the doctor had to say about their recovery and treatment. Belinda remained below, hesitant to invade such a happy family reunion.

Mrs. Draper quite forgot her salts or vinaigrette or any other potions she would generally have resorted to in an emergency, when she saw her eldest son, and she rushed to give him a kiss, the tears of relief for his safe return, even wounded as he was, running down her face.

"Now, Mama!" Ned complained, "you are wetting all my new bandages! And why is it that women always cry when they are happy? I should think you would be smiling at me, and I am convinced I must look terrible, to cause such a flood!"

Mrs. Draper told him they were tears of joy, just as a footman appeared to announce that the Earl of Cannock was below, waiting to accompany Miss Draper on their ride in the park.

"Oh, I cannot go riding today!" Caroline said, smiling fondly at Ned. "Tell him my brother has just returned from Spain and we are all very busy! I am sure he will understand."

Mrs. Draper was not at all sure this was the way to treat such a personage as the earl, and tried to insist that Caro at least go and explain the situation to him herself, but Caro refused to leave Ned's side.

"I am sure Belinda will be glad to do it for me, Mama," she said carelessly, causing her mother to roll her eyes heavenward. She could not change Caroline's mind and soon desisted, for she was much more concerned with her son's injuries, and wanted to speak to the doctor as soon as he finished attending Captain Carter.

The footman went away to ask Miss Wells to relay Caroline's regrets, and Mrs. Draper asked Ned about his companion. "For of course we shall be happy to care for him, Ned," she said in a distracted way, "but it will make everything that much more difficult, and I should prefer to spend all my energies nursing you, my dear! *Your* recovery, after all, is the most important thing to me!"

Ned frowned a little and took her hand. "Dear Mother, let me tell you that if it had not been for Captain Carter, your son would be in no need of nursing! Alan saved my life, and in doing so was severely wounded himself. If he had left me, he could have escaped without any injuries at all!"

Mrs. Draper immediately changed her mind and declared that she was so grateful to the young captain that she would personally see to it that he had the finest care available! She saw that Ned was very tired, and soon shooed the girls from the room to allow him to sleep.

"We will have time to question him later, girls," she said, giving Lizzie a special hug for her care of her brother, "and as soon as I have seen the doctor, I shall come to you and tell you what we must do. Wait for me in my room!"

As her daughters went down the hall, Lizzie said earnestly, "I think we should write to Father at once, don't you, Caro? He will be so glad to hear that Ned is home, and so anxious to hear his condition! I would not be surprised if he set off for London right away!"

Caroline agreed that such a letter should be their first concern, and when Belinda joined them to give her the earl's compliments and assurance that he quite understood why she could not ride, and only hoped her brother would make a complete and speedy recovery, she had quite forgotten him, so deep was she in planning the letter. In this instance, the earl would have understood perfectly.

That evening at dinner, the four ladies discussed nothing but Ned's sudden return, and the bravery of his captain. Mrs. Draper was especially affected by such devotion, and had to pause and wipe her eyes on her napkin before she could continue telling the girls everything she had learned. She had seen the doctor; he promised Ned a complete recovery, with only a slight limp to mar his appearance, although he cautioned Mrs. Draper that it would be a lengthy business, and that Ned would often be in pain. He had taken a ball through the shoulder, and another in the leg, and there had been infection and fever. He shook his head over Captain Carter. The young man had been unconscious, so he was unable to question him, but it appeared that besides the bullet that had creased his skull, there were bad burns on his hands and face, and a stomach wound from a saber, that did not seem to be healing well. The doctor promised to call in the morning, but said he would come at once if there was any change in his patients, for he feared the captain was sinking into a coma.

"Of course," Mrs. Draper told Belinda and her daughters, all wide-eyed with shock, "he has just had a most uncomfortable time of it, first in the crowded ship bringing the wounded home from the battle at Pamplona, then in a hired coach, jouncing over the rough roads. I have great hopes that a few days of quiet and good care will bring about some real improvement in his condition, and if there is anything at all we can do, girls, *anything,* then of course we will do it gladly! To think that he saved Ned, only to be so wounded himself! I love him already, and I shall treat him as my son, and you must treat him as your brother. Remember!"

Eagerly the girls agreed. They had been engaged to go to the theatre with Lady Salton and the duke that evening, but only Belinda went away to dress. Mrs. Draper insisted there was no need for her niece to remain at home, although she had offered to do so and help with the nursing. Mrs. Draper had of course sent a note to Lady Salton; now she told Belinda it would be a kindness for her to excuse the Drapers from the party, in person. She and Caro and Lizzie were to take turns sitting with the invalids until the doctor sent his best nurses to take over such duties in the morning. There would be a footman in attendance to assist them, and since there was nothing to be done but administer some medicine if they complained of pain, or give them a drink of water or change their position in bed, Mrs. Draper felt she and her daughters would be more than capable of handling such chores for one night.

Lizzie went to entertain the duke when he called for Belinda, and Mrs. Draper looked after her fondly.

"Who would have thought that Lizzie would have managed as well as she did, Caro?" she asked. "Mrs. Winsted told me all she did, without once bursting into tears or fainting. I am very proud of her; perhaps she is growing up, after all!"

Caroline agreed and went to lie down on her bed, for her mother was going to attend the invalids till midnight, when she would call Caro. Lizzie was to be summoned at dawn.

Nothing untoward occurred during the night, and when Caroline came to get her sister, she was able to report that both young men had been sleeping almost continually; in fact, Captain Carter had not wakened even once.

Yawning as she dressed in one of her oldest gowns, and tying a big white apron around her waist, Lizzie went at once to the sickrooms. Ned was fast asleep, Stanley sitting beside him watchfully, so she went to Captain Carter's room next door. It was very quiet; so quiet, in fact, that she hurried up to the bed. The slight rise and fall of the bed covers showed that he was breathing, and she took a deep breath of relief herself. By the dawn light coming through the window, and the candle on the dresser, she was able to see her brother's captain, although she had no idea what he looked like without his bandages. She took the chair by his side and studied him. One tiny corner of his head showed he had dark blond hair, but the only features she could see were his closed eyes and part of his mouth. His hands, limp on the counterpane, were also covered with gauze, but his forearms looked strong and capable. As if suddenly aware he was being stared at, the young man stirred and moaned. At once Lizzie was on her feet, bending over him anxiously. He opened the darkest blue eyes Lizzie had ever seen, and stared back at her, perplexed.

"Captain Carter!" Lizzie said. "Can you hear me?"

He tried to sit up and moaned again, and she put both her hands on his shoulders and pressed him back in the bed. "No, do not try to move, sir! I am afraid you will hurt yourself! Can I get you a drink of water?"

The captain lay quiet, those dark blue eyes open wide in wonder. "But do they have water in heaven?" he asked in a whisper.

Lizzie smiled at him. "You are not in heaven, sir; you are at the Draper house in London. And if we have anything to say about it, you are a long way from heaven yet!"

He raised one of his bandaged hands and winced. "Ah, I remember! Yes, some water, please, Miss...?"

"I am Lizzie Draper, Ned's sister, sir," she said and went to the dresser, where she poured him a glass of cool water. Holding up his head so he could drink, she watched him take several sips before he seemed to lose interest. Carefully she lowered him back onto his pillows, and as she went to replace the glass, she heard him murmur, "But I do not believe you, for you are definitely an angel!"

By the time she returned to the bed, he was fast asleep again. She took her seat, smiling a little to herself. Surely the fact that he had wakened and spoken to her was a good sign! She wished she could see what he looked like! His voice, even as weak as it was, had been pleasantly deep. Lizzie was intrigued, and spent the remainder of her duty speculating on his appearance, where he might be from, and who his family was. When Ned woke up, she went to his room and sent Stanley to fetch some tea for them both. Ned said he hadn't had a good cup of tea for what seemed like years. He seemed stronger this morning, and Lizzie was delighted to remain with him while Stanley went to care for the captain, stirring his tea and helping him to the scones the cook had sent up to tempt his appetite.

From a household whose main concerns were invitations to a ball, Miss Wells's engagement, or the number of floral tributes delivered each morning, the Draper house quickly changed to one where the major event of the day was the doctor's visit and the latest news of the invalids. No more bandboxes were carried upstairs to the young ladies' rooms, no more delicious new gowns were delivered from the modistes; instead medicines and nurses went up the stairs, and trays and laundry came down, and the unbroken hush that attends most serious sickrooms prevailed throughout the house.

Not that the girls gave up all their social life. Belinda, especially, continued to go about with her fiancé, and even Lizzie and Caroline went for rides or walks in the park, since their mother insisted they get some exercise every day.

"It will do no one any good, my dears, if you become ill from lack of fresh air! And now we have such good nurses to care for the boys, there is no need for your constant attendance!"

Mrs. Draper noticed the earl had sent flowers and several notes to Caroline, and she was in hopes that the relationship might begin to flourish again, now that Caroline went out in company. She did not notice that her second daughter had not only stopped begging to go to parties, she sometimes had to be ordered from the sickrooms as well, before she would leave; and that she showed no interest at all in a masquerade that was to take place in two weeks' time, and promised to be the major event of an already brilliant season.

Belinda asked permission for them all to go as the Three Graces, and, distracted as she was, Mrs. Draper agreed without questions. Belinda and Caroline informed Lizzie of the scheme and were surprised when she did not seem to care very much about it. Caroline asked her cousin if she thought Lizzie was feeling well.

"I cannot remember a time when she was not in raptures over a coming party, cuz!" she said, shaking her head in bewilderment. "This is most unlike her!"

Belinda agreed absently, but as she was thinking of the duke, she was not properly attending. That gentleman had had the temerity to tell her that the gown she had worn the previous evening was much too revealing, and he would appreciate it if she never so appeared again. Belinda was still smoldering. How dare he? She had tried to argue with him, but he held up a repressive hand and said solemnly, "We will not discuss it, Belinda! Kindly remember that we are in company! Besides, when I tell you that as the future Duchess of Darwood, you are not to be so immodest, I most certainly do not expect any opposition to my wishes!"

Belinda had seethed but, seeing Lady Salton looking at her, had held her tongue. This morning, however, she had every intention of telling the duke as soon as possible what she thought of such high-handed ways. They might be engaged; he did not own her! They were invited to tea at Lady Lincoln's that afternoon, and Belinda was sorry that such a tame occasion gave her no chance to wear her new white muslin, for that was even more daring than the peach silk that the duke had objected to. I shall wear it at the first opportunity, she thought, and I shall dampen my petticoats as well! *That* will show him!

Ned continued to improve every day, causing his mother to send many glowing reports to her husband. Mr. Draper had been unable to leave the estate, but as the news came in that Ned was on the mend so rapidly, he contained his impatience at not seeing his son. Mrs. Draper said that she intended to bring both young men to Hunstanton, where the sun, the salt air, and the quiet of the countryside was sure to hasten their recovery, but that she was unable to leave town until Dr. Booth pronounced Captain Carter completely out of danger and able to travel.

He was recovering too; not as fast as Ned did, but a little each day. Now he could sit up, propped up on pillows for a short time, at least, and he was eating better and was not in such severe pain. The bandages were removed every day so fresh salve could be applied to his burns, but Lizzie was still no wiser as to his looks, for she was firmly put from the room whenever the nurses were caring for him. She spent as much time with him as she dared, talking to him whenever he was awake, and she heard all about his childhood, his home in Kent, and his reason for joining the army, and she in turn told him all about her home and family. They became fast friends, and the captain, who had never seen such a lovely girl, was falling in love more quickly than he was recovering from his wounds. After the noise, the dirt, and the pain and horrors of war, it was not surprising that this beautiful English girl should so attract him.

One morning, after the doctor had left, Lizzie brought him some flowers she had purchased on her walk with Caroline, and as she found him asleep, she went quietly to the table by the window to arrange the carnations and lilies in a bowl. The captain opened his eyes and saw her there, bending over the flowers to inhale their sweetness, and his heart turned over as he watched, not daring to make a sound. As she stood up, she saw he was awake and came to the bed.

"And how are you this morning, Captain Carter?" she asked shyly, her own heart beating a little faster, as it always did when he turned those dark blue eyes her way.

"I am feeling better, thank you, Miss Lizzie," he said formally, a small frown between his eyes. Lizzie was quick to notice it, and thought he must be in pain.

"Did the doctor hurt you this morning, sir?" she asked. "Is there anything I can get for you?"

He waved one of his bandaged hands impatiently.

"No, there is nothing! I am a little tired still; I think I will try to sleep again!"

He closed his eyes and shut out her look of hurt bewilderment. Presently he heard her steal away and he groaned. He could never tell her of his love, he thought sadly. Besides the fact that she was an heiress, and he had but a competency and a small estate, he was sure he was disfigured from his burns. He watched the nurses' faces eagerly when they removed the bandages, and although he had seen no sign of revulsion, he was sure it was only because they were trained not to show emotion. He might have asked for a mirror, but somehow he did not dare. But how could such a dear sheltered girl like Lizzie want a man who was scarred and ugly, as well as poor? It did not bear thinking about! She should marry a lord or a rich man; indeed, Lizzie Draper could marry anyone she pleased. A mere Captain Carter was no fit match for her.

He decided that it was better that she think him cold and abrupt, and return to her beaux. He had heard all about the Drapers from Ned, through many a long night in Spain, when the boy, homesick for England and his family, had poured out his heart. He knew about Caroline, her father's right hand; he knew about Mary Martha's giggles and Andrew's pranks. He felt as if Clorinda was his own dear little sister; and of course he had heard about Lizzie, beautiful, flirting, desirable Lizzie, who, as the beauty of the family, was sure to make a brilliant marriage. He sighed and beat his fists on the bed until the pain reminded him that no good could come of such anger, and that fate had decided that Alan Carter, although deeply in love, should never claim his lady. It was no good to rail that it was not fair; at twenty-eight Carter knew life seldom was. Well, he would get well as soon as possible and then he would leave the Drapers, and if they would not have him back in the regiment, he would retire to Kent. Perhaps there he would learn to forget Lizzie, with her sweet mouth and brown curls and winning laugh, and the way her long eyelashes swept her cheeks when she blushed. He groaned again, for the prospect was not at all inviting, and he did not see how he could ever forget her! He almost wished he had died at Pamplona, rather than have to face such a life of disappointment.

Ned limped in to see his friend, and was sorry he did not appear to be in better spirits, for he had hoped to interest him in a game of cards. He was fast becoming bored with the invalid life, and wished to go home. He had told Caro that he was sure that out of the bustle of town, he would soon regain his health completely, and it waited only until Alan was well enough to travel before they could be on their way. Now it was Caro's turn to frown, and she was glad, without knowing the reason, that her mother had made her accept an invitation to a reception that same evening. It has been a long time since I saw my friends, she told herself. I wonder if Lord Anders has become even more exquisite, or if Mr. Sawyer has missed me.

As she came down the steps that evening and joined the duke, she was glad she was wearing her orange crepe, and that Peggy had done her hair so well. Deep in her own thoughts, she did not notice that Belinda greeted the duke very coldly, and shrugged her shoulders when he would have put her stole more closely about her to shield her from the night air. The duke looked bemused, and, since Caroline was the only one to converse with him all the way to the party, much offended as well, by the time he was helping his love down the carriage steps. He had no opportunity to question her, however, not with Miss Draper waiting for them.

Later, in the garden, he took Belinda's arm and led her a little way from the other guests. The night was warm, and the doors had been left open so the guests could enjoy the fountain and the flowers.

"Whatever is the matter, my dear?" he asked in bewilderment as soon as they were around a bend in the path and out of sight. "You must tell me what I have done! You know I would never displease you!"

Belinda shrugged, and appeared to be completely engrossed in a yellow rose bush. Suddenly the duke had had enough of her silence, and he took her shoulders and turned her towards him, drawing her close and forcing her to look at him.

"Now, Miss Wells!" he said between clenched teeth. "You *shall* answer me!"

Belinda tossed her head. "Oh, of course, Your Grace," she said sarcastically. "Everyone must do as you command! Even to discarding gowns that are not acceptable in *your* eyes!"

"Whatever are you talking about?" he asked, quite forgetting the peach gown. "It would be most improper to discard your gown, my dear! Not yet...not quite yet!" He bend his head towards her and saw her blushing.

"I did not mean it like that!" she cried, but he only laughed and kissed her. By the time they rejoined the others, Belinda had forgotten their quarrel completely, for the duke's whispered lovemaking had so enthralled her that if he had asked it of her, she would have promised never to leave the house in a gown that was not buttoned to her chin.

In the meantime, Caroline was pleased to see Matthew Kincaid at the party, and not adverse to chatting with him when he came to her side. After asking courteously after the invalids and the state of their health, he remained with her for quite a long time, telling her of all the parties she had missed, and all the latest *on dits*. Not once did he anger her by his arrogance, and when he left her at last, she watched his retreating back in some confusion. He could really be very pleasant, she thought, when he forgot his consequence and did not try to manage her affairs. It made him dangerously attractive! But then, she reminded herself, gathering up her fan and going in search of Belinda, I am sure he will do something truly outrageous soon. This pleasant manner is only an act he is assuming! Again she wondered why he continued to seek her out and shower her with attentions. Could it be possible that he was attracted to her? She laughed at such thoughts. The wonderful Earl of Cannock, in love with an insignificant miss from Hunstanton? Impossible! He was merely amusing himself, and thank heavens she was too old and too wise to be taken in by such tricks. When the season was over, she was sure he would make his graceful farewells and never be seen again. She felt chilled at such an ending, and then another unpleasant thought occurred to her. Perhaps, not wanting to be caught in parson's mousetrap and in an effort to foil the matchmaking mamas, he had chosen to make her his companion as a purely defensive move. He must think her in no way a threat to his bachelorhood! This was so lowering that all her enjoyment in the evening left her, and when the earl smiled at her from across the room, she turned her back on him swiftly.

Lady Salton saw it and cackled. "Not going well, Matthew?" she inquired. "Alas that your fatal charms do not seem to be attracting Miss Draper with any success. You will have to try harder!"

The earl frowned down at the old lady. "We shall see, Lady Salton. I do not despair as yet!"

He sounded so determined that Lady Salton laughed again and wished him good fortune. The earl was feeling bewildered. Here he had put forth his best effort to entertain and charm the girl, for he found he had missed her while she was busy nursing her brother. She had also agreed to ride with him the following afternoon, and he had left her smiling and pleasant. And then, a few minutes later, she turned her back on him! Whatever was the matter with her? Women, he thought, who could understand them? He almost wished Lizzie Draper would get in another scrape so he could have the opportunity to help Caro rescue her, but Lizzie was seen even less than her sister these days, to the regret of several young gentlemen who looked for her in vain.

Miss Lizzie was staying very close to home, and very close to a certain bedroom on the second floor of the Drapers' London establishment. In fact, she spent so much time there that Ned asked her straight out, the following morning, what she was about. He was most interested to see her blush, and suddenly he knew what had happened.

"Lizzie, how famous!" he crowed. "No, do not shake your head, for it is as plain as the nose on your face that you are in love with Alan! And does he love you too, little sister?"

Lizzie shook her head, much flustered, and said it was no such thing. "Of course I am concerned with you both!" she said, summoning as much dignity as she could, with her cheeks blazing. "I do not know what you mean, Ned!"

"But even my mother is not as attentive as you, dear Lizzie! You cannot fool me, you know, and why should you want to? Alan is a capital fellow; I wish you both joy!"

"But Ned," Lizzie wailed, dropping any innocent airs, "he has not spoken to me, or acted in any way interested..."

Ned frowned, and then he offered, "I could ask him right out, you know; easiest thing in the world...!"

"No, no!" Lizzie shrieked. "Don't you dare! I should never forgive you!"

Ned shook his head. If the girl was in love with Alan and obviously could not relay this information herself, why did she get so excited when a perfect messenger was found? Why, he could straighten things out in a trice! He half determined to speak to Alan anyway, but Lizzie would not leave him alone until she had his promise that he would not do so. As she closed his door behind her, he told himself that even if he was now pledged to silence as far as Alan was concerned, there was no reason why he could not get Caroline's advice.

When his oldest sister came to visit him later, he was quick to acquaint her with the facts. At first Caroline ridiculed the notion.

"You must remember, Ned," she said, "that Lizzie is forever falling in love! This must be just a passing fancy, because the captain saved her brother and is a hero, and heroes are always romantic! Besides, she has never seen him without his bandages. You must be mistaken!"

Ned assured her he did not think he was. "You know, Caro," he said seriously, "if Lizzie thinks herself in love with a man who cannot dance or squire her to parties, and is too ill to flirt and pay her extravagant compliments, don't you feel that perhaps this time she really is in love? And Alan is older than her usual beaux. True, she has never seen his face; she does not know if he is ugly or handsome, and still she loves him. How can I be mistaken?"

Caroline was much struck by the logic of what he said, and went away to ponder it. She promised to watch Lizzie carefully. It was true that her sister had abandoned all her scatterbrained ways; true that she never once mentioned how she missed the gaiety she had become accustomed to; true that she more often than not refused invitations in order to remain with the invalids. Perhaps Ned was right!

So once again, when she rode with the earl that afternoon in the park, she was far, far away from him in her thoughts, and more than once had to bring her mind sharply back in order to answer one of his questions or contribute to the conversation.

The earl was not slow to notice her abstraction, and gritted his teeth. Caroline Draper was turning out to be a more formidable citadel than he had ever attempted to storm, he had to admit, but it only made him more determined to break down her defenses and make her fall in love with him.

Chapter Ten

Caroline lost no time in seeking her sister when she returned from her ride with Matthew Kincaid. She was almost sure Ned must be mistaken, and that Lizzie was indulging herself in histrionics. Of course it was more exciting to be in love with a veteran of Wellington's campaigns who was a genuine hero as well, instead of listening to some exquisite of the *haut ton* pay you compliments he did not mean. And even though Lizzie had taken on more than her share and had been as competent as either Caro or her mother in helping nurse and amuse the invalids, that must be because she was determined to show her mother that she had changed, and thereby forestall her early removal to the country. As for not showing any great interest in Lady St. Mark's masquerade, two weeks was a very long time in the future for a young miss like Lizzie. Caroline was sure she was not mistaken, and as she left the earl, she did not notice his frown or his terse good-bye, for she was already planning how to approach Lizzie and gain her confidence.

At the top of the stairs, she found her sister just coming out of Captain Carter's room, and said that she wished to speak to her. Lizzie blushed a little but followed Caroline to her bedroom, where the older girl was sure they would not be interrupted.

She had given Peggy the afternoon off, as well as some extra money, so the maid might do some shopping for her wedding, and Peggy had hugged her warmly for her kindness before she hurried off. Caroline had thought then how unfair it was that Belinda could spend whatever she wished for her marriage to the duke, while Peggy had to scrimp and save for even just a little finery. She made a note to ask her mother if they could not do something further for Peggy, for she had been an excellent maid, and had kept Lizzie's adventures with the Baxter twins a secret from the other servants as well. Yes, she deserved some kindness, and Caroline would see that she got it!

Now she led Lizzie to a chair near the window and took the seat opposite. Her sister looked at her curiously.

"But what can you want to talk to me about so privately, Caro?" she asked, her eyes wide with innocence. Then she jumped up and clapped her hands. "I know! The earl has spoken to you at last, has he not? Oh, Caro, I am so excited for you! Belinda and I both think him a definite 'one,' and I knew you would come to agree with us! How famous, and how pleased Mama will be!"

Caroline felt herself blushing as her sister came to embrace her, and put up her hands to hold her away.

"It is not true, Lizzie! Whatever can you mean? The earl is not interested in me at all, nor am I in him! He is merely amusing himself during the season, for he is a great flirt, you know!"

Lizzie looked at her sister's rosy face, which quite belied her stern words, and smiled again. "Well, he has certainly never flirted with me, Caro, but I am not in the least surprised that he flirts with *you!* Anyone can see he is attracted!"

Caroline shook her head more vehemently. "That is not the way of it, Lizzie, believe me! If he has seemed to like me this season, it is only to protect himself from being leg-shackled to some young girl, for I am convinced he has no desire to marry, and is dancing attendance on Miss Draper to save himself from the matchmaking mamas!"

Lizzie would have vehemently protested such thinking, but Caroline changed the subject abruptly. "But come, Lizzie, it is not of myself or the earl that I wish to speak. It concerns you!"

Lizzie sat down again slowly and folded her hands in her lap, a look of great seriousness coming over her face. "Yes, Caro?" she asked quietly.

Caroline leaned forward. "You spend a great deal of time with the captain, Lizzie! More even than you do with your own brother! Why is this?"

Now it was Lizzie's turn to blush. "He is more badly wounded, Caro," she said in a faint but perfectly even voice. "And Mama has asked us to be most particular in our care of him, for what he did for Ned!"

Caroline got up and began to pace the room. "But is there something more between you? I know Mama would be most displeased if she thought you were getting up a love affair right in her own home, and with a stranger, too, no matter what he has done for Ned! You remember she asked us to treat him as our brother!"

As Lizzie bowed her head and turned slightly away, Caroline continued, "After all, my dear, we do not know anything about the man! How do we know he is suitable, or even that he does not have a young lady waiting for him to come home from the wars, a girl he has been promised to all this time?"

"That cannot be so!" Lizzie gasped, stung into speech. "He would have told me! And I at least know something about him, for he has told me all about his life before he received his commission, and his home and connections as well!"

"So I am not mistaken! You have been encouraging him to fall in love with you! Oh, Lizzie, how *could* you?"

At this, Lizzie lifted her chin and turned to face her sister squarely. "I tell you this, Caro," she said in a very serious voice, "I have been encouraging him, that is true, for I am deeply in love with Alan Carter, but you need not fear there has been anything underhanded about it, for he does not care for me, and he has not said one word to me that you or our mother could not hear. He is a gentleman! But, Caro," she wailed, in quite the old way, "I wish he would! I do love him so much!"

"There, there," Caro soothed her, going to her chair and kneeling beside her. "I did not mean to upset you, Lizzie, but—and you must forgive me for saying this—you have been in love many, many times before! How can you be sure that this time it is real? Do you not feel that perhaps it is just that you have been so much in his company, and have not attended any parties or balls since he and Ned arrived? Come, my dear, be honest with yourself! If you were to go to a ball this very evening, how can you be sure that you would not meet some handsome new beau who would intrigue you to the point that you would gladly forget Captain Carter?"

She spoke in a bantering way, but Lizzie shook her head. "I see you do not understand, Caro! There will be no handsome new beaux for me!"

"But you have always been attracted to handsome men, Lizzie, and you have never even seen Captain Carter without his bandages! Why, he might be ugly, or hideously scarred...."

Lizzie smiled a little at her older sister, who before today had always seemed so wise. "It would not matter to me what he looked like! I have fallen in love with his gentle deep voice and dark blue eyes, but more importantly, with his conversation and concerns! You might parade a hundred handsome beaux before me, and I would not be tempted to change my mind!" She sighed a little, and added, "But what good does it do? Alan does not love me; he treats me most formally, and even my broadest hints go un-answered!"

She seemed so sad, that Caroline said, "But he could hardly, as a gentleman, make love to you in your mother's house, dear Lizzie! If he did, it would be the action of a rake!"

"As if I cared for that old fustian, Caro!" Lizzie said passionately. "But what good does it do to re-pine? I shall go on as I have been, and pray that I can somehow make him love me!" She turned to the door, her eyes bright with unshed tears. "Please help me if you can, Caro! If I cannot have Alan, I want no one at all! And I shall go down to Hunstanton when they leave London, so I can remain near him at least!"

Caroline spent some time alone, thinking of all Lizzie had told her. If it had been anyone but her younger sister, she would have been forced to believe such avowed devotion without question, but for Liz-zie to feel so strongly, about an older man who had no social pretensions and who might in truth be in-capacitated for life from his wounds, was a new come-out indeed. She went to her mother's room as soon as she heard her come upstairs from her afternoon engagements, and was glad that she had arrived before Grandish had been summoned to help her change.

"Mama," she said. "Do you have a moment? There is something serious that I have to talk about to you."

Mrs. Draper paused in the act of removing her large sage-green bonnet, with its nodding plumes, and beamed. "Dear, dear Caro!" she said fondly, an-ticipating her daughter's words, for she knew Car-oline had been riding with the earl. "Of course I am not too busy, for a little bird tells me that you have some very exciting news, do you not, my dear?"

"Well, I am not perfectly sure you will find it all that exciting, Mama," Caroline began, but Mrs.

Draper interrupted her with a playful shake of her finger.

"Now, do not try to dissimulate with me! Sit down, my dear, and tell me all about it at once! How did he ask you, and what did you say? Oh, Mr. Draper will be so pleased, for you know how much he liked him! And although I am not especially pleased that he approached you before he had a chance to speak to your father, I am sure we can forgive such impetuousness! Indeed, it shows how deep he is in love!"

Caroline's head was in a whirl. First Lizzie, now her mother. It was too much! "Whatever are you talking about, Mama?" she asked as soon as Mrs. Draper was forced to pause and take a breath. "No one has spoken to me; most certainly not the earl, if that is whom you are referring to! And if he did, I would refuse him, even though I admit he is so attractive, for he is arrogant, conceited, puffed-up, and a know-it-all as well!"

Mrs. Draper dropped her bonnet and reached for her salts. "Caro, I do not know what is to become of you! How can you say the earl is conceited or...or any of those horrid things? Why, he has been so attentive, and he is everything anyone could wish for their daughter! You make me very angry that you do not see what a wonderful marriage you would have, nor how lucky you are to have a man like Matthew Kincaid at your feet!"

She stopped to search for a handkerchief, and Caroline said, as steadily as she could, "Yes, well, Mama, he is hardly at my feet, and besides, it is not my marriage I wish to speak about; it is Lizzie's!"

Mrs. Draper dropped her salts. *"Lizzie's?* Lizzie has not left the house this age! Whatever can you mean?" She clasped her hands to her ample bosom and then exclaimed, "You do not mean to tell me that she has been sneaking away to those horrible Baxter twins, do you? Oh, that one of *my* daughters should be so bold! It gives me palpitations—incorrigible girl!"

Patting one well-upholstered sage-green shoulder

and handing her mother her salts, Caroline said, "Calm yourself, Mama! No, it is not the Baxters, and no, Lizzie has not been sneaking out! Indeed, if you recall, she has been extremely difficult to remove from the sickrooms, and when both Ned and I questioned her about it, she admitted she has fallen in love with Captain Carter."

"Captain Carter?" Mrs. Draper echoed, her mouth dropping open, and the salts rolling off her capacious lap again. "Captain Carter? A mere *nobody*? Why, Lizzie could have anyone she wants, anyone in the world, from a duke to an earl to a marquis! Surely you must be mistaken, Caro; I pray that you are!"

Although delighted to see that this new problem had driven all thoughts of the Earl of Cannock from her mother's mind, Caroline saw she would have an uphill battle to convince her mother that Lizzie was indeed serious. She spent some time with her, and by the time she rose to go and dress for dinner, her mother was resigned.

"If what you say is true, Caro, we must look forward to welcoming an army man into the family, for I am sure it is only his nice conduct that prevents the man from telling Lizzie he loves her. Who could not?" she asked proudly. "She is so beautiful and lively! And although I cannot like it in my heart, I am so grateful to him for saving Ned's life that I shall do all in my power to help him win Mr. Draper's approval. But, Caro," she added sadly, "I had such hopes for Lizzie!"

Caroline soothed, agreed, and pledged her to secrecy for the moment, and then she went away. She decided to question the captain more closely the next time she visited his room.

In the meantime, Lizzie had returned there herself after her talk with her sister. After ascertaining that he wanted nothing fetched for him, she took a seat near his bed and began to chat, determined to find out his true feelings if it was at all possible.

"I wish you might go outside, Captain," she began. "It is such a beautiful day!"

"Since I cannot, Miss Lizzie," he replied, "please do not feel you have to remain indoors too! You at least should be enjoying the sunshine!"

"That is of little importance, since I would so much rather be with you!" Lizzie said, with a melting glance.

The captain bit his lip, his eyes searching her face, but he did not ask her what she meant. Instead he changed the subject abruptly.

Several times she hinted at her deep feelings for him, and each time he turned the remark into something innocuous. Lizzie might say how glad she was they had met, and how it raised her spirits to see him feeling better at last; he only thanked her gravely for her concern. She might say she could not wait to show him Draper House, or talk about the picnics and rides she planned for them both to take together; he replied he would be delighted to be in *all* the Drapers' company, for he felt that Lizzie and Caroline were like the sisters he had never had. Becoming impatient, Lizzie even asked if he had ever been in love; he denied it, his heart beating rapidly as he told the lie.

She sighed. "Indeed, it is not a very pleasant feeling after all, as I have found out!" she said.

The captain longed to put his arms around her; instead he laughed and said, in a bracing way he was far from feeling, "Come, Miss Lizzie! You are in the doldrums for some reason! I am positive one of your beaux is teasing you, and you must curtail your visits to the invalids and go about the town more, so he will have a chance to tell you of his feelings!" This was dangerous ground, and he hurried on before she could speak. "But you have been in love many times, have you not? I am sure you will be again!"

"Yes, Caro thinks so too!" Lizzie told him. "But I know it is not so, for where I love now, I shall always love!"

She peeked at him and saw that he had closed his eyes and turned his head away and seemed to have fallen into a doze. She sighed again as she left the room, shutting the door softly behind her. She had heard the first dressing bell, and knew the nurse would soon return with his dinner and his medicine, and there was no use in remaining with him any longer.

At the sound of the catch, the captain turned back to the door, his blue eyes even darker with the pain of what he had been forced to do. He had to leave the Drapers as soon as possible, for he could not remain feeling as he did about Lizzie and listening to her hints that he tell her what was in his heart. It was more than any man could stand to have her so near, so beautiful and loving, and not declare himself! He promised himself that just as soon as he could manage it, he would take himself off, and when he was gone, Miss Lizzie would soon forget him and find someone more worthy of her love.

That evening, Mrs. Draper was entertaining at dinner before a theater party in honor of the duke and Belinda. Since her son and the captain were on the way to recovery, she felt able to go about in society once more, at least until they should all leave for Hunstanton. It did not occur to her that the duke did not approve of such frivolous entertainment, and had agreed to attend only after some earnest coaxing from Belinda.

Mrs. Draper had asked his advice in making up her numbers, and he was glad to recommend three gentlemen he said he was sure she would find most amiable. That was not quite the word Mrs. Draper would have used after she had spent some moments with the duke's cousin, an elderly clergyman from Leeds, or Mr. Stevenson or Lord Malbert, and she was glad when Winsted finally announced dinner.

Lord Malbert seemed quite taken with Lizzie, but she did not appear to notice his heavy compliments or the way he bent towards her when he spoke. Mrs.

Draper, still thinking of Caroline's amazing revelations, watched her daughter carefully. She seemed listless and pale, even in a most becoming gown of yellow silk.

Across the table, Caroline was having difficulty finding a topic interesting to Mr. Stevenson, who, after admitting he was new come to town, told her he never visited it if he could help it, for he much preferred the country. He proceeded to regale her with all the tedious details of a new drainage system he was trying on his land, and Caroline was able to make a very good dinner while seeming to appear attentive. She was not sorry when her mother gave the signal for the ladies to retire, and she smiled a little when she heard Belinda whisper to the duke as he held her chair, "Franklin, how could you? What sticks!!"

The ladies were not left alone in the drawing room for very long, so Belinda did not have time to do more than make a droll face at her relatives and bid them to be patient.

"You shall see, dear aunt," she said, "how I shall change the duke for the better as soon as we are wed! I shall have to, or you will never want to visit me at all, if all I offer you for amusement are the likes of Mr. Stevenson or Lord Malbert!"

Lizzie smiled a little, but as she had not really heard Lord Malbert, she had no idea whether he was boring or not, and if it had been possible, she would have refused to be a member of the party at all. But when she had said, several days before, that she would so much rather remain at home, her mother told her such behavior would be vastly impolite to her cousin and the duke, and he would be sure to take umbrage at such cavalier treatment. So with her thoughts upstairs in Alan Carter's room, she allowed Lord Malbert to hand her into the carriage, and resigned herself to several more hours of tedium as well as a whole night wasted in sleep before she could see him again.

At least Mrs. Draper and Belinda enjoyed the play. The elderly clergyman shrank to the back of the box, afraid one of his superiors would see him in such a worldly place; the duke remained aloof and superior; and what the other two gentlemen thought, they did not say. Lizzie sat quietly, her thoughts far away; and Caroline, who had seen Mathew Kincaid in one of the other boxes just before the lights dimmed, was annoyed that she was conscious of him even in the dark, and had trouble giving the play her full attention.

Mrs. Draper had noticed him as well, and was pleased she had not given in to an earlier impulse and asked him to join the party. That would have been much too obvious, she thought, and she did not want him to feel he was being pursued! And even if Mr. Stevenson was a bore, there was no way he could know it, from way over there! Perhaps seeing Caroline with another man would bring him to the sticking point.

The duke had planned to take the whole party on to Grillons after the play, for a late supper, but he was so displeased with Belinda's obvious enjoyment of what he considered vulgarity, and her open pleasure at the farce which followed the last act and caused her to actually laugh out loud at some very salacious jokes, that he stiffly escorted the ladies to the carriage and had them driven directly home.

The Drapers said good-bye to their escorts and entered the house, leaving the engaged couple alone on the steps for a moment. The duke bowed stiffly as Belinda smiled at him, her eyes sparkling with amusement, but there was no time to say anything, not with the others waiting in the carriage. She knew very well what was wrong with the duke, and it bothered her not a whit. Franklin would have to learn, she told herself as she made her way up to bed, that he was not about to get his own way in everything, and that she had no intention of allowing him to dictate to her to the extent that his wishes always prevailed. She was sure he loved her so much that she could soon win him over to a more tolerant attitude, and she knew that she loved him just as much in return; much too much, in fact, to permit him to remain so stiff and pretentious and boring!

The next morning, Lizzie happened to be in the hall while Winsted was sorting the post. She was about to open a letter from Mary Martha when she saw him put to one side an official-looking envelope addressed to Alan, and at once offered to take it to him.

"There is no need for you to summon a footman, Winsted," she said. "I have an errand for my mother in the sickroom, and I will take the captain's letter to him!"

The butler bowed, unperturbed, and watched her run up the stairs. Aye, and what are you up to now, Miss Lizzie, he thought, for up to something you most certainly are!

Lizzie knocked on Alan's door, and when she received no answer, made so bold as to softly turn the knob and peek inside. The doctor had already come and gone; perhaps Alan was asleep. She was alarmed to see that the bed was empty, and when she heard a groan near the dressing-room door, she hurried inside. Lying near the foot of the bed was Alan Carter, dressed in his breeches and shirt, with one boot on and the other lying nearby. He appeared to be unconscious, and Lizzie dropped the letter and knelt by his side.

"Oh, my darling Alan, whatever is the matter?" she asked tearfully. There was no answer, so she carefully raised his head and placed it in her lap, and then she reached for his hands and began to chafe them earnestly. Captain Carter came to himself, his head still spinning around, to find Lizzie holding him and exclaiming, "My dearest love, please, please speak to me!"

He opened his eyes to find her bending over him so closely, he could have kissed her easily. At the sight of his dark blue eyes, Lizzie gasped in relief, and then, as if she had read his mind, she placed her lips on his and kissed him softly. He was unable to refrain from kissing her back, but when she lifted her head, blushing at her daring, he said weakly, "No, no, we must not, dear Lizzie! This is all wrong!"

At that, she wiped her eyes and sat up a little straighter, still holding him fast. "It is *not* wrong, Alan, for I love you more than anything in the world!"

The captain groaned again, but when he would have tried to stand, Lizzie would not let him go. "No, stay here! I have waited so long to be close to you!"

He was forced to accede, for the room was still spinning around, although whether that was due to his faint, or Lizzie's closeness, was hard to distinguish. Bravely he tried to reason with her.

"You must help me up, Lizzie; we cannot remain like this! Besides, you should marry a better man than I am!"

"I do not think there are any better men, my dear!" Lizzie said, her eyes shining like stars, and she made no move to help him rise. He frowned and waved an impatient hand. "Please, do not...you do not understand! Why, I am nobody, and Miss Lizzie Draper should marry a duke, or an earl..."

"I would not consider the Prince Regent himself!" Lizzie declared stoutly, "not after falling in love with you!"

Suddenly she noticed his frown and said in a small voice, "Perhaps I am mistaken, Captain Carter? Can it be that you do not care for me, and are trying to temper my disappointment?"

Although he wished with all his heart to deny such a statement, he saw that this was the only way to bring her to her senses, and he nodded. At once, he was released, and she rose and went to stand at the window with her back to him. He struggled to his feet, clutching the bedpost, his heart sinking because he had let her go. There was a long pause; then she squared her shoulders and turned to him.

"I beg your pardon!" she said tightly. "I am sorry I have embarrassed you; you may be assured that such behavior will not be repeated. But why are you dressed? I am sure the doctor does not wish you to leave your bed."

She sounded so distantly concerned that he knew he had succeeded in convincing her he did not care. His life was ruined and he answered her bleakly, the frown darkening his eyes again.

"I thought to leave the house. I have spent too long here, have inconvenienced you all too much! I am grateful for your care, but I wish to remove to my own home."

Lizzie nodded a little. "Of course, Captain, but until you can walk farther than to the end of the bed, I am afraid you will have to curb your impatience and remain with us some little time yet! If it is my presence that offends you, you will not be bothered by it again! And now, I will send the nurse to help you back to bed!"

She swept by him, her head averted so he could not see the tears that were beginning to stream down her face. Sadly, he made no move to stop her, and in a moment he was alone. As alone as if there was no other person in the world, he thought, and indeed, without Lizzie beside him, the world had become a place of dust and emptiness. His only satisfaction was that he had behaved like a gentleman by persuading her he did not love her. Now the way was open for her to marry another. It was a very empty victory. He found hot tears running down his face, that had nothing to do with the pain in his side or his throbbing temple.

When he was undressed and back in bed, he fell into a deep slumber, worn out by his emotions rather than his exertions, and it was some time later that Caroline found him awake, staring with unseeing eyes out the window.

When she opened the door, he turned eagerly, but although he smiled, his face fell. Caroline had no idea what had occurred that morning, for she had not seen Lizzie, who had gone out for a walk with Peggy as soon as she left the sickroom. Caroline thought the captain did not look at all well, and asked him if he were in pain. Not the kind you mean, Miss Draper, he thought, even as he thanked her courteously for her concern.

"I understand the doctor says your bandages may be removed tomorrow, sir," she continued, wondering what Lizzie saw in such a taciturn man.

He stirred a little. "Yes, that is good news! I hope you will not be shocked by my appearance, Miss Draper, or...or your sister either! Doctor Booth seems pleased with my progress, but I am afraid there will be scars."

"We are hard to shock, Captain," Caroline reassured him. "Why, Lizzie and I are country women, not delicate town blossoms! I am sure my sister looks forward to seeing your face at last, after all this time, for she is very fond of you, you know." There, she thought, that should encourage him to confide in me! The captain only frowned and turned away.

She straightened up the room a little, watching him out of the corner of her eye, and when she heard his sigh, she made up her mind to get to the bottom of this, and went up to the bed. He certainly did not look like a man in love, and her heart sank for her sister. When he turned to look at her, she took a deep breath and said, "Can you not trust me, sir? Indeed, I am most anxious to help, and Lizzie has told me of her feelings, but of course if you do not reciprocate them, there is nothing more to be said!"

He looked startled, but as he gazed at her and saw her tender concern and understanding eyes, he wavered. He could not let her think he did not care, so he shook his head, and in no time at all, was telling her the whole.

"Captain Carter, I admire you for your sincere

feelings, and I have to tell you that the Drapers would be honored if you married Lizzie!" Caroline said, cheerfully forgetting her mother's disappointment.

"That is only because I saved Ned, and you know it!" he said quickly.

"Not at all! Why do you continue to insist on being difficult? I see I shall have to tell you as well that I have never seen Lizzie so concerned for another's well-being. I know she loves you deeply; so deeply in fact, that what you did this morning must have hurt her a great deal! Perhaps I had better go and tell her that you love her but only meant to spare her, thinking yourself unworthy. Yes, that is what I should do!"

As she made to leave the room, Alan stopped her by catching hold of her arm. "No, wait!" he said. "I have been thinking—what if I am disfigured? I could not bear it if Lizzie felt she had to marry me, even though looking at me was repugnant to her! Please, do not say anything until after the bandages come off. Then, if it is not too bad..."

Caroline stared down at his unhappy blue eyes and hoped with all her heart his premonitions were unfounded, for she knew now how much he loved her sister if he would give up his own happiness to spare her pain; and for a moment, she felt a pang of envy. What must it be like to be a recipient of such a love, such sacrifice? Lucky Lizzie! She promised him that she would do as he asked, although she knew it would be hard when she saw her sister and her disappointment.

As it turned out, Ned called to her as she was leaving the captain's room, and begged her to stay and amuse him, so she did not see Lizzie until the afternoon. By that time, she was composed, although very quiet and pale. Caroline's heart ached for her, but she had promised the captain! Mrs. Draper, hearing the whole story from Caroline, was moved to tears at such nobleness, forgetting that only yesterday she had called him a nobody.

Caroline also told Belinda when she came in from a card party. Caroline had not had much time for her cousin lately, and thought she looked a little unhappy; she was not so quick to laugh, and there was often a droop to her pretty mouth, and although she always seemed to be coming and going, it was without any real sense of enjoyment. As soon as this affair of Lizzie's is settled, I shall ask Belinda what is wrong, Caroline thought, as she watched the little figure slowly climb the stairs to her room to rest awhile before the evening's party. I knew the duke was a mistake, Caroline said to herself, no matter how she claimed to love him!

The next morning, Mrs. Draper intercepted the doctor in the hall and took him to the small morning room before he should see his patients. Caroline knew she was asking him the extent of the captain's injuries, especially the condition of his burned face, and she was relieved to see her mother's smile when at last she came upstairs with Dr. Booth. They did not summon Lizzie, for it had been decided that they would wait until Alan had a chance to see for himself how badly he looked. Caroline found herself clasping her hands tightly together as the nurse unwound the bandages, and knew her mother was also holding her breath. At last they were off, and the doctor turned the captain's head to the light. Caroline gave a small gasp, quickly controlled, for there was a great livid scar down one cheek, a puckered angry red. She felt her mother stir beside her, and warningly put out her hand.

The nurse handed the captain a mirror and he stared at his reflection, while the doctor rambled on about how lucky he was to have such a small souvenir instead of a much more serious injury; indeed, he might easily have been blinded! Alan did not appear to hear him, for he threw down the mirror with a look of the utmost despair on his face.

At that moment, the door opened and Lizzie walked in. She had meant to stay away, as she had promised, but she was unable to resist the chance to see what her love looked like before he was lost to her forever. Alan turned to her and frowned, his mouth set in a hard line. Caroline held her breath again, but Lizzie—silly, scatterbrained little Lizzie—did not even flinch. She walked calmly up to the bed and said in an even voice that Caroline knew must have cost her a great deal, "But how handsome you are, Captain Carter!"

Mrs. Draper gasped, but Caroline suddenly saw the Captain Carter that Lizzie was seeing. Outside of the scar, he was a handsome man. The face under the dark blond hair had even, very masculine features. Those deep blue eyes were set under a pair of well-shaped brows, his nose was strong and straight, and the mouth above his determined jaw was neither too thin nor too full. Even with the stubble on his cheeks, Caroline knew Lizzie was right.

"Do not mock me, Lizzie!" he cried in a despairing voice. "I have seen what I look like!"

"Oh, you mean the scar?" Lizzie asked, quietly removing the mirror to the bed table. "You might have received it in a duel for it is not that disfiguring, and it will fade in time. Believe me, I was not mocking you, sir!"

As she made to move away, he reached out eagerly to capture her hands. "Do you mean it, Lizzie? You are not just pretending that you do not find it repulsive?"

There was such a note of urgent pleading in his voice that Lizzie was startled, and looked to her mother and her sister. They were both smiling at her, Mrs. Draper through her tears. Really, it was so affecting, she thought. Suddenly Lizzie turned back to the captain and looked at him intently. What she saw in those pleading blue eyes caused her to smile radiantly.

"I was not wrong, then?" she whispered.

"My darling!" he murmured, and then, remembering they had an interested audience, he stopped and blushed. The doctor, who was packing up his bag, pretended not to notice, but the nurse was agog with curiosity, and Mrs. Draper showed no sign of moving until Caroline led her to the door and beckoned to the doctor and the nurse to follow her.

"I think Captain Carter has something to say to Lizzie, Mama," she said, firmly propelling them all out the door. "We can come back later!"

As she turned to close the door, Alan Carter took a moment from gazing lovingly at her sister to throw her a warm smile of gratitude.

Chapter Eleven

Mrs. Draper was in a quandary. She sat at her writing desk, nibbling the end of her quill, and wondered what she should tell her husband. Dr. Booth had announced that since Ned and Alan Carter no longer had any need of his services, it would be better for them to leave the noise and bustle of London and finish recuperating in the country. The captain was well able to stand the rigors of the journey, as long as they proceeded slowly and took many rest stops. The doctor chuckled when he told Mrs. Draper that Miss Lizzie was better medicine than any he had in his bag, and she had to agree with him. The captain had made great strides since becoming engaged to her daughter, and was now able to leave his bed for longer periods of time each day. It made Mrs. Draper misty to see how Lizzie cared for him and would not let him overtax himself, and the loving smiles they exchanged whenever they thought they were unobserved.

Unfortunately Ned was occasionally very bad-tempered when his leg continued to pain him, generally after he stood on it too long. He was so impatient to be home; she almost wished he would stop talking about it so constantly. According to him, everything would be better—his leg, Alan's wound, everything—if only they could go home! But in spite of wanting to grant his wish, as well as introducing Mr. Draper to his son-in-law to be, she hesitated. Surely this was a very bad time to be leaving town! A coldness seemed to have developed between Caroline and the earl; what caused it, she had no idea, but he was not nearly so attentive, and the afternoon rides in the park had stopped completely. Caroline made no sign that she even noticed, but Mrs. Draper thought she seemed a little dispirited.

Suddenly she put down her pen and rang the bell for her butler. On finding out that Miss Wells was indeed at home, she asked Winsted to fetch her. Belinda might be able to help; she was such a wise puss for her age!

When she came in, she kissed her aunt affectionately and asked what she might do for her. Mrs. Draper asked her to take a seat, while she fidgeted with the papers on her desk, managing to drop her pen and knock a small china cupid onto the floor. It did not break. "Not that I have ever cared for it, my dear!" she assured Belinda. Her niece picked it up and put it in a safer position, and then seeing her aunt still frowning, asked her whatever was the matter.

"I just don't know what to do that is best, my dear! Tell me, have you not noticed, as I have, that the Earl of Cannock does not visit as often as he once did? And that Caroline seems downhearted? Belinda, tell me, do you think there has been a quarrel, or that perhaps I have been making air castles to think they would ever make a match of it?"

Belinda had not been so busy trying to reform her duke that she had not seen just the things that Mrs. Draper was mentioning. Now she said, "Yes, I have noticed, and you are not mistaken. Matthew Kincaid does not call, and although he often asks Caroline for a dance, sometimes, if it is just a reception, he does not seek her out all evening. I too have wondered what could be the matter, but when I questioned Caro, she was indignant, and gave me that story about not being taken in by him, and not wanting to marry anyway!"

As Mrs. Draper rolled her eyes heavenward, Belinda laughed. "Yes, and we know, do we not, dear aunt, what a farradiddle that is! But *Caro* does not know! She has always treated the earl so casually that I do not think he knows what to make of her; perhaps he is deliberately witholding his attentions to see if that will make her feel warmer towards him in time."

Mrs. Draper was much struck by this line of reasoning, and brightened considerably. "If only we knew for sure that he was interested, and not merely flirting the season away!" she said finally. "It is too bad that women must pretend to be so indifferent, and never be able to ask a man his intentions!"

Belinda laughed again. "Well, we do have *some* weapons, as you know, but I agree it would be more to the point if we were able to speak our minds! I can never conceive of it happening, however!"

"Lud, no!" her aunt exclaimed. "It would drive the gentlemen away in droves!" Suddenly she sobered and added in a gloomy voice, "But there, my dear, whatever am I to do? Here are Lizzie and Alan, all April and May, and there is Ned begging me to set a date for departure, and I know myself he would recover better if he could see his father and his land again! But how can I drag Caro away at such a time? If she were to leave town now, there is no certainty that the earl would not forget her in a se'ennight! *Men!* And then there is your wedding, and all the shopping and planning, for even though you have convinced the duke that you wish to be married in Yorkshire, you know you must have everything in train before you leave town. I have never visited that part of the country, but I am sure there are no superior dressmakers worthy of a duchess's trade!"

Belinda told her she was quite right in her surmises, and said it would be some time before she was ready to leave town, and then she added, "But aunt, have you forgot Wiggles?"

Mrs. Draper looked confused, and Belinda enlightened her. "You remember, Miss Wiggleworth, my old governess? After that fiasco with the Baxter twins, you thought to use her while you removed Lizzie from town. I know if you wrote to her and explained, she would be glad to come and play gooseberry, and then there is Lady Salton to take us about, and the duke as well. As an engaged lady, I have a little more freedom now, and no one would take it amiss if Caroline and I stayed behind, under such chaperonage!"

"The very thing!" Mrs. Draper declared. "I knew you would help me, Belinda! If you will give me her direction, I shall write today, and as soon as she replies, I can arrange to take the others down to Hunstanton."

Belinda told her where Miss Wiggleworth might be found, but as she was preparing to leave her aunt to her letterwriting, Mrs. Draper vacillated again. "I still wish I did not have to leave Caro! She seems to have no idea how to go on, for all her age, almost to the point of taking a perverse pleasure in cutting up all her hopes! Will you be a dear good girl, Belinda, and see what you can do to help her?"

"Of course I will, aunt! And do not be upset that you will not be on the scene. If Matthew Kincaid sees that you leave town so casually before the end of the season, as if you thought Caro had no expectations at all and cared not a jot whether he proposed or not, it might be a powerful spur to the man! Men do so hate to be chased—but even worse, I have found, is how they feel when no one is pursuing them! It annoys them so! And you may be sure I will do everything in my power to bring them together!"

Miss Wiggleworth replied by return post that she would be happy to come in three days' time, and Mrs. Draper set about moving her household, or at least part of it, to the country. She spent a lot of time with

Caroline, for her daughter would be responsible for closing the London house at the end of the season. Mrs. Draper was careful not to look at her as she remarked, "Of course, Belinda is engaged and there is really no reason why she cannot remove to one of the duke's relatives—Lady Salton, for example—so that is not why I ask you to remain here, my dear. I take it as a great kindness that you would do this chore for me, when I know you are longing to be home as much as Ned is, and never wanted to come up to town in the first place!"

She was glad to see that although Caroline said she was happy to remain in such a good cause, she did look a little conscious, and Mrs. Draper felt better as she bustled away, calling for Mrs. Winsted and waving yet another list in her hands.

Miss Wiggleworth was duly installed in a very comfortable bedchamber on the second floor, and Caroline determined to make her stay as pleasant as possible, even if she had not cared for the woman at first meeting. From the things Belinda had told her, she knew the governess had had a hard life, and that it was difficult to get a new position at her age, now that Belinda did not need her any more. Miss Wiggleworth seemed grateful to have the opportunity to be of service and not to have to remain with her brother and his wife in the crowded cottage in Chigwell. She had never gotten along with her sister-in-law, and felt her brother could have done a great deal better than he had in the choice of a wife, and of course, Maisie Wiggleworth was only too aware of her opinion.

Early one morning, therefore, near the end of June, the traveling party set out for Hunstanton in the Draper coach. There was a vast amount of baggage, as well as all sorts of medicines and potions that Mrs. Draper felt might be needed. Ned, in a sunny humor now that he was going home, laughed till he had to hold his sides when he saw his mother with her collection of shawls and pillows, salts and bottles, and when Alan saw how she was beginning to bridle at the way her son was making fun of her, he hastened to smoothe her feathers by telling her that he sincerely wished she had been with them at Pamplona, for under her excellent care, they would have been completely well in no time!

Caro and Belinda stood on the steps and waved as the coach moved slowly off, followed once again by the lighter coach containing Grandish, Stanley and Peggy. At least two of that party were not adverse to leaving town, for Stanley had whispered to Peggy that he would see to the posting of the banns as soon as they arrived! Peggy blushed and squeezed his hand as he helped her into the coach.

Mrs. Draper felt that in leaving the girls with Yvette to maid them, as well as the Winsteds, she had done all she could to insure their respectability. A governess was all very well; a superior butler and a competent housekeeper were much more impressive!

Lady Salton had agreed willingly to take the girls around, although she had to be coaxed to attend Lady St. Mark's masquerade. Caroline had thought that Belinda might change her mind about their costumes, now that there only two graces, but Belinda had laughed and said that two were better than none, and that she had a famous scheme! Just wait until she told Caroline about it! She looked so much happier discussing the masquerade that Caroline was forced to smile at her. The duke still called every day and sent flowers as well, and her cousin always seemed to be delighted to see him, but still Caroline could not be easy in her mind. She made a note to ask Miss Wiggleworth about Belinda's childhood; perhaps there would be some clue there that would tell her why Belinda did not seem to be as ecstatic as she had been when she was first engaged.

She had actually sighed heavily and pouted when she told Caroline that after the season, she and the duke, accompanied by Lady Salton, were engaged to visit every one of the duke's relatives in the entire British Isles before they were free to repair to Yorkshire and their wedding. Caro agreed that it would be tedious to be paraded before people you had never met, and be expected to do the pretty over and over again at such a time, and Belinda said that it could have been much worse! "At least we are not spending our wedding journey visiting them, which Franklin quite had in mind to do! I told him there was no use insisting on such folly! I will see them as an engaged miss; as a married lady, I want to see the Greek Isles!" She chuckled a little, remembering. "It was not very hard to persuade him, dear Caro! Especially when I pointed out all the advantages of being alone together!"

As the traveling coach lumbered around the corner and out of sight, Belinda took her cousin's hand and drew her back into the house, saying gaily, *"Now,* my dear Caro, *Now!"* She would answer no questions, but beckoned her into the morning room after telling Winsted they did not want to be disturbed. Caro felt a small warning bell ringing in her head, but she calmly took a seat and poured herself another cup of coffee. Belinda joined her at the table, her eyes sparkling with fun.

"Oh, we are going to have a great time of it, Caro!" she exclaimed. "And the first order of business is the masquerade. Let me see, we still have a final fitting on our costumes this afternoon; then, my dear, we are going to Monsieur Henri's establishment!"

"Whatever for!" Caro asked. Monsieur Henri was a wigmaker, but they had never used his services.

"He is going to turn us into a pair of bewitching blondes, my dear, at my orders!" Belinda said. "I have always wished I had long blond hair, instead of these black curls! Won't it be fun? And since we are going to be dressed alike, and heavily masked, no one will know if I am you or the reverse!" When Caro would have spoken, she continued rapidly, "You see, Caro, there is no mistaking even two of the Three Graces if we dress as we have been named; everyone will know us immediately, and where is the fun in that?"

"They will still know!" Caroline said dryly. "Have you forgotten I am several inches taller than you, cuz? We will not fool a soul!"

"I thought of that too! You are to wear your flattest slippers, and I, a pair of very high heels. You do not know what a problem I had finding a pair, now that they are *passé*. Would you believe Yvette had to go to Cheapside to get them? And of course we must separate as soon as we enter the door, and never stand next to each other all evening. I think it might be better to meet Lady Salton there, do you not? The gowns *are* a trifle revealing—such a good thing your mother was too busy to really look at them!"

Caroline put down her coffee cup. "Now, what are you up to, cuz? And do not try to fob me off with any protestations of innocence! I have not lived with Lizzie all these years that I cannot tell when something is afoot!"

Belinda laughed and told her it was a secret, but that she knew she would like it when she discovered it.

As the two of them left the morning room, they discovered Miss Wiggleworth waiting patiently for them in the hall. She took one look at Belinda's face and said solemnly, "'Mischief, thou art afoot!'"

Belinda shook her head. "Dear Wiggles! You do know me so well, do you not? But there is nothing to worry about, for this is very, very good mischief!"

Miss Wiggleworth sniffed and shook a bony finger at her late charge. "Yes, I know you, Miss Belinda Wells, and what I intend to do is to tell your cousin to be on her guard. Miss Draper, you have been warned!"

Belinda changed the subject by asking her governess if she wished to accompany them shopping, but Miss Wiggleworth begged to be excused. As Belinda and Caroline went upstairs to fetch their reticules and stoles, she whispered, "Wiggles hates shopping! I knew it was perfectly safe to ask her to go, and besides, it has removed any suspicion that I am up to the mischief she deplores, at least for today!"

Somehow, Caroline was in high spirits after they left their luncheon party and strolled to the dressmaker's. She had thought she might be downcast after her family's departure, but she felt a new sense of lightness. It was pleasant not to have to worry about the invalids and what the doctor had said; pleasant to have nothing more on one's mind but tonight's rout party and all the other occasions they were promised to. Belinda seemed happier too, and Caroline looked forward to them both holding household for the next two weeks, before she must return to Hunstanton. She wondered what Matthew Kincaid was doing; it had been so long since she had seen him to talk to that she was not even sure he was still in town. Then she remembered Lady St. Marks; surely he would attend his aunt's masquerade. The thought made her smile a little as they entered the dressmaker's.

The fitting went smoothly, and the costumes were promised in plenty of time before the masquerade the following evening. Caroline thought the gowns were very pretty, although she was sure her mother would have frowned at the low necklines and the flimsy draperies that comprised them. They were made of tiers of white gauze, with tiny gold shoulder straps. There were golden girdles to match, and ribbon to wind through their hair. Caroline had found the masks, and Belinda declared them perfect, for they covered all of their faces but their eyes and lips, and she declared that no one could possibly know who they were, no matter how hard they tried to tell them apart!

At Monsieur Henri's, Caroline was surprised to see that the wigs Belinda had bespoke were not at all elaborate, made as they were in a long, loose style that descended almost to their waists. She was also surprised to see what a transformation such flowing blond hair could make as it framed her face, rather than her usual brown curls. She had fallen in with all Belinda's schemes so easily, and yet she felt a flicker of alarm again at their plan to fool the ton, for it now appeared to be well within the range of possibility.

As they left the wigmakers, Belinda said, "I just thought of something else, Caro! Since there will be many people at the ball who do not know that Lizzie has left town, it will be even more confusing! After all, she has not been much in society since your brother and Captain Carter returned from Spain. Perhaps you may dance once as Lizzie, then turn around and waltz as Belinda. What fun!"

Caroline had to agree, and reminded her cousin not to mention her sister's departure that evening at the rout party unless someone should inquire for her especially.

The evening of the masquerade arrived, and Caroline and Belinda dressed in their matching gowns, with much laughter and speculation about the party. Yvonne was there to help them with their toilettes, although she told Caroline bluntly that she was sure they would not fool anyone, even with Belinda's high heels. But when she had adjusted the blond wigs and threaded the gold ribbon through each tress in exactly the same way, she had to admit they were almost identical.

"At least, to a casual observer," Caroline agreed, "but I am sure the duke will know you at once, Belinda. How could he not recognize his own fiancée?"

Belinda laughed. "If he does not, I beg you will not steal his heart, cuz! And you must not give us away by behaving as Caroline Draper, if he should be fooled!" She clapped her hands. "And I shall attach the earl and pretend to be you!"

Caroline frowned and would have spoken, except Belinda went on. "I think it will be I who sits down a great deal. These shoes are prodigious uncomfortable!"

She held up the hem of her gown and extended a little foot in a gold slipper with very high heels covered with diamond chips. "How do you suppose ladies ever danced in them?" she asked in wonder. "I have been practicing, but it is so very awkward, and I feel as if I am about to fall on my nose!"

The two cousins stood together in front of Yvette and asked her if there was anything further they could do to deepen the disguise. Yvette suggested that they speak only in whispers, for Caro's voice was lower than Belinda's. They agreed to do so, thanking her for the suggestion.

They rode to Lady St. Mark's home in the Draper town carriage, for Belinda had arranged to meet Lady Salton and the duke at the ball. He had tried to insist that they needed an escort, but Belinda would not hear of it. As she gave her sarsenet stole to the waiting maid and adjusted her mask, she said to Caroline, in an undertone, "Good luck, cuz! And remember, do not come near me all evening!"

Caroline nodded and Belinda flitted up the stairs with a couple who had just arrived, leaving her cousin to make her own way to the ballroom. Since they had purposely arrived late, this magnificent chamber was filled with a crowd of people, all brilliantly costumed, although some of the gentlemen had merely donned a domino over their evening dress. She was immediately claimed by Mr. Sawyer, whose pirate outfit was no disguise at all, and as he led her to the dance floor, she saw Belinda talking to Lady Salton and the duke. Lady Salton was not in costume, but the duke wore a mask and a pale blue domino. Caroline noticed he was frowning as he stared intently at Belinda, and she smiled to herself. As Mr. Sawyer swung her around, she lifted her hand and waved gaily to the trio. The duke frowned even more heavily, and she felt vastly amused that they had deceived him. Mr. Sawyer was determined to find out which of the Three Graces he had captured, but Caroline answered him in whispered monosyllables, and when the dance ended, he was no wiser than he had been before. Caroline was beginning to enjoy herself immensely as her partner left her in search of another of the Graces.

Noticing that Belinda was dancing, Caroline made her way to Lady Salton's chair, and curtsied. The old lady chuckled.

"Now, is this Belinda or Caroline?" she asked the duke. "I vow, you have fooled us all, although I did think, Franklin, that you at least would have no trouble distinguishing your wife-to-be! It is a definite setdown for you, my boy!"

The duke stared at Caroline's left hand, but since Belinda had taken the precaution of leaving her diamond and sapphire engagement ring at home, he was not enlightened. Caroline saw that the color was beginning to rise in his face, and knew he was not a bit pleased with even such an innocent amusement. She took a seat next to Lady Salton, wondering yet again why Belinda loved him. Before she was forced to converse for too long, the Earl of Cannock came up and asked for a dance. Caroline could feel her face getting warmer as his eyes, under a black half-mask, stared at her intently, going insolently over her bare arms and throat and up to her lips. He nodded to himself, but even though she was almost sure she had been discovered, he said nothing. As he took her in his arms, she tried to bend her knees a little in order to appear shorter.

"You will notice it is a waltz, my dear mysterious lady!" the earl said.

"Why, so it is!" Caroline whispered, trying to look puzzled.

He laughed. "But perhaps I was wrong, and you do not know what I am talking about? I recall an evening when I was accused of always asking a particular lady to dance whenever they played a waltz! Can it be that you are not Miss Draper after all?"

"As to that, sir," Caroline whispered again, "you will have to wait until the unmasking to find out!" She laughed out loud, trying to imitate Belinda's gay trill, and had the satisfaction of seeing those heavy brows come together in confusion.

It was a festive evening, although at one point Ferdie Baxter came up and claimed that she was Lizzie, for even a mask and a wig could not hide the identity of one who had been so dear to him, and so loving as well! Caroline had all she could do to refrain from giving him a blistering setdown, and when he asked her for the supper dance, was happy to tell him she had been engaged by Lord Everest.

After a delicious repast of fancy sandwiches, ices, and jellies, as well as little cakes and comfits, all accompanied by an excellent champagne, she returned to the ballroom and was immediately claimed by the duke. As they strolled to a sofa somewhat removed from the press of people dancing under the many brilliantly lit chandeliers, he said, "I do not know if you are Belinda or Miss Draper, and I see that neither of you has any intention of revealing yourself, but if it is you, Belinda, let me tell you that this has gone far enough! I insist you stop the masquerade immediately!"

He was grasping Caroline's arm in a hard grip, and she made to withdraw it, but he would not let her go. Sitting down beside her on the sofa, he continued, "And that gown! It is a disgrace! Whatever was Mrs. Draper thinking of, to let you appear so lightly clad in public! That my future wife should be seen in such an immodest ensemble!"

Caroline saw that he was convinced that she was Belinda, and her heart sank. When he found out he had been chastising the wrong lady, he was going to be very angry indeed. She would have told him her identity at once, but she chanced to look to the dance floor, and her eyes widened. There, right in front of them, were the earl and her cousin, dancing together and appearing to be excessively friendly.

When the music stopped, Belinda spied her and would have moved away in another direction, but the earl took her arm and escorted her to the sofa, where he bowed to the duke and Caroline.

"Ah, Brownell!" he said blandly, not at all confused by the duke's disguise, nor expecting to be unknown in his own black mask and scarlet domino. "I see you have captured the other Grace that is present. Shall we sit them down side by side and compare them, for I am confused myself as to which is which. Is that Miss Draper with you, or do I have Miss Draper on my arm? Or perhaps it is Miss Lizzie?"

"Miss Lizzie has left London!" the duke snapped.

Thinking quickly, Caroline tossed her head and whispered, "Fie on you, sir, to tell him!"

Belinda, who had been opening her mouth to say the exact same thing, closed it quickly. She had not known that Caroline would be so adept in aping her mannerisms, and she applauded her silently.

"Well, that narrows down the field, at least," Kincaid said, ignoring the duke's anger. "Now we only have to determine which is which! If only they would forget themselves and stop whispering, I am sure we could tell in a moment!"

The duke was looking from one lady to another, his eyes narrowed, and Belinda curtsied quickly. "You must excuse me, Your Grace, sir," she said. "I am promised to another!"

Suddenly she moved away before either man could stop her. The earl stayed beside the seated couple for a moment, and then, after asking Caroline for a dance later in the evening, followed Belinda. Caroline sighed a little. She was left with the duke, and he was not the most pleasant of companions this evening. She wondered why he could not relax and enjoy the evening, for the deception was only an innocent bit of fun! When he would have continued his diatribe, she asked him to fetch her some punch, and although stunned to be ordered about like a servant, the duke complied. By the time he returned with a lackey bearing a tray, her next partner had arrived and she was able to escape. She met Belinda in the lady's withdrawing room later and the two cousins had a good laugh over their successful ploy.

"But, cuz," Caroline said as she adjusted the ribbon in her wig, "I fear you may be in trouble for this evening's work! The duke is so very angry!"

"I know!" Belinda agreed. "Is it not amusing? I have not had such fun in ages, Caro!" She rubbed her feet as she spoke. "In spite of these terrible shoes! But I almost regret that it will soon be midnight and we will be forced to unmask!"

She insisted Caroline leave the room first, and gurgled with laughter as Caroline exclaimed, "I, for one, will be glad to stop whispering, *and* listening to the duke's scolding! He is sure that I am you!"

Just before midnight, Caroline saw her cousin and the earl together again. She was flirting with him, that much was obvious, and the earl appeared to be enjoying it tremendously. He bent to whisper something to her, and Belinda laughed up at him, holding onto his arm closely and tapping him with her fan in mock reproach for his words. Caroline suddenly felt the masquerade had gone on long enough, surprised that she felt such a pang to see the earl and Belinda so friendly. She heard an indrawn breath right behind her, and turned to see the duke observing the couple as well. Just then, Lady St. Mark requested all her guests to unmask and reveal their identities while the orchestra played a fanfare. Caroline felt her heart sinking as she untied the strings of her mask. As soon as she had it off, she turned to the duke and tried to smile. With a muffled oath, the duke left her and rushed up to where Belinda was coyly pretending she could not remove her mask, even though the duke was standing much too close to her to help.

"Belinda!" the duke exclaimed in an awful voice. Several guests turned to stare, and he lowered his voice, although his tone was still angry. "How dare you behave in such a manner? You have been most immodest tonight—imprudent!—unmaidenly! To think that you, the future Duchess of Darwood, would so forget yourself!"

Belinda lowered her mask. "How dare you lecture me, Franklin?" she asked, now as angry as he was. "'Twas just a prank, an innocent prank! You do not see the Earl of Cannock upset because we have fooled him!"

"He is not the Duke of Darwood!" the furious voice answered, causing the earl to raise his brows and stare. Caroline came up just then and put out her hand.

"Oh, pray do not argue here, Your Grace!" she said. "You are attracting so much attention!"

The duke looked around, and then he imperiously took Belinda by the hand and tried to force her to leave the room. "Thank you, Miss Draper. We will retire!"

By now, Belinda was furious. "We will not retire, sir!" she said rapidly. "It is completely unnecessary for us to do so! I shall not listen to any more of your...your pompous scolding!"

The duke drew himself up stiffly. "When I say we shall retire, that is exactly what we shall do! Do not always be setting yourself up against me and contradicting me, Belinda! You will learn, after we are married, that I will not tolerate such wilfulness!"

Belinda was now as white as her gown. "As for that, Your Grace," she said in a low, steady voice, "you will not be called upon to tolerate my wilfulness, as you call it! I am terminating our engagement as of now, and I would appreciate it if you would send a notice to the newspapers to that effect immediately! Your ring will be returned to you tomorrow!"

She turned away, insolently refusing to curtsy, and left them so rapidly that the duke was unable to stop her or to speak to her. Caroline clasped her hands and looked to the earl in a beseeching way, and he held out his arm.

"Come, Miss Draper! I am sure the duke would prefer to have a few moments alone, and we are definitely *de trop!*"

Gratefully Caroline took his arm and allowed him to take her away. Her head was whirling. Now what had they done? And what could she do about it? The earl saw her concerned face, and led her to a chair.

"I see you are blaming yourself, Miss Draper," he said easily. "But whose idea was this masquerade of yours? Was it not your cousin who dreamed up the scheme?" Caroline nodded and he continued, "Perhaps she did it to find out once and for all whether she wished to marry the duke or no. And after listening to him just now, I would be amazed if such a spirited miss would ever have meekly begged his pardon and promised never to do it again!"

Caroline nodded. "I have often wondered," she said, thinking out loud, "what Belinda saw in the duke. He is so starched up, so stuffy, and full of his own conceit! And she is so gay and unassuming, even with all her beauty, wealth, and position. I have to be glad she has broken it off, for I do not think she could be happy with such an arrogant man!"

"Surely more arrogant even than I!" the earl said, causing her to look at him in dismay. He smiled. "Oh, yes, I have been accused of arrogance, as you know," he confided. "But surely I have had a lesson from a master tonight. How Miss Wells ever agreed— well, love is very strange, so they say!"

"Love!" Caroline exclaimed. "How could he possibly love her, to talk to her so? I think he was just looking for a suitable duchess, one whose birth and wealth matched his. As for love, I saw little of that!"

"But then," the earl mused, "you would not be apt to, would you?"

Caroline blushed, and he laughed at her. "I was—

teasing!" he said, as Belinda came up to them, her face white and her eyes full of unshed tears.

"Caro!" she demanded. "Are you ready to go home? I do not think I can bear to remain another moment!"

Caroline rose and curtsied to the earl. "Of course, my dear, I understand. We will leave at once!"

As she moved to her cousin's side, the earl put a delaying hand on her arm and bent his head and whispered, "You will never know how I wish it had been you, dear Caro, instead of your cousin, who had been flirting so gaily with me this evening! I even tried to convince myself that it was so, and that your indifference towards me was changing to a warmer feeling. Alas, that I was wrong!"

His dark blue eyes sparkled with amusement when he saw how confused this statement made her. So I have finally managed to gain your undivided attention, Miss Draper, he thought, and he bowed sardonically when she turned away in distraction and quickly left him without saying a word.

Chapter Twelve

The Draper house became a very gloomy place in the days that followed. At first, Caroline was delighted that her cousin had finally discovered the duke's true character, but when Belinda refused to speak of him at all, and became so very quiet and subdued, she began to wonder if she had been wrong in thinking her cousin not really in love, but only dazzled by the prospect of becoming "Duchess Bel." She saw the occasional melancholy expression on Belinda's face when she thought she was unobserved, although she tried hard to appear normal in company.

Belinda had had to endure a visit from Lady Salton as soon as the announcement that the engagement had been terminated had appeared in the social columns, and that lady had wrung a mighty peal over her head. Or so she had said. Caroline had been banished from the room, and Belinda had been very flushed when Lady Salton finally left, with both her head and her color high. She would not discuss the meeting further with Caroline, which was so unlike her that Caroline began to worry in earnest. Miss Wiggleworth went about shaking her head and muttering quotes from the Bible or her favorite poets, and when Caroline sought her out to ask her opinion of the situation, she did not find the elderly governess much help.

"She was always a most determined piece!" Miss Wiggleworth said in a despairing way. "And she was bound to have her own way in everything! Her father gave in to her shamefully, and now we see the result! She cannot bear to be thwarted, and for the duke to criticize her was too much! Alas, Miss Draper, what we have here, as the poet says, is 'a pair of star-crossed lovers'!"

Caroline went away, somehow wishing she had her mother with her to give her advice. She had always thought her such a flighty person, but she realized now that if anyone would know what to do in this situation, it was Mrs. Draper. But of course she was out of reach in Hunstanton. Since Lady Salton had washed her hands of Miss Wells, Caroline could not go to her for advice, and Miss Wiggleworth was worse than useless; in fact, Caroline thought it would be a help if she would just stop presenting her gloomy views at every opportunity.

Belinda herself took a hand, and one evening at dinner, she spoke sharply to her governess, just as soon as the butler left the room.

"That is quite enough, Wiggles!" she said, her face white with anger except for two bright spots of scarlet on her cheeks. "Neither Caroline nor I care to hear your nattering any more. The duke and I are no more—let us hear you no more as well!"

Miss Wiggleworth subsided meekly.

For the first few days, Belinda refused to attend any parties, and Caroline was sure she would soon be making plans to return to Yorkshire, but one morning Lord Everest came to invite them to a picnic luncheon at his mother's home, a few miles from town. The weather had been unseasonably warm, and Belinda decided that an afternoon in the country would be refreshing, only stipulating that Caroline must find out if the duke had been invited, for if he had, she had no intention of going, no matter how warm it was. Some adroit questioning of Lord Everest produced a satisfying answer, and the two cousins donned their lightest gowns and large straw hats, and were driven to Barnet.

Caroline was delighted to put her worries about her cousin in the back of her mind for one afternoon, although she blushed when she saw Lord Cannock was among the guests. She had not forgotten his final statement at the masquerade. The man was incorrigible, and such an accomplished flirt! She tilted her lemon-yellow sunshade at a becoming angle when he greeted her and offered to fetch her a glass of iced lemonade. Belinda had been claimed eagerly by Lord Everest and whisked away to meet his mother, and Caroline had been glad to see the saucy wink Belinda gave her as she left on this duty. Perhaps she is recovering her spirits after all, she thought, although she knew that Belinda had no interest in Lord Everest, who, in spite of his attentions and obvious delight in her broken engagement, remained forever a "seven."

The earl strolled across the lawn with the lemonade and took a wicker chair by her side, remarking on the beauty of the day.

"I imagine you are planning to return to the country soon, Miss Draper?" he added.

"Why, yes, within a week or two. It really depends on Belinda. I thought after the masquerade that she would want to leave town immediately, but she has not even set a date for her departure for Yorkshire. Until she does so, I, of course, must remain."

"Perhaps she hopes the quarrel can be mended," the earl remarked in a casual way. Caroline did not hear the boredom in his voice.

"Good heavens, m'lord!" she exclaimed, "There is no chance of that! And yet—sometimes I am sure that must be the case. Even though I myself would be delighted to see the back of the man and say a hearty 'good riddance,' Belinda..." She shook her head sadly.

"Do we always have to talk about your family, Miss Draper?" Lord Cannock interrupted rudely. "It seems that every time I am with you, you are embroiled with the problems of one or the other of them, to the exclusion of all else!"

Caroline could not fail to notice his exasperation, and replied in a cool voice, "Do you think so? How very rude of me! And who would you prefer to talk about m'lord? Yourself?"

The frown left the earl's face. "You think to give me one of your setdowns, do you not, Miss Draper, but you will find I am very hard to offend! Yes, let us talk about me—and, perhaps, you!"

Caroline felt they were getting into very dangerous territory indeed. "Do you too plan to leave for the country soon, m'lord?" she asked as calmly as she could. "I have noticed that London is very thin of company lately."

"Soon, perhaps!" he said, those bright blue eyes now twinkling at her. "It depends on circumstances and on another's plans: an aggravating, pretty matchmaker with brown curls!"

Caroline rose quickly, for he was going much too fast for her, and her heart was beginning to beat in an alarming way. It disturbed her that the earl was becoming so direct in his remarks, and carrying a casual flirtation into deep waters.

"You must excuse me, m'lord!" she said. "I see Lady St. Mark over there, and I have been meaning to thank her for the masquerade!"

"Allow me to escort you," he replied, ignoring the nervous fluttering of her fingers as he drew her hand through his arm and patted it gently. "I am delighted that you wish to further your friendship with one of my closest relatives. She was very taken with you at the ball, you know," he confided. "And she considered your costumes the best of the evening. My aunt is always ready for a joke, and the way you fooled the duke amused her greatly!"

Caroline nodded, but she did not speak again until she was seated with Lady St. Mark. The earl wandered away in response to a hail from one of his friends, and Caroline drew a deep breath of relief. Lady St. Mark began to speak of Belinda's broken engagement, saying she was sorry the duke had taken such offense at her party. "He is a stick, is he not?" she asked, and although Caroline would never have discussed Belinda's affairs with one who was almost a stranger, she found herself warming to the concerned, kind gaze of Lord Cannock's aunt, and was soon pouring out the whole story.

"I am in such a quandary, m'lady!" she said finally. "What to do, I don't know! It is obvious that Belinda is not happy, but she will not even discuss the duke, never mind consider a reconciliation!"

"Has the duke approached her?" Lady St. Mark asked.

"No, he has not! He is just as stubborn as Belinda. I thought that he might write when she sent his ring back, but he did not even acknowledge receiving it!"

"Perhaps *you* could write to him," the older lady said slowly, "and ask him if it was delivered safely. You can say that you have been worrying about it, since it is of such great value. That at least will open the door, and if he wishes to mend fences, he has an excuse to call!"

"How very clever!" Caroline beamed. Lady St. Mark was entirely different from Lady Salton, although they were much the same age. She decided she liked the earl's relative very much indeed, and promised to call and tell her what developed.

Belinda was very gay that afternoon, flirting outrageously with Lord Everest, to the great chagrin of his mother, who considered Miss Wells a shameless hussy to try and attach her son so soon after breaking her engagement with the Duke of Darwood. The young man himself was in raptures as he handed her into the Draper carriage at the end of the afternoon, and kissed her hand in farewell. Belinda laughed at his adoring face as they tooled away down the drive, and declared she had had a very good time after all. But sometime later, as they approached the London streets again, Caroline stole a glance at her now-silent cousin and saw her staring out the window of the coach, a little tear running down her cheek. Belinda turned away, and somehow Caroline did not dare to comfort her, but the incident made her determined to write to the duke without delay.

Her note went the next morning, and she was encouraged when the Duke of Darwood presented himself early that afternoon and begged to speak to her. Better and better, she thought, as she made her way downstairs, glad that Belinda and Miss Wiggleworth had gone out.

The duke rose as she entered, and bowed sternly, his eyes never leaving her face, as if he hoped to see some sign of encouragement there. Thinking he was looking very tired and pale, Caroline asked him to be seated, and took a chair near him.

"I am so glad you have come, Your Grace," she began. "I trust the ring was returned to you safely? It has been much on my mind."

The duke waved an impatient hand. "Oh yes, I have it in my care! I wish I did not!"

Caroline raised an eyebrow. "Do I understand you correctly, sir? You wish it were still on my cousin's hand?"

"Of course I do!" he said, and rose to pace up and down, more agitated than Caroline had ever seen him. "But there is nothing I can do about it! She was so vehement, so angry when she returned the ring! I decided she never really loved me, for if she had, she would have considered my feelings, to be made the butt of such a joke!"

Caroline put out a deterring hand. "I am afraid you have not read my cousin's character correctly, sir! I am sure she is still in love with you"—here, the duke whirled and stared at her eagerly—"but she also has her pride. Besides, it really was only an innocent bit of fun, and no one else took exception to it. I am afraid Belinda thinks that you will make her life miserable after she marries you, by being so formal and stiff, for you must know how gay and happy her personality is. If she is forced to live a life of ceremony, always being told what to do, and what is not becoming for the Duchess of Darwood, she will be miserable!"

"But I would change, for *her!*" the duke said with fervor.

"Why don't you tell her so?" Caroline asked. "She will never know otherwise!"

"All the letters I have written, I have torn up. They all sound so stern, so stiff. But, my dear Miss Draper, I assure you that I love Belinda with all my heart. Is there nothing you can do to help me?"

Caroline smiled at him. How different he appeared when he humbly acknowledged he needed assistance! "I will try to think of something, and send you word, Your Grace."

They parted as friends, the duke pressing her hand warmly in farewell, declaring he would be forever in her debt if she could reunite him with Belinda. Caroline went to her room to think, glad she had a few hours of leisure before dinner and the rout party she and her cousin were to attend that evening.

Nothing had occurred to her, however, when she joined the others in the dining room. Since Lady Salton had washed her hands of Miss Wells, the elderly governess had been pressed into service as a chaperone, and although she was dressed in her best black silk, it was obvious from her expression that she was not looking forward to the evening's frivolity. Caroline thought Belinda had a great air of resolution this evening, and it was not long before she knew the reason.

As Belinda helped herself to a dish of peas in

cream sauce, she said, "I have decided that I have spent enough time in London, cuz. And although I will miss you, I intend to begin packing to go home tomorrow. Wiggles has said she will go with me; my only concern is leaving you here alone. Is there no one who could come and stay with you?"

Caroline shook her head, a little stunned by this turn of events. "I am sure there is no need, with the Winsteds here. I will attend no more parties after tonight, for I shall be busy packing and closing the house. But Belinda, are you sure...?"

Her voice died away as her cousin looked at her sharply. "Quite, quite sure!" she said. "I made a mistake, remaining as long as I did! Besides, I am anxious to see my parents and my home, and I intend to plan my next trip. In fact, dear Caro, I would be delighted if you would consider traveling with me, for I am sure you would love the Greek Isles! That is, of course, if you are free to come with me."

Caroline's mind was busy, and she missed the roguish look her cousin gave her. She said only that the Greek Isles sounded delightful, but in her mind she was planning a note to the duke early the following morning, for if Belinda remained adamant about leaving town, there was no time to waste. She helped herself to the veal in Madeira sauce that Winsted was offering, although she had no idea what she was eating. Perhaps by morning she would know what to do.

It was quite obvious to the Earl of Cannock that Miss Draper had something on her mind that evening, for her great air of abstraction, her look of being far, far away, and the necessity of repeating questions made it only too clear that her thoughts were not on him at all. He gritted his teeth and wished he might shake her. She was the most exasperating woman he had ever met! Even his best smiles and most wicked charm and provocative flirting had no power to move her; how could they? She was not even aware of them! Just you wait, Caroline

Draper, he said to himself, as she stared dreamily into space. Someday I will have your complete and total attention, if I have to beat you to get it, and then we will see! Caroline did not even notice when he took his leave of her very stiffly, and after pausing briefly beside his aunt to tell her in a very harsh voice that he would do himself the honor of calling on her in the morning, he abruptly left the party. Lady St. Mark had not missed his conversation with Caroline Draper and was much amused at his thunderous expression; it appeared dear Matthew had met his match at last!

All unconcerned with the earl's bad temper, Caroline sat contemplating a plan that had begun to form in her mind. A plan that would be sure to convince Belinda that the duke still loved her, and had mended his ways as well! If only she could be sure he would do it—aye, there's the rub, she thought, as she took a seat next to Miss Wiggleworth. It was undoubtably what that good lady would have remarked herself—not that Caroline had any intention of asking her counsel.

The duke was not present at the rout, and before very long, Belinda began to complain of a headache and wish she might go home. Miss Wiggleworth was only too happy to comply, and Caroline agreed the evening was a trifle flat, looking around as she spoke, surprised that the Earl of Cannock had left already. Now, when did he go, she wondered?

The next morning, another note from Miss Draper was carried to the Duke of Darwood, and an hour later, while Belinda was busy with her packing, Caroline slipped out of the house and made her way to the park, trailing a reluctant Miss Wiggleworth.

"I am sure I should be helping Miss Belinda," this lady complained, struggling to keep up with Caroline, "and not gallivanting about in the park!"

"You will be doing more to help my cousin by coming with me!" Caroline retorted, taking a seat under a shady tree and looking around. The duke had not arrived; she launched into an account of her scheme to the governess, who forgot herself so far as to let her mouth drop open in shock as Caroline hastily outlined her plan.

"But my dear Miss Draper!" Miss Wiggleworth exclaimed at last. "That is—why, that is positively indecent! And here I thought Miss Wells was a madcap! I was never so surprised!"

"Perhaps it runs in the family!" Caroline could not resist saying, and then, seeing the duke approaching, urgently bade her chaperone to take a short walk while she acquainted the hero of the play with his part.

At first she thought the duke would refuse, for her tale was interrupted many times by his frown or indrawn breath, and once even by a startled "My Lord!" but before long she had him agreeing to the scheme, and was pleased to see a twinkle in those hitherto cold green eyes.

"Do you really think this will do the trick, Miss Draper?" he asked. "I shall feel a complete fool if you have misread her heart!"

"Better to feel a fool than lose the one woman you love!" Caroline said stoutly, beckoning to Miss Wiggleworth, who was hovering nearby. "I want to make you known to Belinda's chaperone, Your Grace," she said, as she introduced them. "It is important she will know you when the time comes."

Miss Wiggleworth curtsied deeply, not immune to the peerage, and said that if the duke considered the plan unexceptionable, she would swallow all her apprehensions. Before she could continue, Caroline interrupted. "Yes, yes, Wiggles, we will take the responsibility! Now, Your Grace, I shall send you word as soon as I can—it could be as early as tomorrow, so you must be prepared!"

The final arrangements were made and the party separated; Caroline smiling, the duke bemused, and Miss Wiggleworth shaking her head.

The next morning, Belinda suddenly remembered

a gown she was having made at Madame Theresa's and asked Caroline if she would be a dear and accompany her to the shop to fetch it. Caroline buttered another piece of toast and said she was very sorry, but she had another engagement that morning and Miss Wiggleworth would undoubtably be delighted to oblige. Belinda sighed. "I was trying to avoid her company, cuz; she has become so depressing! Besides, we have so little time left to be together..."

Caroline felt a pang of remorse at her lies as she shook her head. As soon as Belinda left the room, she hurried to the writing desk and penned a quick note to the duke, which she had Winsted send off by footman immediately. The butler made up his mind to have his wife speak to Miss Caroline, for surely it was not seemly, all these notes to a titled gentleman!

An hour later, dressed in a pretty morning gown of lilac muslin sprigged with white flowers, and wearing a matching bonnet, Belinda set off on her errand, accompanied by her governess. Caroline watched from behind the drawing room draperies and surreptitiously crossed her fingers.

She was in a state of suspense all morning, even after Miss Wiggleworth returned, and it was not until late afternoon, when a note arrived from the duke, that she allowed herself to relax and smile.

The duke said all had gone as planned. He had been waiting for Belinda in a closed carriage at the bottom of the street where the dressmaker had her shop. When he saw Belinda and Miss Wiggleworth approaching, he adjusted his mask and jumped down from the carriage to intercept them. Before Belinda could even think of screaming, he swept her up in his arms and bundled her into the carriage, giving the coachman the office to start by rapping sharply on the roof.

Belinda had landed in a heap on the squabs, her bonnet tipped over her eye and her dress much disarranged. She opened her mouth to scream in earnest, but the duke put a firm hand over it and, grasping her two hands, told her to be quiet or else! Belinda's eyes widened in shock, for she had never been spoken to in such a way. She wondered why she was not especially alarmed; indeed, she felt quite calm, under the circumstances.

The mysterious kidnapper spoke again. "If you will nod your head, promising not to make a fuss, Miss Wells, I shall release you!"

Belinda frowned. There was something familiar about that voice, even muffled as it was by the mask, and suddenly she nodded. She was instantly released. As she straightened her dress and bonnet, her captor removed his mask and smiled at her.

"FRANKLIN!" she said in a shocked tone. "Whatever is this all about?"

"I am kidnapping you, my dear!" he answered cheerfully. "And I warn you, I have no intention of ever letting you go! There is no ransom on earth that could persuade me to give up *this* prize!"

Belinda sat up straighter. "You cannot do that! Why, my reputation will be ruined! I demand to be released at once; where can you be taking me?"

The duke took her hand and, turning it over, placed a kiss in the palm. At this familiar gesture, Belinda felt her heart melting, but she looked at him haughtily and waited for his reply.

"We are going to my grandmother's, my dear. Of course, she is not there at the moment, having gone to drink the waters at Bath. As for your reputation, it will hardly be ruined, even though we are alone, for we are going to be wed as soon as possible! I have a special license in my pocket, and the vicar who has the living has always been most obliging!"

"I refuse! I absolutely refuse! How dare you, Franklin? To think you can just scoop me up, carry me off, and expect me to be all complacency!"

"It was the only way to convince you that I have never stopped loving you," he said in a now-serious voice. "How else could I apologize for my behavior at the masquerade and show you I have changed? And who cares for state weddings and the consequence due the Brownells? I shall have my duchess any way I can, let convention be hanged!"

Belinda could hardly believe her ears. "This is most unlike you, Franklin," she said in a small voice. "And what if I refuse?"

He smiled, not at all disturbed. "You will not refuse, for I am sure you still love me! Shall I try to make you admit that you do?"

He moved nearer to her and slid his arms around her. Belinda tried to draw away but he paid her no heed at all, and bent to kiss her. After a long time, he whispered in a husky voice, "Well, m'lady? What do you say now?"

Belinda did not reply for a moment, but then she raised her head and stared into his adoring eyes. "Yes, I admit I love you, Franklin, but how can I be sure you will not revert to your former ways as soon as the ring is on my finger, and lead me a terrible life?"

The duke laughed. "Then you must point out the errors of my ways, my darling! You notice I do not promise you a peaceful, quiet life; I am sure we will have many a battle royal, but at least we will never be bored! And if I should become pompous again, I am sure you will know exactly how to charm me out of it, will you not?"

Belinda blushed and nodded. As the duke bent his head to her again, she said suddenly, "Wait! What about Caroline and Miss Wiggleworth? They will be so worried about me."

"Not at all! They know all about it; in fact, the plan was all Miss Draper's, and as for that governess with the unlikely name, she also agreed to assist me. I shall have to do something for her in return. Do not worry, my dear, at the first stop I will send a note back to reassure them both that all is well."

"Caro planned this? And Wiggles agreed?" Belinda began to laugh in earnest, but only for a little while, for the duke began to make love to her again, and soon all was quiet in the traveling coach.

The groom on the box above cast a cynical eye at the coachman.

"I'll never get used to the ways of the quality, Tony, never—if I live to be a hundred!" he said. "Behave indecent, they do, if you wants my opinion!"

The coachman agreed, saying he had never thought to see the day the Duke of Darwood would so forget himself.

Chapter Thirteen

The house seemed very large and very lonely without Belinda to keep her company, and Caroline lost no time setting a date a week hence to leave town. She was busy with the Winsteds as well as her father's agent for the next few days, arranging all the details that such a step entailed. There had been one ecstatic letter from the newlyweds, thanking Caroline for all her help and promising to call in Hunstanton as soon as they returned from the Greek Isles. Belinda had added a postscript. "I cannot say that I am sorry we will not be traveling there together, dearest Caro, for you would know it for the lie it is! But I suspect you will soon be traveling too, if not to Greece, then somewhere equally entrancing. See if I am not right!"

Caroline shook her head; matrimony seemed to have made Belinda a little giddy, she thought, as she took the notes addressed to Miss Wiggleworth and Yvette that had been enclosed in hers. The governess was packing her few belongings without much enthusiasm, preparatory to returning to Chigwell and her reluctant relatives, and she read her note eagerly. That evening she was all smiles as she confided to Caroline that the duke had asked her to repair to Kent, where he had instructed his agent to place a very pretty cottage at her disposal for as long as she cared to live there. "And he has promised me an annuity as well!" Miss Wiggleworth beamed. "He says it is for my care of his wife, and for the hand I had in forming her character, but I think that is a whisker, don't you Miss Draper?"

"'Never look a gift horse in the mouth,' Miss Wiggleworth!" Caroline intoned solemnly, but the governess was too happy to notice her mimicry. Yvette had asked permission to join the duke and duchess as instructed, and was leaving in the morning with Belinda's trunks.

The duke had sent announcements of their wedding to the London papers, but as Caroline did not go about in company any more, she was spared the gossip and speculation that this *on dit* inspired. She did not escape a visit from Lady Salton, however. The older woman arrived one afternoon while Caroline was directing the maids in placing Holland covers on all the drawing room furniture, dressed in her oldest gown, with an old-fashioned mob cap on her hair to protect it from the dust. Lady Salton took one look at her and clicked her tongue.

"Is there no place in the house that is not in disorder?" she asked sternly, fixing one small tweeny with a baleful glare, as if the mess were all her fault.

Caroline laughed and took her to the library, ordering a glass of negus for her guest.

"You look a fright, Caroline!" Lady Salton said as she seated herself and began to fan her overheated face rapidly. "When do you plan to leave town?"

"It will be the end of the week, m'lady," Caroline replied.

"Well, I suppose there is no need for you to remain," Lady Salton said in her positive way. "Not now, when the Earl of Cannock has left town!" Abruptly she changed the subject. "Tell me at once what this announcement of Franklin's means! To think that I was not informed! And to marry in such a ramshackle hole-in-the-corner way! Hmmp!"

She was given a condensed and not entirely truthful version of the affair. According to Caroline's account, given with a clear, open expression, the newlyweds had made up their quarrel in London and, not wishing to continue an engagement that they both considered long enough even before their estrangement, had had the romantic notion of marrying quietly at the duke's grandmother's estate. Caroline added that the duke had thought to protect Belinda from any further gossip as well.

"As if that naughty miss needed protection!" Lady Salton exclaimed when Caroline had finally finished. "The whole thing sounds most unlike him; I am sure it was all her idea! I will make it a point to discover the whole when they call on me here in town shortly, so that we can make arrangements to travel around and introduce the duchess to the family, as was originally planned."

Caroline was forced to tell the old lady that the duke and duchess were even then taking ship for Greece, which had the effect of further ruffling her feathers. Maliciously she turned on Caroline and began to berate her for letting Matthew Kincaid slip away.

Caroline was indignant, but she held her tongue and her temper in check while Lady Salton extolled the earl's family and fortune and said that she had never thought that Caroline would be so silly as to whistle away such a catch!

"But I didn't!" Caroline finally said when she could contain herself no longer. "The earl doesn't love me, that is clear, and he was just amusing himself over the season by flirting with me. I am sure he did it to protect himself from the matchmaking mamas who have been trying to trap him for so many years!"

Lady Salton snorted. "What a fairy tale! As if Matthew Kincaid needed protecting from anyone! I should like to see the mama who would dare to try! She would be put in her place at once. Furthermore, no man ever knows when he is in love until it is pointed out to him! And here I thought you were the intelligent Draper girl!"

Caroline said firmly once more that the earl had no interest in her, and she was glad she was old enough not to be taken in by his charms. Lady Salton threw up her hands and declared she washed her hands of such blind missishness.

"Give my regards to your mother, Caroline," she said, as she prepared to leave at last. "Tell her it was most unfortunate that she had to leave town when she did!"

On this cryptic note, she held up her wrinkled cheek for a farewell kiss, and patted Caroline's hand. "You are a good girl, my dear," she said, in quite the mildest tone Caroline had ever heard her use. "I shall miss you, and I do wish your season had had a happier ending!"

Caroline had a lump in her throat, but she put the earl's departure from her mind. She had been dismayed to find how much her spirits had sunk when she learned he had left town, and without even coming to bid her good-bye. Stoutly telling herself that she had been right all along about his character, she reminded herself that it would be most discourteous if she did not call on Lady St. Mark, as she had promised to do, and tell her the story of Belinda's elopement.

Consequently she sent the lady a note and was bidden to tea the following afternoon. Lady St. Mark received her on a small terrace off the breakfast room that was bright with flowers and pretty summer furniture. Caroline admired the love birds in their elaborate cage and took the seat Lady St. Mark indicated. "Tell me at once!" that lady commanded, a twinkle so like the earl's in her eyes, that Caroline immediately recognized it. "I am longing to hear how you solved everything, Miss Draper!"

"It was all due to your suggestion, m'lady," Caroline assured her before she proceeded to relate how she had brought the two lovers together. Lady St.

Mark laughed heartily and clapped her hands in admiration.

"I do so admire you, my dear, for thinking of such a clever scheme! I hope you will allow me to call you 'Caroline,' for I am sure we are going to be very good friends!"

Caroline said she would be delighted, but added that she was leaving for the country at the end of the week.

"Ah, you also?" Lady St. Mark asked, pouring her another cup of tea. "You must know that Matthew has left already, to visit friends in the country. Well, the season is over, and what a brilliant one it has been! I hope you have enjoyed yourself, my dear, and I do so look forward to seeing you next year."

"As to that, m'lady," Caroline replied, "I do not intend to come to town again. I only did it to oblige my mother this year, since she had both my sister and my cousin to present to society, but I shall now retire. Three seasons in London is quite enough!"

She sounded tart and not a little sad, but Lady St. Mark pretended not to hear. "I shall miss you, Caroline, but who knows? Perhaps in a year you will change your mind—about society and many other things as well!"

They parted the best of friends, with Lady St. Mark kissing her warmly and wishing her godspeed.

Suddenly the day of departure arrived, and Caroline, who was a little tired at this point from all her labors, was glad to lock the front door of the house behind her and hand the key to the agent. He helped her into the Draper coach and wished her a pleasant journey, but Caroline stared with unseeing eyes as the coach made its way through the busy streets towards the post road to home. She felt let down and sad that the season was over, and this was so unlike her that she wondered at herself. Prior to this journey, she had always been delighted to return to her home by the Channel, and the company of her family, and most especially her father, whom she had not seen for such a long time. It was very strange! She told herself she should be glad she had been able to help all the others to a happy ending; first Peggy and Stanley, then Lizzie and Alan Carter, and finally Belinda and the duke. Only Caroline was left on the shelf. Sitting alone in the coach, she realized, now that Matthew Kincaid had left London without a word, how much she cared for him, in spite of all her protestations to the contrary. And if she were to be completely truthful, she would have to admit that even with his domineering ways, he had managed to capture her heart—the heart she had always felt to be so impregnable! Captured it, and walked away without even a backward glance. She must forget him, she told herself sternly, and at once, for to love a man who had only been toying with her was disgraceful! She sighed and tried to sleep so she would not have to think of him all the long tedious hours she had before her on the journey.

Two days later, the coach traveled up the long drive to Draper House, and her spirits began to revive a little. Home at last! She had sent word that she was coming today, and her father was there when the steps were let down, to enclose her in a hearty hug.

"My dear daughter!" he exclaimed, holding her away from him for a moment so he could look at her, and with such a fond beaming smile that Caroline felt tears forming, to know that here at least there was someone who loved her so very much.

"Let me look at you, my dear!" he said.

They did not have much time to talk alone, for suddenly Mary Martha was there, and Clorinda, who begged for a kiss and had to be told how much she had grown, and even Andrew, who announced that he had washed his hands in honor of the occasion. They all went into the house together and Caroline felt a great deal better, surrounded by people who loved her and needed her. She went up to see her mother, who was resting in her room.

"Yes, we were at a party last evening," her father told her. "Such raking as we have had! It seems everyone wishes to honor Ned's return and Lizzie's engagement. A fine young man, Captain Carter; I am most pleased! You will see everyone else this evening, my dear!" he continued as she started up the stairs.

She spent a long time with her mother before she went away to dress for dinner. She had thought Mrs. Draper strangely excited, and although it was reasonable for her to be thrilled by Belinda's story, that did not quite explain her behavior. From her, she heard all the news of home; all about Ned and the captain's recoveries, and when Lizzie planned to wed; she heard about Mary Martha's putting up her hair and learning to control her giggles at last, and about the plans to send Andrew away to school in the fall. But there was something else, something she felt her mother was not telling her. Caroline shook her head in bewilderment as she went away to greet a blooming Peggy, who had already unpacked for her and ironed one of her prettiest gowns. Listening to all Peggy's plans delayed her, as did the elaborate hairstyle that her maid insisted she wear.

"But it is only a family dinner, Peggy!" she exclaimed, a little annoyed at all the fussing, as Peggy rearranged the curls at the back. The maid refused to be hurried, and Caroline, who had heard the first dinner bell long before, ran down the stairs and across the hall to the drawing room.

Everyone else was assembled, right down to Clorinda, in honor of her homecoming. But there was someone else as well. Standing by the fireplace with her father, dressed impeccably in evening clothes, was the Earl of Cannock. Caroline thought her heart stopped for a moment, she was so surprised. She felt herself begin to tremble as he gave her that sardonic smile, and she was glad that he allowed the others who had not seen her as yet to greet her first. Lizzie kissed her warmly, and Caroline, even as her thoughts tumbled towards the earl, thought she had never looked so beautiful. And Alan Carter, looking healthy and happy, came to kiss her as well. He had begun to tan again now that he was back in the country, and her brother was almost nut brown from his days outdoors. But even as she noted all these facts and said everything that was correct, she was constantly aware of that tall, powerful figure in the background, and although she was careful never to glance his way, she was conscious that his eyes never left her face. Suddenly she was more angry than unnerved. What right had he to come here and continue the farce? It was bad enough that he had made her so conspicuous in London, with his flirting attentiveness, but to come to her home was a great deal too much, especially since she had, as she told herself, relegated him to the dim and dusty past! And here he was, without so much as a by your leave, arranging everything to his own satisfaction, with no regard for the feelings of others!

Her greeting, when he finally came up to speak to her, was decidedly frosty, and he raised his brows and stared at her intently.

"I would almost think that you were not the least little bit glad to see me, Miss Draper," he murmured, so softly that he was unheard by the others. Caroline withdrew the hand he was holding and tilted her head at him in inquiry.

"How can such an *abasing* thought ever have occurred to you, m'lord?" Her tone was as sweet as her eyes were cool, even though her heart was racing so fast that it seemed to take her breath from her throat. "Of course, when the Earl of Cannock appears to honor those less exalted than himself, they must naturally be thrown into transports of delight!"

"I'll throw you into transports of delight, my girl," the earl said between gritted teeth, "if you do not stop this foolishness!"

Now it was Caroline's turn to raise her brows. Just then Winsted announced dinner was served, and as she turned away, she could not resist throwing a challenge back over her shoulder. "I should like to see you try! Perhaps then you might once, just once, have a humbling experience!"

Suddenly the earl grinned at her, that slashing smile that was so white against his tanned face. "Oh, I intend to try, believe me!" he promised her softly, and then he added, "And I have no intention of being 'humbled,' so beware!"

Before Caroline could think of a retort, he left to take her mother in to dinner. She realized that she was still trembling, although she felt a strange surge of elation at his arrogant reply. As she took her place at the table, she was glad that it was impossible to continue thinking of him, surrounded as she was by her family. The talk was lively and full of laughter. She learned that Lizzie and Alan were to be married in a week's time; that they had only waited to be sure she would be present as the maid of honor before setting the date. She found out there was to be a ball for them in a few days, to honor their marriage, and that Mrs. Draper had invited all the neighborhood, as well as several of the family to come and spend the week and attend the wedding. She heard about Ned's new sloop and her father's new horses. She was pleased to see Mary Martha chatting easily with Alan and the earl, and not once did she hear a single giggle! In fact, she thought, as she observed her sister, she has grown up, while we were away, into a complete young lady, and a very pretty one too. With her hair up and the roses coming and going in her cheeks, and her sparkling eyes, she was a match for Lizzie any day. Her attention was drawn to Clorinda, who told her that she had named her new pony Matty in honor of the earl, for he had arrived on her birthday and was the first person she had seen while she was trying to think of a name. Caroline was amused that the mighty Earl of Cannock had a pony named after him, and such a name as well, and she stole a glance at his face to see his reaction. He grinned at her, not at all dismayed by this dubious honor.

With the dessert, Mr. Draper suddenly tapped his wine glass and the animated conversation died away. Standing and smiling at them all, he raised his glass and said, "A toast!"

Obediently everyone lifted their glasses and looked at him expectantly. "I give you a toast, my dears, to Lizzie and Alan!" he proclaimed as he smiled at them both. "To the happy couple—and to love!"

"To love!" everyone echoed, and although Caroline tried to keep her eyes lowered, she felt them drawn as if by magnets to the earl's face. He was not sipping his wine, he was watching her; and when he caught her glance, he raised his glass a little higher, in a private toast to her. Caroline felt herself flushing. What would the man do next?

It seemed an age before the ladies retired to the drawing room, and Caroline went to sit beside her mother and ask why she had not mentioned the earl was visiting, and to what purpose. "I suppose it slipped my mind," Mrs. Draper said vaguely. "There was so much to tell you. We were delighted to welcome him, for you know how much your father liked him this spring, before we went to town."

Caroline had to be satisfied with this ingenuous explanation, but she made very sure she was busy with the children, setting up a game in the corner of the drawing room, when the men reappeared. Alan went at once to Lizzie, Ned and her father continued discussing the barley crop in the northwest field, and the earl smiled at her, well aware of her plot to avoid him. He sat beside Mrs. Draper, chatting easily until the children were sent to bed. At that, Caroline had to return to the others, but she was careful to take a chair somewhat apart from her mother and the earl. He did not seem at all disappointed by her tactics, she thought, a little indignantly.

In spite of her long journey, Caroline spent a restless night, her sleep interspersed by fragmentary dreams she was glad she was unable to remember as she woke in the summer dawn. Suddenly she knew she had to get away for a while, and, dressing quickly, she stole through the quiet house, where everyone else was still asleep, to the kitchen, where she begged a cup of coffee from the surprised cook. As she walked briskly to the stables, she was relieved to be outdoors; perhaps a fast ride would help to clear the cobwebs from her head, especially one most persistent and unwelcome cobweb!

She turned her mare to the sea and rode along the shore, enjoying the bracing salt air and the early-morning flight of the gulls, searching the damp sand left by the ebbing tide. When she reached the Head, she turned for home reluctantly, and then she saw a figure on horseback cantering towards her. Her heart took that now-familiar leap as she recognized the earl.

"Servant, Miss Draper." He smiled, tipping his hat as he reined in beside her. Caroline was forced to slow the mare to a walk. She nodded distantly.

"I see you are not an early-morning chatterer!" he remarked politely. "But perhaps you would rather be alone?"

Caroline bit back her retort. No, you are not going to trick me that way, she thought, for it would be impossibly rude to reply to a guest of her father as she wished she might do.

After waiting for a moment for her to speak, the earl continued, looking carefully past her, out to sea, "I shall remember. No transports of delight until after breakfast!"

Caroline's hands jerked at the reins, and her horse skittered a little, sidestepping towards the earl's bay. He put out a strong hand and grasped her reins. "Easy, my dear! The mare is still fresh!"

She tried to move away, but he would have none of it, and before she knew what was happening, he had both sets of reins in one big hand and was drawing her towards him with the other. His arm stole around her, and for a moment he stared down into her startled eyes before he bent his head and kissed her. Caroline did not even try to escape, for she knew it would be impossible, twisted sideways as she was in the saddle, and any sudden move would be sure to spook the mare. She thought she would faint before he raised his warm lips from hers.

Handing her back her reins, he moved his horse a little away.

"Perhaps before breakfast after all!" she heard him say, his harsh, deep voice a little shaken.

At last, Caroline found her voice. "How *dare* you?" she demanded.

"But I told you I was not the sort of man to trifle with, I believe, my dearest Caro! Come, admit that it is you who is to have the humbling experience after all!"

"Never!" Caroline exclaimed.

"Do you mean to tell me that, after returning my kiss so warmly—you did return it, my dear—you now deny that you are attracted to me? How unnerving to find yourself in love with an untruthful lady!" He had his voice under control now, and quirked one dark brow at her, his blue eyes blazing with what she thought was laughter at her expense. She was suddenly furious, although whether at the earl or herself, she could not say.

"Not before or after breakfast, or any other time!" she said as firmly as she could, and before he could reply, she kicked the mare to a canter and rode away. She was glad he did not catch her up, which she knew he could do easily, and when she reached the stables, she leapt off the mare and ran to the house as if the devil himself were after her.

As the day of the ball drew nearer, Caroline was much too busy helping her mother to have time to ride. The earl made no move to seek her out or try to catch her alone. Sometimes she would feel his eyes on her, but he behaved so politely and so distantly to her that she was sure he was regretting his early-morning lovemaking. As much as I do, she told herself stoutly.

One morning, as she and Lizzie were counting tablecloths in the linen room and setting aside those that needed some small repair, Lizzie asked her shyly if she felt any differently about Matthew Kincaid.

"Not in the least, my dear!" Caroline said briskly, feeling as much the liar as the earl had claimed she was. She shook out yet another cloth and went over it carefully.

"I only ask," Lizzie persisted, "because I am so very happy myself. Oh, Caro, you do not know how wonderful it is to be in love! Why, Alan is everything in the world to me, and I would so like to see you have that joy as well!"

"Perhaps I will, dear sister," Caroline said, smiling a little at Lizzie's flushed face and glowing eyes when she spoke of Alan. "But *not* with the Earl of Cannock!"

Lizzie shook her head in disbelief. "I do not understand! He is most definitely a 'one,' and everyone else likes him—Father, Mother, the girls, even Andrew!"

"Perhaps our personalities do not suit, Lizzie." And then, to change the subject, she asked, "Do you think we should include this cloth? There is a small darn here in the corner."

Just as she had planned, Lizzie was drawn off the scent, much to her sister's relief.

Family members assembled, flowers were brought in from the garden and palms from the greenhouse, silver was polished, and the prisms of all the chandeliers were washed until they sparkled. As the ball drew nearer, Caroline saw the earl only at dinnertime, and it was easy to avoid him; she had only to turn away to make sure Great Aunt Mabel had her shawl, or that Cousin Hargate was not trying to argue politics with Uncle Wentworth. She knew the earl had been invited to remain a guest until after the wedding, and she was glad there was so much to do that her inattention did not appear rude.

The awaited morning dawned clear and sunny, and Caroline knew it would be a delightful evening. It was neither too warm nor too chilly, and she was glad she had suggested to her mother that they have some chairs and tables placed on the terrace, and some colored lanterns lit about the rose garden, in case the guests wished to stroll about between dances.

That evening, Lizzie was breathtaking in her white silk gown trimmed with old lace, with rosebuds in her hair. At her corsage, she wore a ribbon with the colors of Alan's old regiment. He himself looked extremely handsome in full regimentals, which he had donned for almost the last time, for the War Office had refused to reinstate him after his injuries, and he and Lizzie planned to travel to his estate and begin their life there immediately after the wedding. Caroline thought that even with his scar, considerably less noticeable now against the tan of his face, he was a happy man, as he bent over her sister with an intimate smile.

Caroline herself was dressed in a very becoming gown of palest ecru brocade, shot through with gold threads. Because the fabric was so elaborate, the gown was cut very simply, with a deep neckline and the tiniest of sleeves. She wore gold slippers and her amethyst jewelry, and both her father and mother thought she was stunning. So too did the Earl of Cannock as he approached her to ask for the first dance. And the third, and the fifth, and the ninth!

"No doubt they are all waltzes, m'lord?" Caroline tried to tease, determined to put their relationship back to its earlier, easier phase. "You know I cannot give you so many dances! It would cause all kinds of gossip and set everyone's backs up!"

"In the country, Miss Draper?" the earl asked, content to follow her lead. "Surely you are allowed more freedom here in your own home, and with an honored guest of the family as well!"

If that isn't just like him, she thought, as she agreed to three. He will never forget his consequence! She went away to remind Mary Martha not to forget the plate of cakes and ices for Clorinda, who had been so disappointed she was not old enough to attend the ball. She found her flirting with Lord Bernard, a very young peer who seemed stunned by his good fortune, and Caroline drew Mary Martha aside.

"Behave yourself!" she said sharply. "Such flirting is not at all the thing, and I want nothing to upset Lizzie's evening. You are much too young to be setting yourself up with a beau in any case!"

Mary Martha tossed her head, a gesture so like Lizzie's that Caroline was startled. "Oh, do not be so starchy!" she exclaimed impatiently. "Where is the harm?"

Caroline could have told her, but she saw her mother beckoning to her, and had to go and see what she could do to assist her. It was Great Aunt Mabel again. She had to be installed in the most comfortable chair, and not near a draft, or too far from the music, and she had to have her shawl again, and—and—and!

Caroline was almost glad when the earl came up to rescue her. As they reached the dance floor, the orchestra began to play a waltz, and she had to laugh at his air of quiet satisfaction. She realized she was enjoying the evening very much. There was a bubble of anticipation underlying her surface calm, almost the way she had felt as a small girl on Boxing Day, when she woke early and lay in her bed, wondering what presents were waiting for her. Anticipation, and an exciting premonition of danger as well!

Some time later, as the orchestra began a lively schottische, she looked around to be sure Mary Martha was not romping on the dance floor, and was startled to find that her younger sister was nowhere in sight. Her lips tightened as she made her way to the hall, where Winsted was stationed so he might oversee the footmen. When she asked if Mary Martha had come past him, he shook his head. "I have not seen her come this way, Miss Caroline."

Caroline smiled at him and went around the dancing couples to the terrace. There were some guests here enjoying the soft breeze scented by the garden, and watching the small sliver of moon sailing in the sky, but Caroline felt a pang of apprehension as she scanned the terrace and was unable to see her sister. Discreetly edging her way to the steps, she slipped down them to the darkness and started for the rose garden, wishing she had never suggested to her mother that they use the terrace and the gardens as part of the ball. It made it entirely too difficult to keep track of Mary Martha, who, she was beginning to discover, was as much of a scamp as Lizzie had ever been. As she picked up the hem of her gown to keep it from the dewy grass, she jumped a little to hear a harsh, deep voice behind her.

"No, do not tell me! Let me guess! You are going in search of yet another errant sister, are you not, Miss Draper?"

Caroline whirled to see the earl leaning on the terrace wall, staring down at her knowledgeably. She flushed, glad he could not make out her face in the dim moonlight, and then he came lightly down the steps to join her. He took her arm before she could protest, and led her towards the lake.

"But I am sure she must have gone into the rose garden, m'lord," she objected as he continued in quite the opposite direction.

"Know she did. Saw her with that silly young chub who has yet to develop a jaw," the earl said calmly, not slowing his steps in the slightest.

"But why are we going this way?" Caroline asked, bewildered and a little frightened as well.

"Because, my dear Caro," he said, tightening his grip on her arm, "I have no intention of allowing you to become embroiled with yet another silly Draper miss! Are you the only sister with any sense? Besides, I have been relegated to the background on so many occasions, while you rush to their rescue, that even if I were the most conceited man in the world, I would be quite humble by now. And since the morning after you returned home, you are constantly disappearing into the kitchens or the still room or the butler's pantry because of this wedding of Lizzie's. I am sure I wish all your family well, but Miss Caroline Draper will not be available for the next hour! You rode away from me that morning, but I insist on speaking to you now, and what is more, you will listen!"

"How masterful of you!" Caroline exclaimed, skidding to a stop on the wet grass. "Let me go at once! Let me tell you, m'lord, I do as I wish, and if I do not wish to speak to you, I won't! I answer to no man!"

"You will answer to this one!" he said grimly, propelling her up the steps of the little gazebo near the lake and forcing her to sit down on a marble bench. He stood over her, with his hands on his hips, and demanded, "Why is it that you strive so hard to make happy endings for everyone else, and yet do not make the slightest push to contrive your own? Especially since that happy ending involves me?" he added, a little ruefully.

Caroline felt breathless but she answered him fiercely. "I do not know what you mean. I only want to live my own life, not be at the beck and call of some man!"

The earl laughed, but it was not a pleasant sound. "Let us consider that, then. Is it preferable to be at the beck and call of your family instead? To be only a beloved daughter, a watchful sister, and dependable aunt as you wither away into old age, without any real happiness?"

Caroline clenched her fists. "You are so arrogant! Who is to say that marriage to such a man as you would ensure my happiness? But of course you cannot conceive how it could be any different, that there is one lady who is immune to your charms, who cares not a whit for your compliments and attentions and—"

But she got no further in her tirade, for the earl exclaimed, "You lie!" and, taking the seat next to her on the bench, pulled her into his arms and began to kiss her. His lips were as warm and insistent as she remembered, and his powerful hands held her close to him; so close, in fact, that she could hear his heart beating through her thin ball gown. Her own heart beat as rapidly in response. When she was finally released, her head was reeling, and she was glad he did not move away, for she needed that broad shoulder for support.

"Marry me, Caro!" he said, in an ardent voice she had never heard before.

"But I do not wish to marry!" she cried. "Nor do you!"

"Of course not," he agreed; "I always make it a habit to go about the countryside proposing to ladies I do not wish to marry! And if you do not want to marry either, why did you return my kisses so sweetly, and why do you remain in my arms? Explain that if you can, dear Caro!"

"Matthew, please!" she said. "I am so confused! Why, you have flirted with me all season, but you know you had not the slightest desire to marry me! It was because you knew I was safe—an old maid, in fact—that you fixed your interest on me!"

"Yes, your mother told me that was how you considered yourself, oh, foolish Caro!" He laughed at her, and then he added more seriously, "Perhaps in the beginning I only meant to teach you a lesson, and then, when you continued to hold me at such a distance, you became a challenge! Now, however, it is a great deal more than that—a very great deal more! Couldn't you tell my feelings that morning on the beach?" His hands, traveling up her bare arms in a gentle caress, were warm and insistent. Caroline closed her eyes, for his dark, handsome face was so close, her senses were swimming. He chuckled and released her, getting to his feet and moving away, as if to give her time to compose herself. She swayed on the bench and regarded him with dismay.

"Say you will marry me, Caro!" he repeated gently. "I have your father and mother's blessing; indeed, that is why I came back to Draper House, you know, to ask for your hand. And if you marry me, you will save yourself all these endless family entanglements! To think you were about to rescue Mary Martha from tripping down the garden path in the dark with that unsuitable young man! Why, she has another year before she will be presented to society. Think of all the scrapes she will get into in that time! And then there is still Clorinda to come! No, I do not intend to wait until you have everyone settled to your satisfaction, my beautiful match-maker! You must marry me now!"

He dropped his bantering tone and said simply, "I love you, my dearest, and I promise you will be happy—and so will I! I know you think I am arrogant and overbearing, but it was only to protect *you*, to help *you*, to keep *you* from worry! Come, tell me, would it be so hard to let me love you—and take care of you—always?"

He did not approach her, but seemed to be waiting for her to make up her mind, and Caroline looked at him in wonder, for she had heard the love in his voice and felt herself responding in a way she had never imagined she could. She rose from the bench and went up to him shyly and said, "Since it appears you were right and you can so easily transport me to delight, what can I say but 'yes, m'lord'?"

He turned her face to the moonlight, and what he saw there made him catch his breath and draw her close to him once again. As she put her arms around him to hold him nearer still, she hoped that Mary

Martha would be able to manage with only her mother to guide her, but in a very few moments, it suddenly did not matter to her, not even one little bit!

ABOUT THE AUTHOR

Barbara Ward Hazard was born and raised in Fall River, Massachusetts. After receiving a B.F.A. in advertising design from the Rhode Island School of Design, she worked as a technical editor, an advertising artist and an advertising freelancer.

In 1968, Barbara Hazard began studying oil painting with Amy Jones and since then has sold 25 major works and had two one-woman and numerous group shows in North Westchester and Vermont.

Her interests, besides her family, include paddle tennis, cross country skiing, quilting and sewing, pro football, classical music, painting, and reading.

Writing, she says, is the most satisfying and the easiest of anything she has ever attempted. She looks forward to many more years at the typewriter.

She is married and has three sons, Steven, David and Scott.

Let COVENTRY Give You
A Little Old-Fashioned Romance

FAWCETT COLUMBINE
COOKBOOKS

ROMANCE From Fawcett Books

☐ A NECESSARY WOMAN   04544 $2.75
    by Helen Van Slyke
    Mary Farr Morgan seemed to have everything—a handsome hus-
    band, successful career, good looks. She had everything except a
    man who could make her feel like a woman.

☐ THIS ROUGH MAGIC   24129 $2.50
    by Mary Stewart
    A pretty, young British actress goes to Corfu for a holiday, and
    finds herself tangled in a web of romance and violence.

☐ THE SPRING OF THE TIGER   24297 $2.75
    by Victoria Holt
    A tale of intrigue and love. A young woman goes to Ceylon and
    finds herself in a marriage of thwarted passion and danger.

☐ THE TURQUOISE MASK   23470 $2.95
    by Phyllis A. Whitney
    Something hidden deep in her memory was the key to Amanda
    Austin's past. She didn't know it was also the key to her future.

☐ THE RICH ARE DIFFERENT   24098 $2.95
    by Susan Howatch
    This is the story of a young Englishwoman whose life, loves and
    ambition become intertwined with the fate of a great American
    banking family.

Buy them at your local bookstore or use this handy coupon for ordering.

COLUMBIA BOOK SERVICE
32275 Mally Road, P.O. Box FB, Madison Heights, MI 48071

Please send me the books I have checked above. Orders for less than 5 books
must include 75¢ for the first book and 25¢ for each additional book to cover
postage and handling. Orders for 5 books or more postage is FREE. Send check
or money order only. Allow 3-4 weeks for delivery.

Cost $_____   Name_____

Sales tax*_____   Address_____

Postage _____   City_____

Total $_____   State_____ Zip_____

*The government requires us to collect sales tax in all states except AK, DE,
MT, NH and OR.*

Prices and availability subject to change without notice.